AVATAR DREAMS

**Sci-Fi Stories
Showcasing the
Coming Age
of Avatars**

Foreword by
Ray Kurzweil

Edited by
Kevin J. Anderson
and Mike Resnick

Scientific Editor
Dr.² Harry Kloor

WFP
WORDFIRE PRESS

Cover art and design by Amy Collen, DesignWise Art

Edited by Kevin J. Anderson and Mike Resnick

Dr. Harry Kloor, Scientific Editor

Kevin J. Anderson, Art Director

Published by
WordFire Press, an imprint of
WordFire, Inc.
PO Box 1840
Monument CO 80132

Kevin J. Anderson & Rebecca Moesta, Publishers
WordFire Press Trade Paperback Edition 2018
Printed in the USA

Join our WordFire Press Readers Group and
get free books, sneak previews, updates on new projects, and other giveaways.
Sign up for free at wordfirepress.com

Created with Vellum

CONTENTS

INTRODUCTION, BY HARRY DOC KLOOR

AVATAR DREAMS

This anthology started last year, but its roots actually began many decades ago.

Growing up, I had the good fortune of having a mother who had written a science fiction novel, *My Beloved Troshanus*, while carrying me. Some would say I had science fiction in my blood; certainly, a steady diet of it since childhood. My desire to create avatars was initiated by two books: Poul Anderson's *Call Me Joe* and Ben Bova's novel, *The Winds of Altair*. I was eight or nine, and don't recall which book I read first—but I became fascinated by the idea that one could inhabit another body. I was attracted to the idea that humans could transfer their mind and consciousness across vast distances and be somewhere else; to obtain a new body—a better body perhaps, or just a different one.

As a child, I envisioned a world where we could move instantly around the planet—even the stars (not grasping the limitations put on us by the speed of light), by moving our consciousness into robotic and android bodies. The idea of being able to go anywhere, become anyone and do anything was very freeing, opening my eyes to the infinite potential available, were we to have unlimited bodies.

During my teenage years, this appetite for science fiction grew, as did my love of science. I excelled in science and technology and even went so far as to build a simple computer via a kit requiring hexadecimal programming, which proved to be a royal pain in the ass. I quickly realized how enormous the gap was between science and science fiction. Fortunately, after a period of disappointment in the limitations of current technology, I came to understand that computers grew in power exponentially, and when interfaced with other technologies, they grew exponentially in capability. We were a long way from being able to build avatars, but given exponential growth, I thought we could achieve it during my lifetime, and was hell-bent on being the one to ultimately create them.

In the decades following that childhood dream, I spent my time building up the necessary skills and relationships needed to create an actual avatar. In my twenties, I shifted my thoughts away from the idea of transferring my actual consciousness into a robotic body, realizing we have something I like to call *Awareness Consciousness* (AC). AC, which is driven by your senses, is what makes you think you're in your body. Simply put, because you see, hear, talk, touch, move, smell and taste through your body, you have the perception that you are in it. Shift these senses elsewhere, and part of your awareness consciousness shifts as well. This is experienced in virtual reality all the time now, and to a far lesser extent, when watching a movie or having a video chat. The more senses you shift and the more actions are done at a distance in a natural, organic way, the more your AC shifts.

It is far easier to shift AC than your actual consciousness. This approach makes avatars possible now, versus waiting a much longer time for science to figure out how to transfer your consciousness into a machine. Now, mind you, it still requires a whole host of exponential technologies to create working commercial avatars—from robotics, haptics, partial artificial intelligence, IOT (internet of things), VR/MR/AR, deep machine learning, high-bandwidth wireless communication, etc. Thirty years ago, this technology was still in its infancy, so I had to bide my time and let exponential technology do what it does best—mature.

Flash forward to May 2016: Peter Diamandis asked me if I would come back to XPRIZE for the purpose of taking over the ANA team, one of nine teams competing to create a new XPRIZE. The team's prize designs would be voted on at the Annual Visioneering Summit at the end of September. The ANA team had been struggling with a molecular teleportation concept, which wasn't working. Normally, I don't return to organizations I've helped launch. Having been in the original founding team of five that created and shepherded the Ansari XPRIZE, I initially said no. But if you know Peter, no is not an answer he accepts, so he countered with an irresistible offer—freedom to change the prize concept to whatever I wanted. So, I agreed to become the Bold Innovator, and changed the prize concept to Avatar XPRIZE.

Marcus Shingles, having taken over the CEO position, had the brilliant idea of allowing sponsors to fund the nine teams in the development of their XPRIZE-worthy concepts. Our team started three months behind, with four left to go. We were up against teams proposing prizes on cancer and ALS that traditionally get a lot of "heartstring" votes. And the concept of avatars seemed fantastical. Turning this around seemed unlikely. But I was fortunate to have Ione Istrate and MacKenzie Ward, XPRIZE fellows, Brandon Alvis my editor, Amy Collins and Seth Rowanwood my artist team, and Jun Suto and Tammy Stockfish, XPRIZE staff, Ray Kurzweil, Anousheh Ansari, Neil Jackcobstein, advisor to help design the prize, as well as my film, TV, VR and animation friends to help explain it. Together, we created a series of kick-ass videos, and brought to the USA two Japanese robotic systems to demo the concept of avatars. We figured we had a fighting chance.

September 29, 2016 arrived, we did our stage presentations, and pretty much everything that *could* go wrong, did. None of our videos played, the sound system for us failed, but worst of all, the avatar concept fell flat. The next day, after the votes were tallied, we were running dead last.

So, we threw the playbook and four months of preparation out the window, shifting our approach away from canned presentations to interactive demos. This new approach included putting dozens of Visioneers into our demo robotic avatar, shifting each person's awareness consciousness across the room into a robot. Among the 80 or so plus Visioneers whose AC we moved included Dean Kamen, Rod Roddenberry, Peter Diamandis, Anousheh Ansari, Pharrell Williams, and the Duchess of York. We also adapted our approach to explain on a personal level how the avatar systems worked and the impact they would have on the world.

Ultimately, the avatar system I envision consists of two systems. First, the avatar control unit—I like to call this the SOUL (Sensor Operation User Link) system—and the second, the actual Avatar Unit. The SOUL consists of a VR/audio system that enables you to see and hear through a robot. Then, a microphone system that enables you to speak through the robot, a haptic system that allows you to feel through the robot, and finally, a motion capture system that enables you to move naturally and have those movements translate into robotic motion. The avatar is the robotic system that has all the counterparts to the SOUL, allowing you to move, touch, see, hear, and talk through the robot. The technologies required have all evolved to the point that integrating and adapting them will lead to commercial avatars in the next decade. Keep in mind, with this type of system, you shift your AC, and it takes zero training time to use the avatar, because it takes no time to know how to use a surrogate body.

The Visioneers initially thought our avatar presentation was about travel, but travel is only a small part of what avatars will be used for. Avatars will impact every part of our lives and create the next golden age of mankind by democratizing opportunity and access. Since the dawn of man, we have concentrated into cities, and those cities have had greater opportunities and access to better resources and talent. Public concentration has also led some to greater poverty, escalating crime, and infrastructure problems. But in the Age of Avatars, *where* you live will no longer limit your access to where you work, play, learn, or contribute. A doctor will treat patients anywhere in the world, a teacher can be brought into any class room, and at the same time, a worker need no longer leave his country to find work opportunities—they can work one day in Tokyo, the next in New York, all from the comfort of their home —regardless of where that home may be located. The limitations of locality will vanish, and be replaced with the abundance of the entire global community.

Many of the prize concepts that were competing sought to solve one of the UN's Sustainable Development Goals (SDGs) (un.org/sustainabledevelopment/sustainable-development-goals/); these goals range from ending poverty and providing quality education to better health and work opportunities. The SDGs are difficult to solve, but not because there is not enough money. About a trillion dollars a year is now given to those in need. Nor is it lack of know-how or equipment; there is plenty of that. The scarcity is in the distribution of skilled people. There are not enough doctors, engineers, technicians, teachers, or experts who are willing to go where they are needed, and for good reason: they have their own lives and problems. Through avatars, this is solved because skilled people need not expend days of travel time to reach and return from remote lands where they can at last lend a hand. Instead, from the comfort of their home or office, they could donate a day once a year, or a few hours each month—as an avatar. There is plenty of skilled labor willing to help if we erased the burden and danger of travel. I envision a billion avatars or more across the world—with a UN Charter that gives operators access to the necessary bandwidth to operate their avatars, in exchange for donating the use of the avatar once a week for social good.

Avatars will not only be effective tools in solving the SDGs, they will bring the world closer together, literally and figuratively, while preserving diversity. Avatars will have partial AI (an AI sub-consciousness), allowing you to speak and understand any language, including its context. It's considerably more difficult to start a war when coworkers, teachers, doctors, and friends live all around the world. Before conflicts overheat and melt down into war, people will step in as avatars to safely interpret what is going on—a worldly deterrent to the escalation of conflict.

And yes, for those of you who are already dreaming bigger —humanoid avatars are just the start—I see the Age of Avatars filled not only with a billion-plus humanoid Avatars, but countless other forms, big and small, real and fantastic. Personally, I am looking forward to my own Dragon avatar, as well as a microscopic one so I can swim through the human body. And the earth is just the beginning—in the Age of Avatars will exist throughout our solar system—albeit controlled from nearby locations until we can transfer full consciousness into them and back. And while we will begin with a combination of systems from VR to motion capture, eventually we will evolve to brain interfaces that provide a purer experience. But for now, I'll look forward to the first avatars being simple humanoid robots that I control via a SOUL system.

All these factors were presented, and ultimately led the Visioneers to vote heartily for the ANA Avatar XPRIZE to become one of three prize concepts voted ready to launch. But being ready to launch and launching are often two different things, which is why I also convinced ANA to pledge, on stage, $22M to fund the prize purse and operations of the ANA Avatar XPRIZE. One year later, at the following Visioneering event, on October 7, they fulfilled that pledge, delivering on stage the check for $22M. This prize will formally be announced to the world on March 12, 2018 at SXSW. It is the first new prize since 2015.

For me, this anthology is the fitting way to begin the Avatar Revolution (go to avatarrevolution.com to help bring about the platinum age of avatars); and the perfect way to announce the launch of **Beyond Imagination**—an avatar company founded by myself and a league of extraordinary luminaries that will bring generic robotic avatars to the entire world to enable anyone, to travel anywhere in three minutes or less, to erase the limitation of locality, to solve the SDG's, to bring prosperity and abundance to all. (Go to beyondimaginationco.com to learn more.)

This anthology, the company Beyond Imagination, and the Avatar XPrize mark the first shots of the Avatar Revolution. A revolution that I will continue to lead until a billion plus avatars exist throughout our solar system. I invite all of you to join, so that we together, can bring about the Age of Avatars.

FOREWORD, BY RAY KURZWEIL

I AM AN AVATAR

"I was smitten. I never wanted to leave this world, one more beautiful than I could have imagined," recalled a woman who recently had her first full immersion experience in October of 2016 in a multiplayer VR world called QuiVr. "Virtual reality had won me over, lock, stock and barrel," she continued.

Her epiphany was short-lived as the virtual hand of another player named BigBro442 started to rub her virtual chest.

"Stop!" she cried. But his assault continued and intensified.

"My high from earlier plummeted," she wrote. "I went from the god who couldn't fall off a ledge to a powerless woman being chased by another avatar."

Finally, after being chased and harassed around the virtual cliffs and ledges of the QuiVr world, she yanked off her headset.

I had several reactions to reading about this incident. First, dismay at the pervasive misogyny and harassment directed at women which is only intensified in the anonymity of many virtual environments and other forms of online communication.

The other reaction is especially relevant to this book. I have written that virtual environments are inherently safer than real ones because you can hang up if the experience is not going to your liking. Indeed, she did ultimately leave the QuiVr world, but a week later wrote, "It felt real and violating ... the virtual chasing and groping happened a full week ago and I'm still thinking about it."

Putting aside for the moment the important issue of harassment and assault in both real and virtual spaces, this incident illustrates a key lesson about the increasingly virtual world we will be inhabiting: *we readily transfer our consciousness to our avatar.*

Like a child playing with a doll, we maintain some level of awareness that the virtual world is ever so slightly more tentative than the real one, but we have little resistance to identifying with our virtual selves. I have always felt that the term "virtual reality" is unfortunate, implying a lack of reality. The telephone was the first virtual reality enabling us to occupy a virtual space with someone far away as if we were together. Yet, these are nonetheless real interactions. You can't say of a phone conversation, "Oh that argument we had," "That agreement we made," "That loving sentiment I expressed," that wasn't real; that was just virtual reality.

We have now had several decades of experience with avatars representing us in virtual environments and these are now becoming immersive with 360 degree three-dimensional virtual environments. Of even greater significance, however, is that we are now embarking on an era in which avatars will also represent us in real reality. That is the subject of this compelling and creative collection of stories compiled by Kevin J. Anderson and Mike Resnick.

A major issue concerning avatars in the real world is the phenomenon of the uncanny valley, which is the sense of revulsion that occurs if a replica of a human (whether a computer-generated image or a robot) is very close to lifelike, but not quite there. Thus far, we have largely stayed on the safe bank of this valley. In the movies, computer-generated actors such as Shrek are decidedly not trying to look human. This is beginning to change. In the 2016 Star Wars movie, *Rogue One*, Grand Moff Tarkin, the Imperial leader of the Death Star, was computer generated due to the death in 1994 of Peter Cushing who played him in the earlier Star Wars movies. For me, he was in the uncanny valley and looked creepy, but not everyone agreed. Many critics applauded how realistic he appeared. Thus, we're approaching the safe bank of the uncanny valley when it comes to animations. There will always be controversy as we get close to full realism.

However, when it comes to robotic avatars in the real world, we're not yet approaching the uncanny valley. I've given multiple speeches using a technology called the Beam Robot, which is a simple human-sized device consisting of a wheeled base holding a display of a person's face at a normal face height. As a user, I can roll out on stage after I am introduced and give my talk, and then mingle with the audience afterwards. There are significant limitations in that I am always afraid I am going to zoom off the stage as I cannot see where my virtual bottom is. When mingling, I cannot shake hands or give and receive hugs. Nonetheless, I do feel like I am at the venue and am able to put these restrictions temporarily out of mind.

Over the next five to ten years all of these limitations of robotic avatars will gradually dissolve, just as fully virtual environments have gone from the simple worlds of Atari 8-bit games to the compelling three-dimensional virtual environments of today. As we do so, however, we will need to be wary of the uncanny valley.

I've described one way to leap over the uncanny valley in an issued patent titled "Virtual Encounters" (U.S. Patent Number 8,600,550) that will allow you to hug and otherwise physically interact with a companion in real reality even if you are hundreds of miles apart. If a third party were to witness such an interaction, they would see each party with a robotic surrogate. However, for the participants, neither party actually sees the robot they are with. Instead, they experience their human partner.

To envision this, let's call the two parties John and Jane. John sees out of the eyes of the robotic surrogate with Jane, and similarly, Jane sees out of the eyes of the surrogate with John. They hear out of the ears of the surrogates and feel (using tactile actuators such as piezoelectric stimulators on their hands, arms and other body parts) the physical sensations detected by the physical sensors on the surrogates. The physical movements of the two human participants direct the movements of the corresponding robotic surrogate. So each party feels like they are with their human partner and does not see or detect the presence of any robots. Given our readiness to transfer our consciousness to avatars that represent us in another environment, both parties feel like they are truly with their human partner. Once perfected, it would be just like being together. The two robotic surrogates are simply a communication channel incorporating all of the senses. This concept can be extended to more than two participants.

The scenario described in this patent is one approach to being somewhere else using avatar technology. Another approach is to transfer ourselves to remote robotic substitutes that will appear real to other real people in a real environment. Through accelerating advances in robotic, sensory, communication, and virtual reality technologies, we will be able to instantly exist in multiple places at once and overcome the limitations of today's state of the art.

The latest XPRIZE, called "Avatar XPRIZE," envisions "limitless travel by teleporting one's consciousness into a physical avatar body that will enable people to instantly be in multiple places at once, literally." I worked on this prize with Harry Kloor, who led the effort.

The technologies to realize this vision are rapidly coming into place. Start with today's Beam robot and replace each of its components with technologies that are already coming into place. For example, replace its wheeled base with walking legs, a capability that Boston Dynamics and a number of teams have already demonstrated.

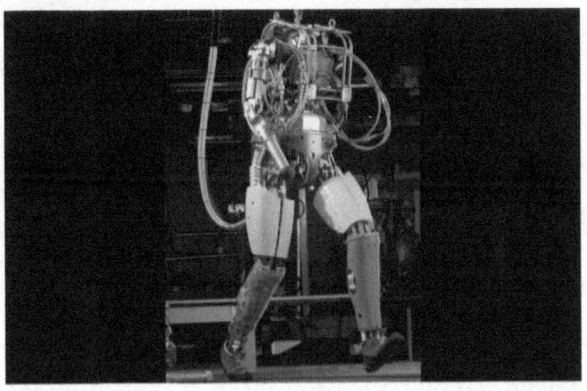

Robotic walking legs by Boston Dynamics

Now add robotic arms that you control with your own arms, another already available technology demonstrated, for example, by Dean Kamen's "Luke Arm," which is intended as a prosthetic for amputees. This technology has already received FDA approval based on its ability to allow users without biological arms to "prepare food, feed oneself, use zippers, and brush and comb their hair."

**Mr. Fred Downs using a prototype of the LUKE arm
developed by DEKA Research & Development**

Replacing the avatar's head with something realistic is the
most challenging aspect of the Avatar XPRIZE, but consider
this robotic head created by communications and biotech-
nology pioneer Martine Rothblatt, in collaboration with
Hanson Robotics Ltd., called "Bina48," based on Martine's
wife, Bina:

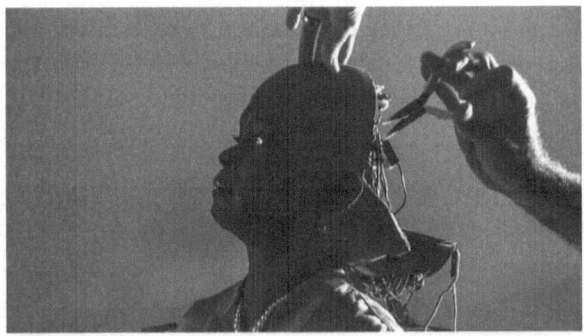

Martine Rothblatt and Hanson Robotics Ltd.'s Bina48 Robot

Bina48 is able to respond to questions using its own AI, but it could also be used to project the presence of an actual human.

In five to ten years, these types of technologies will be perfected and seamlessly integrated into an avatar technology that will enable us to do virtually all of the things we do now by traveling to a different location. They will be designed to look and feel human. We will then be able to prepare and serve a meal, subsequently clean up the table, mingle with guests, hug and kiss a friend, perform rescues, conduct surgeries, engage in sports competitions, and do a myriad of other tasks just as if we were there.

And as a result of the fifty percent deflation rate that is inherent in all information technologies, this capability will ultimately be inexpensive and ubiquitous. Consider that your smartphone is literally a trillion dollars of computation and communication, circa 1965, yet it costs only a few hundred dollars today and there are now two billion of them in the world.

The stories in this outstanding and highly imaginative volume bring these diverse scenarios to life. In Kevin J. Anderson's "The Next Best Thing to Being There," a robotic sherpa guides climbers on Mount Rainier, which illustrates one important application of robotic avatar technology, which is bringing remote expertise to challenging environments. Francesca, the wife of one of the climbers, is experiencing the climb virtually through the sherpa avatar and shares the shock of the actual participants when an avalanche suddenly strikes. As the ensuing crisis develops, the avatar takes on a different role, which is as a remote physician attending to the injured climbers, and directed by doctors far away.

We already see doctors performing virtual surgery using avatar technology. For example, a human doctor remotely doing eye surgery by entering a virtual environment in which the patient's eye becomes as big as a beach ball, thereby enabling the intricate surgical maneuvers required. Surgeries can now be performed by doctors who may be thousands of miles away, allowing medical expertise to be instantly transported to remote areas where medical services are scant.

In Tina Gower's "The Waiting Room," a woman whose physical body has failed her is able to explore the world and seek a relationship with her children by using an avatar that represents her in a physical reality that she would otherwise not be able to navigate with her physical body. Not only does the protagonist of the story successfully transfer her consciousness to her avatar, but we the reader do so as well. We readily accept her avatar as being the heroine. The story brings up the issue of what we should do with our physical bodies as we spend more and more of our time in the future inhabiting avatars in both virtual and real reality.

This then is where we are headed: a future that integrates real spaces with virtual and augmented realities, and a world in which I can effortlessly transfer my consciousness and experiences to an avatar that represents me. This will ultimately be so realistic that I will find myself reminding my friends and colleagues that *I am an avatar.*

THE NEXT BEST THING TO BEING THERE

KEVIN J. ANDERSON

THE NEXT BEST THING TO BEING THERE

BY KEVIN J. ANDERSON

The immersive view of the rugged mountainside vanished as a white wave of snow and ice swept over them, experienced real time by thousands of spectator-participants worldwide—armchair mountaineers, tourists, schoolchildren.

And Francesca.

The avatar tumbled, rolled, slid with sickening disorientation through the kinesthetic sensors. The optics became a whirlwind of pummeling snow; sensor touches conveyed the pounding pressure before the governing software dampened the input; haptics added a vertigo of falling.

"What happened?" Francesca cried. "What the hell happened?"

Her two young daughters were screaming next to her in the soft chairs of the control lounge. The media representatives connected to the SHERPA avatar flailed their hands against the unexpected avalanche that had struck the climbers on Mount Rainier.

In a separate room, some of the reporters tore off their interface sets, but Francesca maintained her telepresence connection as the rolling roar slowly ground to a halt. The SHERPA synthetic used its reactive software to stop its fall and anchor its polymer body in the sliding ice and snow.

Once stabilized, SHERPA scrubbed powdered snow away to clear its field of view, then used autonomous systems to dig itself free. Francesca experienced every moment through her passive interface, as well as the biting cold on her skin, the pressing weight of the snow.

Under a brilliant blue sky, she could see the breathtaking expanse of the glaciated volcano, the dazzling ice field, the gray rock jutting out of the white sea. Tens of thousands of virtual spectators experienced the same thing. The bright sun, uncommon for the Pacific Northwest, had made for spectacular visuals and a perfect ascent of the mountain, but several days of warmth might have melted just enough snow to make the ice field near Disappointment Cleaver unstable for the crossing.

Dr. Carlos Kingman, the program director, was shouting, and Francesca experienced a disorienting duality—hearing his panic next to her in the control lounge, while her real focus remained high above 13,000 feet. In a subwindow in the upper left corner of her field of view, she saw Kingman run to the summary screens.

"Full assessment—now." He whirled, his deep brown eyes wild, his coffee-colored skin darkening with urgency. He yelled to his techs: "Use the disconnects, interrupt the educational feed. We don't want the schoolchildren to see this."

The participating reporters in the secondary lounge were already uploading commentary filled with questions and speculations, even though they knew nothing. Kingman knew nothing. Francesca knew nothing.

Dizzy and stunned from experiencing the avalanche, she gathered up the two young girls, wrapping her arms around Tanya and Tammy. A separate part of her experienced the avatar climbing out of the fallen snow, recalibrating itself and getting its bearings.

She was too confused in the first minute to understand the implications, but then the realization plunged down like a different kind of avalanche. She peeled off the optic interface and stared at Kingman. She had seen no sign of her husband or the mountain guide accompanying the robotic avatar. "What about Stephen? And James?"

She glanced at James Tobler's slender wife Nouri, who sat in another lounge chair, her knees drawn up to her chest, huddled in shock. Nouri still hadn't figured it out.

Francesca raised her voice. *"What about Stephen?"*

Mount Rainier in Washington State, 14,411 feet high, had always been a bucket list item for her husband Stephen. He was outdoorsy and fit, though he had put on a little weight since the birth of their daughters.

Francesca and Stephen had met through a common love of hiking. Living in Colorado, they had set out to complete all five hundred miles of the Colorado Trail, which they did. Together, they climbed all 58 of the 14,000-foot peaks in Colorado—the Fourteeners. As a young couple, fully in love, they supported each other, learned skills together and ticked the peaks off their list, one by one. Stephen had even dropped to his knee and proposed to her on the summit of Mount Sneffels.

They were both schoolteachers, a career choice with the added advantage of summers off—hiking season, mountain climbing season. After Tanya was born, though, Francesca retired from her teaching duties, while Stephen was promoted to vice principal; the resulting raise allowed her to watch their daughter, and then, a year later, Tammy as well.

They had done so much before they started a family, but

Stephen occasionally dreamed of climbing either Everest or Kilimanjaro—admittedly unrealistic goals—as well as Mount Rainier, also difficult, but much more accessible. He and Francesca both knew it wasn't likely to happen.

Then last year, during a backyard barbecue with a few neighbors, Stephen had waxed poetic about mountain climbing in general and Mount Rainier in particular. Their neighbor, Carlos Kingman, had been intrigued with the conversation.

While Francesca rounded up the girls and let them play an inept but entertaining game of croquet in the backyard, Kingman lounged back in a lawn chair and looked at Stephen. "I bet there are countless people who would love to make the climb, but simply can't arrange the trip, or who aren't physically capable. What if you could do it?" Kingman raised his eyebrows. "What if you had the chance to climb Rainier, and tens of thousands of others could join you for the experience?"

"Sounds like an awfully crowded trail," Stephen joked.

"I meant figuratively. What would it take for you to do the climb?"

"Other than getting in better shape?" Stephen cocked an eyebrow. "There'd be a lot of logistics planning, and I'd need the time off from school. It's typically a three-day expedition, led by a professional guide. Even from the highest trailhead, the ascent is still nine thousand feet—a lot harder than any Fourteener in Colorado." He sipped his beer with a wry expression. "Believe me, I've looked at all the details. I've dreamed. I've tried to make it happen. But ... family obligations, you know."

Kingman wore a secretive smile. "I think there's a way we could make it happen, with the full support of your school. It would be an educational opportunity you could share with the world, and I'll have the funding. It would be a pilot project, a great demonstration of the Avatar work—a surrogate experience for students all around the world, and an opportunity for as many frustrated mountaineers who would like to subscribe." He began talking faster. "We have a brand new telepresence unit that would be perfect for this use."

As she gathered up the croquet balls and made sure the girls didn't accidentally hit each other with the mallets, Francesca could tell that Stephen was excited by the idea. He tried to cover it up with skepticism. "Using an avatar? You mean, people would sit at home and experience a real, gritty mountain climb without having to lift a muscle?"

"That would be for the subscriber base of spectator-participants," Kingman said. "But somebody actually has to do it. You and a guide would accompany the avatar. Schoolchildren and paid participants would be connected via the SHERPA synthetic and experience everything you do." He grinned.

"SHERPA? Is that an acronym for something?"

"Of course it is," Kingman said with a chuckle, "but don't ask me what the letters stand for. Somebody was being cute." He set his own beer aside and stood from the lawn chair. "This would be a wonderful opportunity to show off the remote educational capabilities as well as the virtual tourism aspects the technology offers."

In the dozen years since the awarding of the Avatar XPRIZE —a bold initiative that encouraged the development of remote operation and experience via sensory technology—various "avatars" had blossomed throughout the industrial, creative, medical, and service worlds. The rapid development and widespread uses were far beyond what had been envisioned by Dr. Harry Kloor, the instigator and lead of the XPRIZE. Now, in 2036, avatars in all their forms were penetrating everyday life. Francesca had been aware of Dr. Kingman's engineering work, but had not thought much about it. Neither had Stephen, but he was obviously intrigued with this new idea.

SHERPA was a sophisticated unit that would do more than

just carry their packs and supplies; the robot was also a climbing partner that allowed Francesca and their daughters to virtually ride along. The plans came together smoothly, generating a great deal of media excitement.

Their experienced guide up Rainier, James Tobler, had summited the mountain more than fifty times. After a year of planning, Stephen and the robot set off from the Paradise trailhead on the first day, starting at an elevation of 5,000 feet in the thick forest. Guided by James, they headed across the Muir snowfield to the Muir Camp hut at 10,000 feet.

Classes tapped in, with thousands of students virtually participating in the climb; Stephen paused to give lectures, turning to face the avatar so he could explain geology, climate, or weather patterns on the mountain. Nearly 40,000 paid spectators worldwide also subscribed, paying a fee to vicariously experience the climb of Mount Rainier.

After a brief sleep in the cold Muir hut, they headed out at midnight under a full moon, ascending the glaciers. Thanks to the specialized permits Kingman had obtained for this project, their group had the normally crowded trail to themselves. James, Stephen, and SHERPA had reached the high point of Columbia Crest just in time for a breathtaking sunrise—all alone on the mountaintop, but silently accompanied by countless spectators and virtual companions, as well as Francesca and the two girls.

It had been glorious. Francesca had reached out, briefly allowed to use SHERPA's interactive interface. With the avatar's haptic sensors, she could take Stephen's hand and share in his victory from the summit.

Kingman had been delighted at the demonstration of SHERPA's abilities. A complete success, showcasing beneficial aspects of innovative avatar technologies inspired by the XPRIZE competition. The control lounge was filled with shouting celebrations.

But on the descent, while the three traversed the ice field near Disappointment Cleaver, disaster struck ... while the whole world watched, and participated.

As SHERPA oriented itself in the broken snow, recovering its bearings on dangerous ground, Francesca remained connected, desperate to help, but she experienced it only as an observer. The two girls were terrified. Tanya was trying to comfort her little sister.

As Kingman barked orders, his staff jacked into the active interfaces. "How much damage did the avatar suffer? Did we lose any physical integrity? Is the first aid suite intact?" He ran to the external readout deck, calling up screens, staring at diagnostics. "I need remote emergency physicians, now! Bring in our team of active medical responders."

"We have to find the two men first, sir."

"Then find them!"

Still listening to the diminishing rumble and slide of displaced ice chunks, Francesca asked, "What can I do to help? How can I pitch in?"

Kingman was hyperfocused. "We're still assessing. We don't know what's happening yet."

Francesca was desperate to do something, but she was too far away. She was just a former teacher, former hiker, and now, a mother. Unwilling to interfere with the avatar team in the crisis, she withdrew to the background. She watched through the optical sensors as SHERPA searched for the two men in the avalanche field.

"Cycle through wavelengths," Kingman said. "We've got to find them. If they're buried under the snow, we have only a few minutes. We know exactly where they were—run a back projection."

James Tobler's wife Nouri shook herself and stood from her own seat. "Where's James? They're buried!"

Francesca spoke aloud to the room, even though her eyes saw the silent, bright ice field and the gray comb of rock. "Is Search and Rescue on the way?"

"Full teams from Paradise Base Camp are heading up on foot."

She knew how many miles that was. "They'll take most of a day!"

"The weather's good. We are also trying to launch helicopters. Rescue teams should be able to drop down on ropes— if we can find Stephen and James on the snowfield."

Francesca watched through artificial eyes as SHERPA cycled through the spectrum, using various E-M windows to search for the two men who had been tossed about on a wave of ice and snow. They would leave a significant thermal trace with their body heat, unless they were buried too deep.

SHERPA scrambled through the loose, cold rubble, scanning along the obvious avalanche path, looking up the slope to where the climbers had been. The avatar projected their drop path based on their precise last-known positions. The technicians jabbered, going over rough calculations.

Francesca felt adrift in the middle of the activity, but she kept looking, then spotted a bright smear in the garish infrared imaging. "Look, over there!" In her mind and ears, she heard countless other participants also identifying the heat signature—a human-shaped lump buried only a few feet beneath the fresh blanket of snow.

SHERPA bounded over on artificial hands and legs, extruding traction crampons. The robot was designed for agility on rough terrain, and during the climb from Paradise and across the glaciers to the summit, it had learned and adapted to the terrain. Now, the avatar raced toward the thermal image. Digging furiously, it used polymer hands to scoop and shove the snow, exposing the head and shoulders of one of the men.

Nouri let out a sudden cry from her chair and, through the optical sensors, Francesca saw that it was James Tobler. The man wasn't moving, and his head was bloody. Moving gingerly, SHERPA cleared away more debris to free the fallen guide and stabilize him on the uncertain slope.

"Get the emergency surgeons jacked in!" Kingman said. "Use the medical sensor suite to check him out. Is he still breathing?"

"He's still breathing," one of the techs said. "Getting vitals now."

Francesca felt the control shift in the avatar body as medical teams took over the manipulation. She watched its robotic arms move, detected sensors activating, first aid apparatus locking into place from embedded channels in the robotic arms.

SHERPA rapidly pushed through layers of clothing to assess cardiac activity. Simultaneously, the avatar detected breathing with no atypical sounds or gurgling. Airway, check. Breathing, check. The full electrocardiogram revealed no arrhythmias. With one polymer articulated hand, it pulled open James's eyelids to assess the pupillary response.

In the background audio track, one of the physicians announced, "Both pupils are equal and responsive. If there were stroke or bleed, they'd be different, or they wouldn't constrict. Brisk—they look good. Good chance there's just a concussion. What's the blood pressure?"

The remote doctors used the avatar's embedded equipment to inflate securing pillows that stabilized his neck, packing quik-clot on the superficial scalp bleed. SHERPA held its hand just above James's elbow and remained completely still for an eternity of 30 seconds, detecting the sound of the blood flowing as the robot gradually released its hold on the elbow and assessed blood pressure.

"Blood pressure is low, but in the normal range," the remote physician announced. "Doesn't seem like he's lost much blood."

Francesca was glad to see the guide cared for, but she longed to take control of the avatar and keep searching for Stephen along the avalanche path. He was buried out there somewhere.

Though she remained immersed in the connection, Francesca felt the warmth of a body, two bodies next to her. Her daughters were curled up beside her in the wide, comfortable experiential chair.

"Where's Daddy?" Tammy asked. "Is he going to be all right?"

Despite the other connections through SHERPA, Francesca used real nerves and skin, a true sense of touch with her daughters, not through any haptic interface. She pulled the girls close and hugged them. "I hope so."

Kingman touched his ear, listened. "Helicopters are ready to launch soon. We'll have them on scene as quickly as possible."

"Will it be fast enough?" Nouri Tobler asked in a rough voice. "Will James survive?"

The physicians took full control, worked to stop the bleeding from the head injury, ran a final check. "He has the best possible chance," Kingman said.

"But where's Stephen?" Francesca still attempted to look through the corner of her eyes, SHERPA's eyes. The optical sensors scanned, and at the periphery she saw another thermal image. "Off to the left. Up on the slope near those three exposed rocks."

SHERPA's head swiveled, and all spectators could see the smear of body warmth, and more than that—movement. It was Stephen, clawing free of the snow that had buried him. "He's alive!" she cried, then squeezed the two girls curled up against her. "Daddy's alive."

Stephen got his head and shoulders free. "Over here," he gasped, his voice weak.

"We have to get to him." Francesca struggled to move inside the avatar body, but hers was only a passive interface. The physicians had taken full control tending to James.

"If your husband is moving, that's a good sign," Kingman said.

Francesca longed to scramble across the ice field and pull Stephen out of the cold, smothering embrace. She would use the robot's body, the artificial limbs, the haptic sensors, to wrap her arms around Stephen and hold him—use the robot's waste heat to keep him alive.

Stephen pulled himself farther out of the snow, propping himself up. He brushed ice chips away and coughed. Francesca recoiled to see blood splashing out of his side, a bright red stain on the freshly exposed white snow.

SHERPA's optical sensors swiveled back to the still-unconscious form of James. Inside the link, the coordinating surgeon said, "That's good for now. Let's go check the other patient."

After ensuring that James was stretched out and in a place where he wouldn't slip down a slope even if he moved or rolled, SHERPA covered him with a thin thermal film to keep him warm. Then the avatar dug polymer hands and feet into the loose snow to make a cautious ascending traverse across the field to where Stephen struggled to extricate himself.

Suddenly, large chunks of frozen debris slid out from under Stephen's hips and he began to slide down the slope. He yelled, and Francesca yelled with him. He reached out his gloved hands, flailing, trying to slow his fall. He left more blood on the snow.

The avatar shifted its approach to intercept Stephen, working itself downward and across as snow slid under its textured feet. Stephen spread himself out, increasing his surface area, halting his fall. Finally, the unstable snow chunks caught on a rock ledge, and he came to a stop. He groaned in pain.

SHERPA picked and climbed its way over to him. From where he sat slumped on the ledge, Stephen looked gray, and his face was slack. He panted hard. He managed to sit, then pulled on the rock, trying to drag himself upright, but the effort was too much for him.

Through the eyes of the avatar, Francesca saw a wide maroon patch on his clothing, wet, soaked with blood from an injury in his left mid-torso. A large wicked shard of ice had pierced him like a crystalline spearpoint.

Breathing fast and ragged, Stephen reached out to grip the avatar's body. "I'm here. I'm okay."

"Help him!" Francesca shouted into the passive link.

The medical team took over, assuming full fine control of the medical suite in the artificial body. They scanned Stephen's vitals, assessed his injuries. "We can't remove the ice shard. Pack gauze around it so we can apply pressure."

"Traumatic injury, upper quadrant."

The doctors had been reporting through the speakers in SHERPA's plastic face, but Francesca said, "Let me talk to him."

Kingman nodded, gestured to one of his techs. Her audio link became active. "Stephen—it's Francesca! I'm here."

"You're very far away." He sounded disoriented.

"Not as far as you might think. It's the next best thing to being there." She reached out, used SHERPA's polymer hand to clasp her husband's arm. "Hold on. Helicopters are on their way, a full rescue crew. It won't be long."

"I'm fine," he said. "I hate to have the whole world watching this. Don't want to go down in history ... as a klutz."

"Sorry, but we have to do our work," one of the physicians cut in over her private audio interface. "We need control back."

She said quickly, "I'm here, Stephen. The doctors have to take over now, but I'm watching. I'm with you."

"Yeah, a doctor would be a good idea." He forced a wheezing laugh. The spreading bloodstain in his side was growing ominously larger around the gauze and the ice shard.

Francesca retreated into the avatar's background as the surgeons took over. She had always been an active person, wanting to participate. She had climbed so many mountains with Stephen, summiting one Fourteener after another. Once, alone on the top of Mount Lindsey after a grueling hike, with the Sangre de Cristo range all around them, they had decided to make love in the rocky windbreak shelter. What could be more romantic? But they had been so sweaty and so exhausted, the experience had left much to be desired. They spent more time gasping for breath than gasping with pleasure.

Once the girls were born, Francesca had become a mother instead of a mountain climber, caretaker and teacher of her own daughters instead of classrooms of students. She had been happy with her life and with herself. She had been proud of Stephen.

But they both jumped at this chance Kingman's avatar program offered. Stephen could at last climb Mount Rainier, and she could be with him—and Tanya and Tammy had climbed the mountain, too. Connected through SHERPA, they had all stood on top that morning, surrounded by rocks and the sweeping plunge of the crater, the vast fields of the mountain's multiple glaciers.

As the sun rose on the top of the world, Stephen and James had thrown their arms up, howling into the thin air with excitement, and all those many thousands of spectators and participants linked in through the avatar connection did the same as SHERPA raised its synthetic arms.

The Rainier summit was the highest high ... swept away only hours later in a roar and sweep of falling snow.

"Is ... James all right?" Stephen gasped to the avatar as the remote physicians poked and prodded at his wound, muttering amongst themselves as to how best to treat the injury. He slumped back to a sitting position against the rough volcanic rock. "I'm dizzy ... but I can help. With SHERPA I can work my way over to him." He pressed a hand against his stomach.

The emergency physicians were using the avatar's full capabilities. They had a backchatter on their own channel, but Kingman allowed Francesca and Nouri to listen in. One of the doctors spoke through SHERPA. "You need to stay put. Mr. Tobler has a concussion, but he is stabilized. We're more concerned about you now."

"I'm better off than he is," Stephen insisted. "Francesca, are you still there?"

"I'm here. And so are the girls. The helicopters are on their way. They'll be there soon."

Kingman signaled to her in the external real-world window in a corner of her field of view. "Two hours," he mouthed.

"They'll be there in an hour, Stephen. Just hold on."

He made a weak sound. "I'll hold on." The remote physicians tried to hold him down and keep him still. Their backchatter became ominously quiet.

Francesca continued, "Just relax. Let them tend you." She could feel Tanya and Tammy snuggling next to her, as if they could get closer to their distant father that way.

Kingman touched her shoulder and signaled for her to drop out of the immersive link. As she came out, disoriented to find herself in the mundane control lounge, his grave expression made her feel sick. "What's the matter? Everything's all right now. We've got them."

"I won't lie to you," Kingman said. "It's far worse than it looks. I ... I want you to know."

"But Stephen's conscious. He's talking. He wants to go help James."

The lead scientist swallowed hard. He looked at her, looked away, then with a visible effort turned back to her. "The ice shard, that wound in his side—he has traumatic internal injuries. The physicians think it's a splenic laceration, but it may have hit the aorta, and there's no way to block it off. He's got so much adrenaline he may not feel pain, but he's bleeding a lot." Kingman swallowed again. "In fact, his systolic blood pressure has dropped 20 since the first reading, in only a few minutes. That's a strong indicator he may be bleeding out. SHERPA's sensors and diagnostics are quite sophisticated, but the medical suite can't stop internal hemorrhaging on that scale."

Francesca felt cold, couldn't formulate a question. Finally, she said, "But you have the very best telepresence doctors. Bring in any specialist to link up to the avatar. They can be right there."

"We have access to the world's best expertise, but he's out on a snowfield. In order to have a hope of saving him, the surgical environment is ... is just not there. Best case, the helicopters couldn't get him to a real hospital in under two hours." The man shook his head. "Maybe the doctors are misinterpreting the signs, but if the internal injury is what we suspect, it ... it may be fast."

Her world collapsed and broke apart. "How long?"

Kingman just looked at her. "Our experts might be wrong, but prepare yourself. SHERPA has administered epinephrine, but the blood pressure isn't responding. The remote medics have done everything they possibly can."

"No, I don't accept that!" she said. "He's right there!" That's when the girls started crying, but she wasn't sure whether either of them understood what was going on. Her voice hitched, and she struggled to be strong. "Can I talk to him?"

Kingman drew a breath. "I can do more than that. I can let

you be with him, through the avatar. SHERPA will project your face, your voice. With haptic sensors, you can hold him."

Francesca felt cold, a layer of ice around her growing panic. "What about our daughters?"

Kingman didn't hesitate. "They can be there, too. We've deactivated the public connection, and no one else is watching him right now except for the doctors and you. The media is clamoring."

"I don't want reporters with my husband as he dies," she snapped.

"No, it'll just be you. You, and Tammy and Tanya."

Tears streamed from her eyes. "Let's hook up the girls again. We don't have much time."

Tanya and Tammy crowded next to her on the padded seat while a technician hurriedly reapplied the contact web to the girls. Kingman said, "I'm going to drop you into avatar mode again. The physicians will back off."

Francesca braced herself, thought about the summits she and Stephen had achieved, the high points of their lives—and not just on mountains. She thought of the open air, the expansive views, the exhilaration of endorphins, the fresh sense of accomplishment. Now she was so far away ... but through the haptic sensors she could feel him so close. SHERPA's hands were her hands, and she was with Stephen again.

"Something isn't ... right," Stephen said. He seemed very dizzy and disoriented, lightheaded. "I'm hurt bad, aren't I?"

She wouldn't lie. "I'm sorry."

"I thought so. Helicopters coming?"

"They're on the way right now."

When Stephen looked up at her, his expression fell. Through the projected overlay image on the avatar's face, he could read her real thoughts. "Won't get here in time."

"There's always a chance, Stephen! Always a chance."

"I see your face. After all these years ... I can read you."

He would not have wanted her to sugarcoat the situation. With so little time left, he deserved to know, to face his fate, to be with them. "They think you have severe internal bleeding."

"I feel ... loopy."

She squeezed, and SHERPA's hand clasped his arm. "I wish you were here," he said.

"Actually, I wish you were *here*. Just one of the armchair mountaineers letting someone else take the risk." Her voice cracked.

"I like to do things for myself." He spoke slowly, as if each word were a heavy weight to be lifted out of his mouth. "Is everyone else watching, too?"

"No, just us ... and the girls. Tanya and Tammy are holding you along with me. Can you feel this?" She squeezed again. "They have the touch sensors, too. We're all here."

"Good, I'll take that. Better than dying alone on a mountainside."

"You're not alone. We're here." Francesca leaned forward in the control lounge chair, and SHERPA's arms extended on the ice slope, embracing Stephen, wrapping around him and holding him. She could feel his solidity, feel his touch. Through the avatar's haptic sensors, they were right beside him. The girls felt the same thing.

Francesca was shuddering and trembling as she stifled her sobs so Stephen wouldn't notice. "I love you." He grew quieter, but he was smiling, comforted to have them next to him.

Francesca held him. His daughters held him. With a simple adjustment, the whole world could hold him in his last moments, but for now she had him to herself. They were there for him, and Stephen went quietly under the cold, bright sky after summiting a mountaintop he had always wanted to do—with his family.

In the control lounge, the three remained connected to SHERPA long after he was gone. It wasn't until the audio pickups brought her the sound of approaching helicopters in the high, thin air did she relinquish control so the telepresence physicians and the Search and Rescue teams could save James.

They would also bring Stephen's body back to her, but through the avatar she already had an experience that was far more meaningful, far more precious to her, and she held onto that, even as she let go of her husband.

COACH

BY MIKE RESNICK

COACH

BY MIKE RESNICK

When one of your oldest friends invites you to watch a football game with him, it's usually a very pleasant gesture. But when he's Howard McKeever and he owns the Impalas and he's offering to share his private, enclosed, air-conditioned booth with you, you don't even think twice, you just mutter the equivalent of "Yes, please!" and make sure you show up in the right place at the right time.

"Hi, George," he greeted me when I arrived ten minutes before the opening kickoff on game day. "Been a long time."

"Six years," I replied. "You're looking good."

"I'd look even better if these bastards would start earning their salaries," he said. "Second highest payroll in the league, and we're three-and-seven." He snorted in frustration. "Go figure." Suddenly he noticed a KR233 robot standing in the doorway. "That yours?"

"No, not really," I said. "It belongs to the stadium, my son-in-law is avataring into it at the moment."

"Big Nick Kurumbu?" he said. "Yeah, I heard about that. Kid's got my sympathy. How long's it been?"

"A little over two years. He was driving home from practice

his senior year, and some drunk jumped the center strip and collided with him."

"It's a real shame," said Howard. "Two-time All-American. Hell, I was hoping he'd play for the Impalas when he got out of college."

I sighed and shook my head. "He's not playing for anyone from the neck down, not now, not ever."

"I wish you'd stop talking about me as if I wasn't here," said KR233.

"You're *not* here," said Howard. "Your robot is."

"My avatar," said KR233. "We've got a brain-machine inter-face, so I have complete control of this baby."

"Robot, avatar, same damned thing," said Howard.

"Not really. In fact, if it'll make you feel more at ease, call me Nick. After all, that's who you're talking to."

Howard stared at KR233 for a long minute, then shrugged. "Have it your way. I'll be damned if I'm going to argue with a robot." He held up a hand. "Yeah, I know—an avatar." He turned to me. "So, what's Metal Nick"—he jerked a thumb in the avatar's direction—"doing here?"

"The Impalas aren't on TV," said KR233, "so I'm joining you via my avatar body."

"Yeah, we're blacked out," growled Howard. "We didn't sell out, so no local telecast." He stared at KR233. "Maybe I ought to have *you* playing fullback," he said. "I'll bet you don't go in for knee surgery the first time you're hit."

"Yeah, I read about that," I said.

Howard made a face. "A seventeen-million-dollar-a-year free agent, and he blows his knee out on the third play of the season opener." He shrugged. "What the hell. Bring Metal Nick into the booth. Leave him standing outside the door and you can bet someone will walk off with him."

I turned to KR233. "Come on in," I said. Then, to Howard: "He won't be a distraction. He'll just stand or sit, whichever you prefer, and not bother us. He's just here to watch the game with me."

"Once we're down a score or two, which usually takes all of ten minutes, I could use a little humor up here," said Howard. "Can the robot tell jokes?"

"*He* can't do anything," I said. "But Nick can tell jokes."

"Especially if you like dirty ones," added KR233.

Howard turned back to the field. "Damn, those Archdukes have great uniforms. I've got to talk to our board about that. If we can't thrill 'em with touchdowns, we should at least be able to please 'em with our uniforms. There's nothing *distinctive* about them. I mean, take one look at the Rams' or the Bengals' helmets and you know what team they belong to."

He pressed a buzzer for a steward, for all I knew the only one in the whole stadium, and ordered a whiskey sour. "You want anything, George?"

"I'll have a beer, thanks," I responded.

"And I assume Metal Man doesn't drink."

"Actually, this unit has full taste receptors," said KR233. Or, to be more accurate, said Nick through KR233. He smiled through his avatar. "I'll have a single malt, on the rocks."

"Great," said Howard. "Just what we need up here, a drunk robot." He looked down at the field. "About time," he muttered as the teams lined up for the kickoff. The Archdukes' kicker drove the ball into the end zone, and the Impala receiver caught it.

"Take a knee!" muttered KR233.

But instead of kneeling down and having possession start on the 20-yard line, the receiver elected to run the kickoff back. He got all the way up to the 12-yard line before he was tackled.

"Dumb," said Howard and KR233 simultaneously.

The first play from scrimmage was a pass that the defensive back batted down.

"Stupid play," said KR233.

"Nothing stupid about it," I said. "Just a forward pass that didn't work."

"The refs should never have allowed it," said KR233.

I frowned. "Why the hell not? Since when have forward passes been illegal?"

"The left defensive tackle jumped across the line before the ball was snapped, and the refs should have blown their whistles."

"Are you sure of that?" demanded Howard.

"I could have you relive my entire experience if you wanted me to send you my avatar experience of the game, but here, this is faster."

KR233 turned to the one solid wall in the glass-enclosed room, his left eye became a projector, and he cast the play up onto the wall—and sure enough, the Archdukes' left tackle was moving across the line a fraction of a second before the ball was snapped.

"Son of a bitch!" snapped Howard. "It's bad enough that none of these milquetoast millionaires can run or hit! Do the goddamned referees have to be against us too?"

The next play was a handoff to the fullback, who ran right up the middle for a gain of three yards.

"Damn!" snapped Howard.

"Jim Brown he isn't," I said with a smile.

"Then why do I have to pay him as if he is?" said Howard.

I knew my son-in-law Nick, and I was sure he wanted to lecture Howard as to why salaries had skyrocketed in the century since Jim Brown had played football. I put my finger to my lips in the hope that he'd see it before he spoke, and was much relieved when he had the avatar turn back to continue watching the game.

They sacked our quarterback on the third play, and the Impalas had to punt. The Archdukes got possession on their

40-yard line, ran off half a dozen plays, and settled for a field goal.

Howard checked the scoreboard—not the score, but the official clock. "Well, we made it almost five minutes before falling behind," he said bitterly. "That's better than usual."

The Archdukes kicked off, and this time the ball sailed out of the end zone so the returner *couldn't* make the same dumb mistake he'd made on the game's opening play.

The Impalas went into their huddle, then lined up with the quarterback in T-formation, hunched over the center.

"Not smart," said KR233.

"What are you talking about?" I asked.

"The nose tackle is six foot nine or ten," replied KR233, "and the quarterback is giving away eight inches, possibly nine. He'll have about one second, one and a half tops, to find his target before the nose tackle's head, shoulders and arms obscure his vision. He should be standing about five yards behind the center so that he has time to spot his target and find a secondary receiver if the primary one is covered."

And sure enough, the quarterback took the snap from center and was sacked before he could spot his target.

"Anything you want to tell us about the next play?" I asked.

"They'll be expecting a run, of course," said KR233—actually, it was Nick who was speaking, not KR233, but I don't know an easy way to say his voice was coming out of the avatar's mouth—"since the passing game has been totally ineffective." He paused. "The offensive line has been ineffective as well, so the choice is obvious."

"Not to me, it isn't," said Howard.

"Go into the T-formation," said KR233. "The quarterback takes the snap and backs up quickly. The offensive tackles hit their men just once, enough to buy the quarterback an extra second, and as the defense is converging on him and all the downfield receivers are covered, he throws a short pass, behind the line of scrimmage, to his running back."

"They'll see the running back isn't blocking and will stick a man on him to cover him," I said, disagreeing with him.

KR233 shook his head. "The running back will be giving up about one hundred pounds to any defensive lineman. They'll expect him to move out of the way rather than risk injury trying to block someone who's all muscle and almost twice his size."

As he was explaining it, the Impalas tried a handoff to their halfback and gained less than a yard.

"Learn how to block, goddammit!" yelled Howard at the top of his lungs. I know the booth was supposed to be airtight, but I couldn't believe some nearby fans didn't hear him. (In fact, I had a hard time believing that his shout couldn't shatter glass.)

The Impalas punted it away again, and the Archdukes took possession at midfield.

"Stupid," muttered KR233 when both teams lined up.

"What's stupid this time?" I asked.

"Let them finish this play first," said KR233. "The way they're playing they'll be stupid again next play. You can bet the farm on it."

The Archdukes ran for three yards, where the huge Impala left guard nailed the runner and damned near took his head off.

"Okay," I said, when the Archdukes went back into their huddle. "They held him to a three-yard gain. What's so stupid about that?"

"Number 67"—the Impalas' huge left guard—"keeps lining up just a foot or two to the left of the Archdukes' center. There's no rule that says you can't have an unbalanced line of scrimmage, that both the Archdukes' guards or both tackles can't move to the same side of the center." KR233 paused for a moment. "And if they don't present an unbalanced line, number 67 alone will deny them the middle of the field all day long."

They tried another run, to the side of the line opposite where Number 67 was charging, and gained a couple of yards. They then completed a 12-yard pass on third down, which bought them a new set of downs. When they lined up this time, number 67 found himself facing an unbalanced line.

"*They* can learn from their mistakes," complained Howard. "Why the hell can't *we*?"

The unbalanced line provided the necessary protection, and the Archdukes ran off tackle for 14 yards and another first down.

If an avatar could look smug, it would. So it did, its face exactly mimicked every facial expression Nick was making back home a thousand miles away. It was also delivering perfectly every hand gesture and body motion Nick imagined in his mind, even though his human body back home was fully paralyzed. His mind interface made this body a fully articulated one for him.

Howard turned to me. "Wanna buy a team—cheap?"

I smiled. "How many hundreds of millions of dollars is cheap?"

"Less than it was this morning," he said bitterly. "Maybe I *will* put your robot into the game in the second half. He can't be any easier to catch and tackle than the running backs I've already got."

"I rather suspect it's against the rules of the game," I said. "And I'm sure it's against whatever rules govern avatars when they come off the assembly line."

"Actually the avatar laws allow us to do anything we want with an avatar body, but the league has yet to catch up with the times. Otherwise, I would be out on the field right now," confirmed KR233.

"What the hell *do* you guys do anyway?" asked Howard,

groaning as the Archdukes ran the ball inside the Impalas' ten-yard line. "What's more important than winning a football game before 60,000 impassioned fans who shelled out good money to watch them?"

"Avatars can do anything the people running them can do. A surgeon's avatar can perform microsurgery, an artist's avatar can create an oil painting, a handyman's can fix a broken furnace," replied KR233. "There are limits to what they can do, of course, but for the most part those limits are defined by what the human directing the avatar can do. As I said, if his human counterpart is a painter, an avatar can create an oil painting—but he can't create a Mona Lisa." He paused. "An avatar can also give a normal life to a paraplegic. *That* I can vouch for."

"Enough," growled Howard. "I'm properly impressed. I read about you guys in the papers, and every now and then I see you acting as superheroes on video." He sighed deeply. "Now if you could just play quarterback, or maybe middle linebacker ..."

"You know," I said, "actually, if they change the rules to keep up with the times, Nick's avatar *could* play on either side of the ball. Of course, the league would have to install a limiter, so that it couldn't run any faster or hit any harder than Nick could before the accident."

"Too bad," replied Howard. He turned to KR233. "I'll bet you'd have enjoyed it."

"To get back on the field again?" replied the avatar, his metallic tone suddenly almost wistful. "Hell, I'd kill for that." A long pause. "But I'll settle for this. I have, for all practical purposes, my life back, I can act and feel through this body, just as if it was my own. I hate to think how people had to suffer before avatars were created, or before the brain/avatar interface that allowed them to use them."

"I'm sorry," said Howard. "I spoke without thinking."

"It's all right," said KR233. "I might wish otherwise, but things are what they are." He held his hand in front of his face and wiggled his fingers. "I know it sounds crazy, but I can actually *feel* through these fingers. They feel completely like my own, obeying my every thought and impulse. It's my real fingers that are dead to me. Through this body I am fully alive." A pause. "They tell me next year they will add smell receptors to go along with the taste ones."

"Make your lips a little softer than metal and you can even kiss a cheerleader," said Howard.

"I'm a married man," said KR233. "But when they learn to make 'em softer, I'm going to make up for lost time kissing my wife, and much much more."

(I crossed my fingers and hoped he was right.)

The crowd suddenly erupted in strenuous screams and boos, and we turned to look at the field, where the Archdukes were all celebrating and congratulating each other as the scoreboard proclaimed that the score was now 10 to 0.

"Still, you'd have made a helluva ballplayer," said Howard regretfully.

"I *was* a helluva ballplayer," said KR233, unable to keep the bitterness out of his mechanical voice. "Before the accident."

The Impalas ran the kickoff back to their own 28-yard line, actually got a couple of first downs, then had to punt. The Archdukes called for a fair catch, and took over possession on their own 20. The offense lined up, and the quarterback began calling the signals.

"He just changed plays," announced KR233.

"How do you know?" I asked.

"I can read his lips," replied KR233. "'Omaha, Boise, Pittsburgh, Tampa,'" he quoted. "Omaha is meaningless. He begins every call with Omaha. Boise means he's changing plays from the one he called in the huddle. Pittsburgh means it's a pass, and Tampa identifies the receiver."

And sure enough, it was a pass to the tight end.

"So what else can you tell us?" asked Howard.

"From now on," said KR233, "at least until he thinks the Impalas have figured it out, Tampa signifies the tight end."

"And you could see that from up here?" demanded Howard. "With no binoculars, no telescope, no nothing?"

"I can see using various enhancements that have been built into what you would call my eyes, yes," replied KR233.

"Could you get that information to the idiot head coach?" continued Howard.

"We're enclosed in a booth up here," replied KR233. "I suppose I could use hand signals, if he's got a clear view from the floor of the stadium. But if course, if he can see me, so can the opposing coach."

"Have we got a line from here to the bench?" asked Howard. Neither I nor the avatar knew, of course, so he opened the door and signaled to a security guard.

"No, not to the bench, sir, not directly," replied the guard. "But you can contact the offensive coordinator, who's three booths down from you, and have *him* contact the bench."

Howard shook his head. "No, it'd take too long."

"Too long for what, sir?"

"Never mind," said Howard, closing the door and facing me and the avatar. "We'd only have a second between you reading his lips and us adjusting our defense," he explained unhappily. "It'll take longer than that for you to pass the word to the coordinator, him to contact the sidelines, and then to get word to the men on the field."

"Too bad," I said with a shrug, because to me, unlike Howard and Nick and 60,000 fans in the stadium, football is not the be-all and end-all of my existence.

The rest of the first half went pretty much the way it had started. Nick kept talking to us through KR233, telling us what plays and formations had been called as opposed to which ones *should* have been called, which tricks—all of them legal—the opposing coaches and players were going to try, the kind of analysis you expect to hear in the locker room the morning *after* the game, not while it's still being played.

We were five minutes into halftime, and KR233 was explaining why certain plays which the Impalas hadn't tried yet would almost certainly work, when Howard held up his hand.

"Okay," he said. "I've heard enough."

KR233 immediately froze and fell silent.

"Is something wrong?" I asked.

"Of course something's wrong!" snapped Howard. He pointed to the scoreboard. "We're losing 24 to 3, for Christ's sake!"

"I hope you're not blaming Nick or the avatar," I said.

"Don't be a fool!"

Howard opened the door and summoned a security officer. "I want to see Bill Traynor, *now!*"

"*Coach* Traynor?" repeated the guard, surprised.

"You know any other Bill Traynor who's likely to be on the sidelines on a Sunday afternoon?" demanded Howard.

"No, sir," said the guard uneasily.

"Send two men down to get him, just in case he wants to spend halftime telling the team that he's got faith in them and 21 points is nothing to make up."

"Yes, sir," said the officer, saluting.

"That's not all," said Howard. "Tell our offensive coordinator to vacate the booth he's in and join the team down on the field for the second half."

"Yes, sir," repeated the officer, looking at Howard as if he'd gone a bit crazy, but saluting anyway.

"What's this all about?" I asked.

"You can't possibly be that stupid, George," he said. He turned to KR233. "Nick, KR, whichever the hell you are, before the start of the second half I want you to go three booths down from here, where the guard is telling the offensive coordinator to leave, and sit down wherever you have the best view of the field. The microphone you find there will connect you to the sidelines. I'm not sure who you'll be talking to yet, but you'll be calling all the offensive and defensive plays. Do you understand what I am saying to you?"

"Yes sir!" replied KR233. "Thank you! I'm very excited!"

"Robots don't get excited," said Howard.

"I am not a robot. I am—"

"I know, I know," said Howard wearily. He turned to me. "I don't want any misunderstanding or potential revolt on my hands, so I'm going down to the locker room to explain what's happening and to designate someone to talk to Nick and pass his calls on to the field."

He walked out the door, turned to his right, and was soon out of sight.

"This should be interesting," I said to KR233.

"Challenging, anyway."

I frowned in puzzlement. "Challenging?"

"The Impalas are down by 21 points with only 30 minutes left to play. I don't know if I can make them 22 points better than the Archdukes in that span of time."

"Too bad it's not like horse racing," I said. "We could make the better team carry lead weights in their shoulder pads."

He made no reply. We sat in silence for a few minutes, and finally I turned to him. "If you're concentrating on the second half and I'm distracting you ..."

"Not at all," he said. "I know what plays I'm going to start with, and I'll make adjustments as the other side does ... and if they make no adjustments I won't have to."

"You expect it to be that easy?"

"Like I said before, there is nothing easy about overcoming a 21-point deficit in 30 minutes. I'm going to be responsible for calling the right plays and formations. I am *not* responsible for executing them."

"That sounds just a bit egomaniacal," I said. "Meaning no offense."

"If a man with no feeling and no movement from the neck down can call the plays for a pro football team, isn't he allowed just a bit of egomania?"

"Certainly you are," I said. "And I apologize."

"No need to. It's easy to see *this* me"—he tapped his metal chest with his metal forefinger—"and forget who the *real* me actually is."

We sat in silence for a few more minutes, each with his own thoughts. Then Howard returned.

"Okay, move," he said to KR233. "The half starts in about three minutes."

My son-in-law the avatar stood up and walked out the door without a word.

"I hope to hell I haven't just flushed the franchise down the toilet," said Howard grimly.

"We'll know soon enough," I said as first the Archdukes and then the Impalas emerged from their dressing rooms and took the field.

"Here we go!" whispered Howard as the Impalas kicked off. "Keep 'em crossed!"

Well, you've all seen the papers by now. We intercepted two passes, caused and recovered three fumbles, and outscored the Archdukes 42-3 in the second half, winning the game 45-27. The crowd went crazy, tearing down the goalposts, lifting half a dozen Impalas onto their shoulders and marching them around the field, cheering wildly when Howard opened the booth's window and waved to them.

Finally, Howard summoned a guard.

"Get me that robot from three booths away!" he said excitedly.

KR233 was marched into our booth a moment later, and Howard threw his arms around the avatar's lean metal body.

"You're my head coach from this day on!" he bellowed enthusiastically.

"He's not yours," I pointed out gently.

"He will be!" said Howard. "I'm paying Traynor, that idiot he's replacing, eight million a year, and he's got five years left on a seven-year contract. If I can pay fifty-six million dollars for a loser, you can bet your ass I'll pay whatever your son-in-law is worth for a winner." He paused. "I know he can't move. The *real* him, I mean. Can he speak?"

"Only through the avatar," answered Nick.

"Then it's settled. I can't have a coach who can't communicate. Whatever they want for the damned machine, I'm buying it. If there's a better one on the market, I'll buy it for him." He turned to the avatar. "What do you say, Nick baby?"

"I'm thrilled and honored," was the answer.

"Okay," said Howard. "I'll let your father-in-law make all the arrangements for getting you a place near the stadium, and you tell us what you'll need in your office and the locker room, and within a week we'll supply it."

"I don't need anything. The avatar is my eyes, my ears, my mouth, my body. My participation will be the same whether I'm with my wife in our apartment or living alone ten states away."

Howard frowned. "Are you sure?"

"I—that's me, Nick, not KR233—am a thousand miles from the field right now as we're speaking," was the answer.

"Okay," said Howard. "One more thing."

"Yes?"

"I can't have every player calling you KR233. It sounds like a goddamned comic book, and it lacks respect. And no one remembers who Nick the All-American is—or was. So from this minute forward, your name is Coach."

"I *like* that name," said the avatar. (Excuse me. That should be "said the coach.")

THE WAITING ROOM

BY TINA GOWER

THE WAITING ROOM

BY TINA GOWER

I pace in a room. The "waiting room" the counselors call it. The couch is beige and it somehow matches the pink checkered wallpaper that lines the bottom third of the wall and kisses the dirt colored Berber carpet. On one end of the room is a mint green door where visitors enter and the other end is a white door that I've never opened. A blip in the television is the first hint at imperfection in the virtual room; a faint beeping in the dead space of silence another.

It's four in the afternoon, or at least that's what my brain tells me. My hands ache from the memory of sweeping the floor from Rylan's art projects gone astray. My mouth opens to remind Kelly to finish her homework. My stomach growls, a hint of early hunger. It's Tuesday, so the kids will be expecting burritos.

Except I'm not there, I'll never be there again, because of the biking accident. The virtual therapy to wake me from my comatose state is failing and all I can think about is if the kids are going to get burritos for dinner or if Michael, my husband, will get pizza again. Is Kelly finishing her homework? Is the house covered in the scrapings of art projects?

The light above the green door flashes, meaning I have a visitor. I open it expecting the counselor, but instead it's a new face. A woman with black hair pulled tightly in a bun and a grey suit—I wonder if this is what she's wearing in real time or how the hospital programmers want her to appear.

"Good evening, Ava, I'm Maria. I'm here to discuss your case," the woman says. Her voice is perfectly modulated, no hint of sympathy, just straight business. I wonder if she is a program and not a real human.

"Are they going to turn off the simulation?" I ask.

"No need to worry just yet. We're working on those details with your insurance company. I'm here to discuss your options."

"My *options* feel limited. I was unaware I had any options beyond waking up and now that it seems I'm not going to—"

"We can't predict when a patient will wake after a traumatic brain injury as extensive as yours."

A flicker of sadness crosses Maria's face before she wipes it away just as quickly. Perhaps she's not a robot.

"But the best outcome is in the first four weeks. The counselors—"

"—Are only spouting statistics and projections. Mrs. Dryer," Maria says and clears her throat. "I'm here to discuss quality of life. We have a number of programs for patients in your situation. Our hospital just received an X-games grant and we have three avatars specifically for this type of therapy."

"Avatars."

"Yes."

"So I'm to go about my daily life, take my children to school, feed them, all while my body is here in the hospital."

"Not exactly." There's a flicker of something across her face. Nothing terrible, but enough to nag at my mother instincts. "Your navigation will be limited. You won't be permitted to leave the grounds. The program is very new."

Her lips twitch at the end of her delivery. Maybe it's only that she knows this offering will disappoint me. Anything short of waking up in my own body in the next few minutes won't impress me.

"Then what's the point? Why can't we continue to meet with my family in the virtual reality waiting room?"

Maria paces the room, her fingers tapping her chin as if forming her next response. And the line between her eyes tells me it's not going to be anything I want to hear. "I'll be frank, our virtual reality program will be phasing out. Even our avatars may not be able to stay, depending on hospital politics. You should reconsider."

I cross my arms, my neck straightening at her implication. "Do you mean this might be my last chance to say goodbye?" Maria doesn't respond, but her silence is answer enough. "If my insurance covers it, I'll do it."

She nods and reaches for her temples, where in the real world she's wearing a VR headset, but here, in the waiting room, she's exactly how she'd appear in person without all the plastic, wires and gear. In theory, I'm still considering the possibility she's a robot.

"Wait!" I call to her before she disappears. "I want to talk to Michael."

Her eyes meet mine. There's a flicker of recognition, so I know she heard me, but she quickly looks away before her image blinks out.

I've seen that look before. That disappointing tilt of the head, shoulders creeping up to the ears, and pursed lips—the look Rylan or Kelly give me before they're about to lie to me or give me some bad news of their behavior at school. And a zing of panic flutters in the center of my chest and ripples outward before my consciousness cuts out. My last thought plays on repeat.

Maria isn't telling me something.

It's seven in the morning. At least the heaviness in my eyelids insists that's the time. Usually, Michael will get up early on school mornings and kiss me awake. I pack the lunches before I go to bed; I've never been a morning person. I keep my pajamas on while I make the three-mile drive to drop the kids off at school. With the kids safely off to start their day, then and only then can I return home to finish getting ready.

But Michael doesn't kiss me awake. Not today.

"Note. Movement in the arm and feet," A low toned voice says. It's as though I'm underwater.

"We've got frontal lobe activity. 7:18 AM."

"Should we unstrap the restraints?"

"No, not yet. Let's see if we achieve full awareness."

I wiggle my fingers. I'm a little unsettled when something mechanical responds for me. There's a delay, then the hard, cold metal rubs against my fingertips. My butt is warm against the flat surface as if I've been sitting here a while.

"Ava? Ava?" A man's face focuses into view. "My name is Dr. Hernandez. I'm one of the neurological engineers assigned to your case study."

I pull my arm to bring it in front of me; a protective instinct Michael would always point out. My hand catches and I'm unable to move the limb. "What is this?" I tug again. Not too hard. My muscles don't seem to be working right. It's as if I'm floating in water. I frown at the restraints.

Dr. Hernandez reaches forward and unstraps the cotton fabric laced around my wrists. "That odd sensation you're feeling will go away after a few sessions. Your brain is still mapped to expect muscles to move your arms and not metal and plastic. Let's see if you can stand." He clasps both my hands in his.

I rise. Normally I'd ask more questions than this, but I

expect I'm in a state of shock. This is a real room. These people are really here. No VR headsets. No blips from the programming of the waiting room. Although, this is some other kind of waiting room. Sure, there are cords neatly wrapped across the floor, machines blinking, and a team of bored teenagers. At least one open mouthed fellow stares at me from his corner, his eyebrows glued above his hair line.

"Holy shit," The boy whispers from his station behind a panel.

"Mr. Eng, do we have a problem?"

"No, Dr. Hernandez. Levels are normal. It's just—they said it wouldn't work."

"Well, Mr. Eng, *they* are obviously not among the top three neurological engineers in the country."

I take a few steps forward. My legs are like stilts on a unicycle under a lake. Not really, but it's the best I can think of. "Where's Michael? I'd like to see him. Is he outside?"

"Michael?" A girl with a clipboard furrows her brow at the doctor.

"Her husband." Dr. Hernandez keeps his concentration on my movements. "One more step, Ava. Do you feel any resistance?"

The students eye each other in some sort of secret conversation with sad, pitying eyes.

"What?" I ask. "What is it? Why are you all looking at each other that way?"

"She has visuals," a girl with orange hair and an elaborate tattoo of roses down the left side of her neck announces from her station. "You heartless idiots."

"Shit."

"And auditory."

The group of them zipper their lips and gazes bounce around each other, the floor, the ceiling. I remember being that curious student at one time. I'd gotten a programming degree, but didn't use it much after the kids were born.

"I'll go get her counselor," one of them offers.

My stomach—is it my stomach still?—anyway, something twists in my gut and I don't need the counselor for confirmation.

"When? When did he stop visiting me?"

No answer.

"What year is it?" My mind races through all the science fiction catastrophes. The year is probably 3042. Humans are living on some desolate planet. They've retrieved my consciousness from some database, and people have all grown tails. This is a computer geek nightmare. I freeze, unable to move forward another inch. I mean, I could, but I've decided I don't want to. "Put me back. Back into whatever database you've taken me out of."

"Ava, can you touch your finger to your nose?"

I cross my arms. "Yes. I can." The doctor opens his mouth to clarify. "No. I will not perform your monkey-do tricks until you answer my questions."

The door softly clicks open. Sounds are becoming more clear. It's Maria. Her hair is grayer than her VR avatar and she wears thick square glasses. So not a robot. Unfortunately, I cannot say the same about me.

"Ava, it's a pleasure to meet you in person." She squeezes her eyes shut and shakes her head. "I mean outside of the virtual waiting room." She holds out her hand.

"I'd like to see Michael."

"That can be arranged at a later date, but Ava—" She glances around the room. There's some throat clearing and then the teenagers hop over wires and machines, tripping over each other to escape the room.

It's Dr. Hernandez, Maria, and me left in the room.

Maria keeps her expression—devoid of any emotion—

trained on me. "We need to discuss a few things. The passage of time to be precise. It took longer than we expected to gather the funds and secure a grant. Not to mention getting clearance from your doctors and the neurological engineers to deem you a candidate for the study."

"How long?"

"A few years." She pauses. Her cheek twitches. "But—"

"How many years since the bike accident."

"You must understand that passage of time is different in the VR program. You wouldn't have felt differently if you had no visitors—"

"How. Many."

"Twelve, actually."

"Twelve. That's quite a lot more than *a few*," I point out.

Dr. Hernandez lets out a half-laugh that I'm not so sure isn't actually a cough. "She's funny."

Maria ignores the doctor. "Your husband filed for divorce and has remarried. However, he signed over your medical files to the research committee before doing so. Now that you're able to communicate you may dictate your own care." She smiles now, taking in a huge breath as if this is the best news of all.

Hooray. I suppose she hoped I'd shake with excitement. "My children?"

"They are doing well," she answers quickly. "This is a lot to take in—we should adjourn and give you some time to adjust."

"I'd like to see Rylan and Kelly."

There is a gasp in the corner of the room. Orange-haired girl. Her eyes are as large as silver dollars. I hadn't realized she didn't leave with the rest of what I assume were interns.

She recovers, going back to her numbers, but sensing the adults in the room staring at her, she straightens. Her gaze darting to each of us. "Dr. Hernandez," she stutters over his name before pulling it together. "Ava's brain activity is within the normal range. All our research suggested—"

"Thank you, Rosaline. I believe we've already established this earlier."

"Sorry, sir." She ducks behind her computer, tucking her body completely out of sight, and peeks at me from her station.

I bring my focus back to Maria. "Of course." I lay my hand on my forehead as if clearing my thoughts. "I'd love to take a moment to adjust. If you'll excuse me." I look to the back of the room to the one person I currently trust. The only person to show many any humanity. "Rosaline, is it? I'm assuming you're to show me to my room?"

She nods, but her attention is on her superiors.

"Very well." Maria claps her hands together. "Dr. Hernandez and I have some paperwork."

They leave the room quickly enough, but it's as if years pass before I finally have my freedom. Twelve to be exact.

The room is finally empty except for me and my new best friend. There's a buzz while my head adjusts to look her directly in her eyes. A display pulls up, measuring her pupil dilation, her sweat and rise in cortisone levels. I don't need it though, I've always been good at reading people. "We need to talk."

For the next several weeks I'm a perfect avatar experiment. I do the assignments as they say and each night before Rosaline—that's the girl with the orange hair and rose tattoos—disconnects me, she whispers a new bit of information.

My daughter she found easily, on a nursing internship in Africa. My son, however, took some digging.

"I think I found him. He goes by Ry and your maiden name, Baxter."

"We used my maiden name as his middle name. Something we did back then," I confirmed.

Rosaline smirks. "Back in the day?" She can barely contain the smile on her face. "That was twelve years ago. We still do that."

The girl can't be older than twenty-two. I wonder what her favorite cartoon was when I had my accident, but I don't ask. She's a nice person. She treats me like a human and not like an experimental machine without a past or emotions.

"We can't be sure," Rosaline says, "that it's your Rylan. He's an athlete. Professional extreme obstacle course triathlons. Base jumping without chutes, running into the ocean during a typhoon and swimming into the swelling tide kind of stuff."

"Oh my god. That can't be possible." Rylan had done the usual: baseball, soccer, swimming. Base jumping? Swimming into the ocean during a storm? No. No human could do that.

Rosaline's hand lands on my shoulder. "Do you want me to look into it? We only have one shot at this. He'll be in Chicago next month for a competition. He'll be within a few blocks of the hospital. If we're going to risk my job—"

"No." I shake my head. "It can't be him. Those activities are too risky. Rylan was an athlete, but—"

Rosaline lets out a breath. "I keep forgetting. You don't know. Avatars—Ry, the man I'm describing to you? He doesn't do those things using his own body. He's jacked in. He's got an avatar like yours but not medical grade. Athletic grade. You know, to withstand that kind of force from a jump, water sealed, able to withstand extreme temperatures?"

I don't respond. Instead I look down at my own robotic body. Somewhere my body is laying out on some hospital bed, kept alive by machines.

Rosaline scoffs. "I forget how much has changed in the last decade," she says, misunderstanding my somber moment. "I should probably be hinting to Dr. Hernandez about some kind of culture shock counseling for you. But wires, circuits, and fiber optics are more my thing, not so much emotions." She taps around on her tablet. "It's hard to find what he looks like outside of his avatar, but here."

She turns over the tablet and it doesn't register at first, but then I see it. His hair and eye color is different. But since violet isn't a normal color for either feature, I assume those have been modified. It's the tilt of his lips, the uneven flat slant when he smiles for a camera. He never did like the attention. His eyes still squint when he's hiding annoyance. He's an older version of Rylan, but he's mine. A mother should recognize her child and it irks me it took me a second to register. As if even in that millisecond I'd betrayed some ingrained parenting instinct.

I don't realize how long it takes me to respond until I see Rosaline's eyes widen as she leans forward to check my brain activity. She's checking to see if I'm still active. I give her a slight nod. "It's my Rylan. You found him."

She pulls the screen away from my view as I feared she would when I answered. I nearly ask her to upload it into my processor so I can access it later. But it might be weird. My son, this man, doesn't know who I am anymore. He doesn't even know I'm in this experiment. Maria had explained that the counselors and social workers had advised the children stay involved with my care and be allowed to see me, but Michael and his family had strongly decided against it. "Move on,", Michael had said. Michael didn't want our children to cling to false hope and hang on every technology breakthrough. He didn't want to parent through a VR headset for one hour a week for twenty-six weeks because that was all our insurance would cover. Michael had always been a technophobe. He could barely handle his phone settings.

All this information had been laid out for me as if a paragraph synopsis of a thousand-page novel were enough. There's a lot missing. Like the emotion and heartache that I'm experiencing, but no doubt Michael and the kids have already processed years ago and accepted. Am I making a mistake by reaching out to Rylan?

"You'll have a short window. Every Friday at three in the morning we have a security backup. There's a half hour where the research facility doesn't have as much security."

I lift my robotic body from the chair. My limbs hiss and tick as I walk to the window. "What about the outing? Didn't Dr. Hernandez say the team would be taking me outside next week?"

"Timing's bad. You'll have a full group of scientists and a handful of tech geek media following you around. There won't be a great opportunity for you to escape. And also, the competition Rylan is in won't happen till next month."

"Maybe on another outing?" I worry about Rosaline and putting her job at risk for me. The way Maria describes the situation, it's as though I'm selfish for wanting to reconnect. Not really, not exactly. Maria makes all the right empathetic gestures. My vision lights up detecting each facial feature and her sincerity. Her words are appropriate, but it's the dull shine in her eyes whenever I bring it up. Like the one piece she can't hide from me.

"If this one is successful then, yeah, there will be others. But it'll be a while before you and I are allowed one-on-one outings into the public. It's spendy and a risk to the facility to bring the avatar outside."

My gaze focuses on the children playing at the school yard across the street. My favorite time of day. To think I once dropped my own off at school and cheered inside at the few hours of freedom. Now I wish I could have watched them play, volunteered in their classroom, or watched a little more carefully for that car that sped through the light—the one that destroyed the future I should have had.

Rosaline's hand lightly touches my arm. "I'm sorry."

Her apology brings me back into the room. "For what?"

"I meant to say each time we bring *you* out. The avatar is a part of you. I didn't mean to make you feel like a machine. Or that the avatar is more important in some way. You are powering this avatar. You're real."

I place my hand on hers. "There's no need. You have been nothing but kind." Now's when I should tell her not to risk her career for me. I might get ten minutes at most with Rylan before my escape is known. If I were less desperate, if I were a better person, I might have the strength to stop her from this mistake.

But she takes care of that weakness when the alarm on one of the devices she wears goes off. "Oh crap. Gotta go. See you tomorrow, Ava."

She's gone before a goodbye leaves my lips. Just like my children when I'd drop them off at school. I remember the day they stopped turning around for a hug. At the time, I patted my back for allowing them the space to grow independent. Now it only made me feel alone.

It all seems so ridiculous. Breaking out of the research facility. Why would such extreme measures be needed? I request a meeting with Maria and she shows up with my file and medical information.

My fingers ball into fists. "I'd like to send a letter to Michael and my children."

"That's fine. It will be arranged."

That's it? Too easy.

She lets out a long sigh of relief. The emotional interface is all over her body language. "Is that all?"

"No." I hesitate. "There's something else." I scan her perspiration levels, which are heavy in stress hormone. "Why are you nervous?"

Maria's fingers twitch folded across her lap. "It's just that I'm afraid for you. The others in the experiment didn't make it this far. We've put a lot of money into the program and there have been complications."

"Complications?"

"How do you feel, Ava?"

"I feel like I'd like to speak to my family. I've been in this avatar for two weeks and done all the verification, tests, and whatever you've asked of me. You said you'd discuss my family and I'd like to move forward with a plan to meet with them."

"Of course. And this letter is the first step." She makes a note in her file. "I have to say, I should have never worried. You're stronger than the others."

"Stronger? What do you mean?"

She sets her files aside on the table. "The reason I'm so careful that we follow the process is there is a real danger of you developing severe depression. Others who have gone through this program have ... not worked out."

I don't ask her to elaborate. I imagine the worst.

She places a hand over mine. My sensors read it as warm. The touch also communicates to my emotional interface that she is genuine. The tight wall I've built when I'm around her cracks. Slightly.

She smiles, but it doesn't reach her eyes. "If you're feeling overwhelmed, please let us know."

She pats my hand one last time and when it's clear I don't have any other questions, she leaves.

It's been three weeks since I wrote the letter that was delivered to my ex-husband and children. As requested, the counselors on staff also sent it via email. Due to privacy laws and paperwork, a personal visit from research staff isn't allowed.

Maria shakes her head, clearly having expected this outcome. Rosaline continues to plot my escape to see Rylan, but I'm doubting that plan more each day.

"You have one chance," Rosaline explains. "You should take it. Those letters get ignored all the time. It's disgusting the amount of spam we get at the research hospital. And the scammers? They are just as terrible. Your kids might think it's someone out looking for money."

"We'll see," I say and stare out the window, watching the children play at the school. I wonder if my children know I'm still thinking of them.

"Here," Rosaline motions for me to step into the specialized shoes I will need to wear on our outing. I have to practice walking in them and prove I won't tip. Since I'm a comatose body hooked up to machinery and my consciousness is shoved into this avatar body, the neuro link is sketchy. Sometimes, I apparently "space"—meaning, it takes me a while to respond either verbally or physically to commands. However, due to some kind of brain science magic curtain, I'm unable to detect when it's happening and unaware of the occurrence. So Rosaline has been working with me to develop tricks so I know when it is happening. The more cues I can establish that it's about to happen, then I can bring the avatar into a safe position to rest in until I come back online.

I feel the blip on my visual just before I lift my leg. I bring my leg back into place and bend my knees, then turn my face to the clock.

For me, it's a second. Nothing has happened, but the clock now jumps five minutes.

I go to lift my left leg again to allow Rosaline to slip on the boot.

"Good!" she praises me. "You're getting much better at detecting the neurospace. What was your cue this time?"

"The corners of my visual read out were getting fuzzy. It was a lot like a television losing reception."

She makes a face at that. Her brows scrunch together.

"Like when you're watching a digital and the video stops but the audio continues to play? Or you're at a cheap coffee shop that doesn't have adequate Wi-Fi."

Her face lights up with recognition at my meaning. She jots down my description in the notes. "This is going to help a lot more patients when we're cleared for more funding."

Other patients. It reminds me of what Maria said a few months back. "Would it be possible to speak to them? The others?"

As I'm asking Rosaline's expression goes blank. She blinks and keeps her gaze on the computer screen in front of her. "I haven't worked with the others. They assigned me as your one-on-one."

My emotional interface lights up with all kinds of worrisome reports. I want to bat it away, I don't need it to explain her body language to me. "Please tell me."

Rosaline takes a deep breath and stares at her screen for a few minutes. I watch the digital clock in the corner to be sure I didn't space while she explained my question. But there's been no time jump.

"The others we've revived haven't remained viable." She lets out a rush of air. "I'm sorry, Ava." She shakes her head. "This is why it's important to see your son." Her gaze won't leave mine. "Do you understand?"

I don't. Not really. How can I possibly understand something she isn't saying. She leaves the room before I can question her meaning further.

I sneak out the night before Rosaline had planned. But I follow her instructions, the ones we'd practiced. Ry's team is set to train tonight at the auditorium. Fewer crowds, less chance of being spotted. I disable my GPS and go through my shut down process just as Rosaline taught me, but I cut off monitoring. I hold still for the last nurse check. She scans my vitals and moves along. Now it will appear as if I'm plugged in for the evening. They won't know I'm gone until the first nurse check at three in the morning. A three-hour window. I make it count.

Sneaking out of the hospital isn't as easy as I'd imagined. I can't be spotted. Hundreds of thousands of dollars of robotics is difficult to hide when my consciousness is rolling around inside it. The best bet is to not allow myself to be spotted. At midnight, this wing of the hospital is vacant, just as Rosaline said it would be. I manage to make it to the elevator and wait by the janitor closet until the front desk man leaves for a bathroom break. Then I run for it. The door slides open.

Freedom.

Public transportation isn't an option. Avatars roaming the streets isn't common and would create a lot of curiosity and questions. It takes me two hours to walk what I remember of the streets of Chicago to find the auditorium. It stands several stories tall—newly built, the size of three football stadiums, brick façade, with metal designs and sculptures from local artists. The skygram is already projecting a hologram advertisement for the games. Flashes of giant machines clashing, tiny microscopic bugs navigating what looks to be the inside of a human vein. I'm amazed at how far technology has come in the last decade. To those living it, it must have seemed like nothing. A blip in the radar, much like my grandfather describing the calculator. "One day it's an abacus, the next, everyone has a counting machine at their desk," he used to say.

I scan the names at the front for Ry Baxter. He's one of the first listed. I swell with pride. The doors are open as men and women in track suits stream in and out, with teams of people in suits carrying laptops and other electronic equipment.

A security guard stops me at the gate. "I'm sorry. Avatars must be entered through the lab at the side of the building. We can't allow for practice maneuvers in the lobby, we have some delicate displays."

"I'm not here to enter the games," I look around, hoping to find the boy with violet hair and eyes whose smile is flat for the cameras. "I'm here for Ry Baxter. He's my son—"

She glances down as I speak. "Where is your badge? I'm going to have to ask that you leave the building; the games are not open to the public—"

"Please, I must speak to him. It's very important and I don't have a lot of time."

"His mother? Ry Baxter's mother is dead." She shakes her head, leaning her head into a walkie on her shoulder. "We've got a fan break in at the lobby. Possible assist." She looks at me. "Please ma'am or sir, I must ask you to step out of the building."

I can't. Once the hospital finds out how I managed to escape, they'll never be as lenient with me again. "Just let me speak to him for a minute."

"One minute. Everyone always wants one minute with the athletes." She uses her body to back me up and away from the groups who've stopped to watch the drama.

She reads off my serial numbers at the back of my shoulder into the walkie, and presses something there that is out of my reach.

That's the last thing I remember.

I didn't know my body had been kept in the same research facility as this machine, the avatar. Not until I'd overheard Dr. Hernandez discussing some medical details to a nurse in charge of my care. Don't know the protocol, and don't care, but it's my body and I decide I'm going to go see ... myself.

It's not much. An emaciated body hooked up to tubes at my neck that force me to breath. I'm tempted to pull all the plugs. The urge is unbearable. Maybe this is what they meant by the other patients not working. Eventually we all find out that this isn't a miracle. Avatars are no substitute for real life. When Rosaline takes my robotic hand, the sensation triggers, but I know it's not real. It's not my real hand. And Rosaline isn't the hand I want to hold. But it's all I've got. For now. Until I convince them to unplug me. Rosaline asks me to reconsider.

I don't answer. I don't squeeze her hand back when she squeezes mine.

I ask for the paperwork to end the experiment. Dr. Hernandez takes his sweet time. There is a lot of cajoling. I'm the only viable conscious they've managed to extract. *Please*, they ask, *for the sake of science will you reconsider? There are a lot of future lives at stake. Other families that will never have to go through what I did.*

That reason gives me pause. If I must live this half-life, then at least I can convince myself it's for a reason. But they can find another Guinea pig. I'm done.

"One more day," Rosaline begs me. "One more."

I do it for her. Because she's risked so much for me and didn't even know me. Her empathy is inspiring. I'm glad they never found out she'd helped me. I told them I asked her questions and eventually figured out the escape plan on my own. Before I was comatose, I'd had a programming degree after all. They buy it.

The next morning Rosaline convinces me to walk the obstacle course with her, practice my walk and narrowing the neurological to mechanical delay. "What's the point?" I want to say. But she has a hopeful look on her face and her eyes brim with unshed tears.

I'll call Dr. Hernandez later with the news of my decision. They will let her down easy.

She coaxes me along in silence. Holding out her hands when she thinks I might teeter on the obstacle course. This is what my son does, what he learned to do maneuvering in this machine. It takes some time to practice the nuances that are not true to life. And Kelly? She's a nurse in Africa. I feel a stab of frustration that they couldn't reach her either.

"Mom!" A voice rings out and its familiar tones set off a memory of Kelly crying for me when I lost her at a fair. "Mom!"

Rosaline's shoulders sag with relief. "Over here." She waves the woman down.

I blink with confusion. Rosaline is too young to be a mother. But when I turn, I see Kelly. Her hair is a darker shade of blond. Her chin has a tiny silver scar. She'd fallen at lacrosse practice and took a stick to her face. I'd never been more frightened.

"Mom?" Kelly's gaze meets mine. "I came as soon as I could." She turns to Rosaline. "Are you Rosaline?" She hugs her. "You're an angel. My god, they'd told us her consciousness was no longer viable for the VR. This is a miracle. Ry is on his way. He said that someone came to one of his tournaments claiming to be you and we thought it was some sick joke. I remembered the email I'd gotten from the hospital. We thought they wanted a donation or something because of Patty. Patty is Dad's new wife. She's a lawyer, but she was a child star and made a ton of money." She presses her hands to her cheeks. "My god, I'm babbling. I babble when I'm nervous."

"You did that when you were little."

She smiles a watery smile. "I did. I did." She chokes on a hiccup. "I just never believed I would ever see you again." She throws herself into my arms.

The sensation registers a half second too late, but after twelve years it seems like a minor compromise. "I love you. I'd do anything to find you if it was within my capability."

"I know. I know." She saws in breath between sobs. I see a purple haired man pausing at the end of the hallway, watching us, unsure. That's my Ryland: always hesitant. I wait for him to join us. Let him take his time.

"I have so much to tell you. I'm just. It's all just." She's unable to talk through the tears. "I'm. I'm ..."

"It's okay. No rush." I rub her back, letting her body sink into the avatar and if I close my eyes I remember what it felt like to have her in my arms.

Dr. Hernandez pulls Ry aside and answers his questions. Until eventually, my son collapses into my arms too.

"I can't believe they didn't tell us the second you were awake. I never stopped hoping, Mom."

"Don't worry," I whisper into their ears and look to Rosaline and Dr. Hernandez. "We have all the time in the world now."

THAT OTHERS MAY LIVE

BY KEVIN IKENBERRY

THAT OTHERS MAY LIVE

BY KEVIN IKENBERRY

A rms churning through cool, clear water, Devin Morris approached the black-line wall of the lap pool and flip-turned. He pushed off and held a sleek, gliding form as long as his taxed lungs would allow. He came up to the surface and turned his head to the left to breathe. A blurry figure dressed from head to toe waved at him. Not recognizing them, Devin kept swimming. Two strokes later the figure was still there and waving frantically. Devin stopped and brought his head out of the water.

"Doctor Morris!"

Dammit. Every freaking time!

"What is it, Henry?"

Sergeant Jesse Henry was a burly Kentuckian with a perennial scowl and five o'clock shadow, but he was the best corpsman on base and wouldn't have tracked him down without good reason.

"Sir! There's a priority one call for you. World Med."

Devin clenched his jaw. The last time they'd called, eight months and six days earlier, they'd been unable to save Sharron. "Sitrep?"

A situation report was the Marine Corps way of saying "give me the five W's"—who, what, when, where, and why. Henry shook his head. "They've got another one, sir. A Strep-A derivative, R2021-X, that's not responding to any form of antibiotic regimen."

R2021-X. The same one that killed Sharron.

"Where?" Devin ducked under the lane ropes and dog paddled over to the ladder.

"Japan, sir."

Devin inhaled and let it out slowly. "Good, we'll have Mark Four avatars in place there and—"

"They want a nano jump, sir."

"What?" Devin froze on the swim ladder. "That's still in prototype stage—nowhere near FOC."

Full operational capability was the long-dreaded litmus test for all military programs. Nanotechnology wasn't new, since its widespread evolution in 2017, but avatar linkage into a device smaller than a blood cell was deemed theoretical at best. "The Commandant himself is on the line, sir. They want a Marine to lead the fight. He's sending you in."

Devin climbed up the ladder and found his towel and water bottle on the bench. "Go back and tell them I'm on the way. I'm going to get—"

"Sir? Respectfully. The Commandant is on the line waiting for you to speak with him, right now."

Devin nodded. "Secure line?"

"I've got it fed to my car outside." Henry said, walking away.

Devin followed in bare feet. Getting dressed, or even a good hot shower, would have to wait. The Commandant of the Marine Corps was on the line and it didn't matter that Devin called him Dad, or had while Sharron had been alive. Devin looked up into the Hawaiian sky through the open roof of the natatorium. Storm clouds brewed on the windward side of the island to match the ones churning in his mind.

"Devin?" The older man hadn't changed much in the last two years. The deep lines at the corners of his eyes were more pronounced, but his electric blue eyes belied the smile on his face. "How are you, son? Been a long time since we talked. Margaret wants you to come for dinner next time you're on the mainland."

"Sir." Devin said. "Please give Margaret my love. I'll do what I can."

"How's my granddaughter?"

Devin smiled. "Growing like a weed, sir."

He could see the four stars glinting on his former father-in-law's shoulders. The sun was down in Washington and he was undoubtedly pulling another late night. Thirty-five years of them wasn't enough. "Give her my love, will you? Right now, we have a situation in Japan that needs your experience and attention. I trust you'll be able to handle this."

Devin flinched at the insinuation. Just as quickly, he flushed with sudden anger and somehow managed to bite it back. "The links will be better in Japan than they were in Nepal, sir. There shouldn't be an issue this time."

The Commandant bit his lip and nodded, looking away from the camera. Devin knew exactly where he was looking. Across the Commandant's office on a credenza was a framed picture from their wedding. Sharron dancing in the arms of her father.

The Commandant looked at him with misty eyes. "I'm sorry, Devin. That was uncalled for. I know there was nothing anyone could have done."

"Yes, sir." Devin said.

The Commandant waved a hand in front of the camera. "Let's get back on track. You need to get into a Mark Four avatar immediately. Sergeant Henry says there is one ready to go."

Devin looked at Henry, who nodded. "That's my understanding, sir. What's the brief?"

"You'll get the specs and the history when you're in phase. We're linking with a team from all over the world. Paris, London, Rome. We've got an R2021-X Strep A variant in Japan. They've caught it early. Something's not right, though."

"It's still localized? Has necrotizing fasciitis set in?" Devin asked. Streptococcus-A, when found inside the human body, could either become the all-too-familiar strep throat or blossom into a skin-eating nightmare. The chances of the latter were one in a hundred thousand. For all its problems, Methicillin-resistant staphylococcus aureus or its little brother would have been easier to deal with than R2021-X gone wild. There had been over 10,000 cases in the last several years with a 100 percent mortality rate. "What's not right?"

"The team on the ground is racing to save the girl's leg right now. There's been almost no medicinal effect from our strongest antibiotics. World Med has recommended a nano-jump to get in and directly flood the bacteria with antibiotics. They have eight vehicles, six operational and two backups, tested and in place, ready for delivery via PICC line."

A peripherally inserted central catheter usually fed through a superficial vein like the cephalic vein in the arm directly into the superior vena cava. It was the fastest way to the bloodstream.

Devin squinted. "We're not going to deliver straight to infection site?"

"They aren't sure the damned thing hasn't infiltrated other parts of the body. Your jump is part reconnaissance and part surgical strike." The Commandant smirked. "We used to use those words in a whole different way. Nature took the war inside."

Devin sighed. "Why me, sir?"

The Commandant took a deep breath and leaned toward

the camera. "World Med wants a military presence to command the battle space. You've got over 5,000 hours avatar time, Devin and you're a Marine." The old man sighed. "And, this is what killed our Sharron, son. That makes you the right man for the job."

Inside the Mark Four linkage, in his still-wet swimsuit, Devin closed his eyes and relaxed. After three deep breaths, he felt ready. "Engage the connection."

<<Identification, please?>> The link's interface was a woman's happy voice.

"Morris, Devin. Alpha six niner zero Juliet."

<<Please wait.>>

Devin waited, eyes still closed. Connection, even to the most frequent avatar users, sometimes brought disorientation. Vomiting in a Mark Four linkage system was not something he wanted to clean up afterward.

<<Connected.>>

Devin opened his eyes and looked left and right. His avatar was clearly not the nanovehicle. A collection of five avatars in human form sat around a small, round table. They looked at him.

"Hi, this is Major Devin Morris, United States Marine Corps, from Kaneohe Bay, Hawaii. Sorry I'm late. Who is in charge?"

A light-skinned woman with shocking red hair smiled across the table from him. "I believe that would be you, Major." She spoke in a lilting Irish accent. "My name is Doctor Siobhan Murphy from Dublin College of Medicine. I'm the pharmacological vehicle commander, and deputy commander for this mission."

Devin nodded. "Right, Pharma and Control 2. Welcome

aboard, Siobhan."

"Thank you."

He pointed at an Asian woman to Siobhan's left. "Next?"

"Ryoko Matsuyama. Tokyo Medical Center. I'll command Laboratory One, with Pharma 2 as my alternate duty."

A white-haired man to Ryoko's left spoke next. "David Aldin. Trinity University, Melbourne, Australia. I've got Lab 2, but I'm grapple and capture."

Better you than me, pal.

"You've done grapple and capture on a bacterium before?"

"First time for everything, mate." Aldin grinned. "Just don't make any jokes about wrestling crocodiles."

"Because you're Australian?" Devin blurted.

"Precisely." Aldin winked at him.

Devin looked to his right. A dark-skinned man spoke slowly. "Sanjay Chandraspalipamari. Mumbai Directorate of Internal Medicine. I have the primary uplink node aboard."

"And last, but not least?" Devin looked up at a trim woman with sleek, dark hair.

"Joanna Abello. I believe you'd call me the Heavy Weapons Officer." She smiled. "Pharmacology alone isn't the answer when dealing with these things."

Devin blinked. "Weapons? Beyond drugs? What are you talking about?"

Joanna smiled at him. After a split second, he decided it was a friendly one. "Information by direct fire, Major Morris. Penetrometers and sensors. Electrical stimulus, as well. Something to bite the bug back, so to speak."

"They've caught this infection exceptionally early," Siobhan said. "We actually have a chance to find a way to kill it."

"And we have two spare vehicles, just in case," Aldin said.

A chime sounded in the virtual room and a new avatar winked into existence. "Ah, good. You're all here."

A beautiful woman with dark skin and ethereal green eyes

smiled at them. Devin heard at least two other people draw in a quick breath. The Nobel Prize winner didn't really need her introduction, but nodded to each of the team graciously. "I'm Doctor Mary-Ellen Imdiche, Mossell Bay, Namibia. I am on-site with the patient in Sapporo. I'd like to bring you up to speed on the situation."

Devin realized she was looking at him and waiting for a response. "Go ahead, please."

"We've isolated a Strep-A R2021-X variant. There's much more to this, but our theory is we have two bacteria strains in a symbiotic relationship. We simply do not have the time to separate the weaker majority from the super-resistant minority in a lab, so we've ordered an in situ evaluation and attack. That's why you're here."

"How are we going to tell which is which? Flood the site with antibiotics and see what survives?" Devin asked. "Or is there something more precise?"

Joanna turned toward him. "Antibiotic microballs. We'll fire them into the bacteria at close range."

"Like tank rounds?" Devin grinned.

"Something like that," Joanna replied.

"We'll be able to determine the bacteria that are unfazed easily from those affected. Your team will move in and secure the bacteria and extract its DNA. With a viable sample, we can reverse engineer it and create a tailored virus delivered by bacteriophage." Imdiche smiled at them. "Now, in the grand old days of spaceflight, when we sealed astronauts atop chemical rockets that were vertical bombs, they would have called me a capsule communicator. So, I'll be your CAPCOM and your link to the on-site medical team for this mission. I recommend you disengage and take advantage of food and water for the next fifteen minutes. Relieve yourselves if necessary. When you return, we'll load you directly into your vehicles."

She looked directly at Devin. "Devin? Won't you stay for a

moment?"

One by one, the other avatars winked out, leaving him alone with Doctor Imdiche. Her avatar walked across the room and sat in the chair Sanjay had occupied a moment before. She reached out a hand and lightly touched his arm. A tingle of electricity ran down his back. The sensation was almost real, but not real enough. "I wanted to say I am sorry for your loss."

Devin tried to swallow. "Thank you," he managed to stammer. "Sharron was too young for something like this to happen."

"You've been through a difficult time." Mary-Ellen said. "When Commandant Jenkins recommended you, I did not hesitate. You understand that this condition must be dealt with swiftly and that age can be a factor."

Devin nodded. "How old is the patient?"

"She's nine." Mary-Ellen said. "She doesn't understand the severity of her condition, but she is ready. We told her that your team is coming. She believes you're all superheroes."

He mentally reminded himself to arrange a neighbor to pick up his daughter from school. "My daughter would agree with her."

"How old is she?"

"Eleven." Devin said. "She was almost nine when her mother died. I imagine that if all goes well, she'll want to meet our patient."

"They'll be fast friends, I imagine." Mary-Ellen said. "Prepare yourself, Devin. We'll need everything you can bring to the fight."

Devin opened his eyes to a whitish-gray blur. Flexing his fingers, he reached for the controls to the vehicle. "It's like a fighter jet."

Mary-Ellen replied on a private chat channel. "Very much so. Do not try to control it just yet."

Devin frowned. He could see the wraparound instrument panel clearly. There were two manipulator arms in front of the vehicle that would be controlled by slipping his arms into long gloves. Beyond that, the vehicle was simple and clean of distractions. The absence of life support systems made it easier to get only the key components down to the nano level.

"Team, this is CAPCOM." Mary-Ellen said. "We have you in delivery fluid and standing by for injection. In front of your left hand is the throttle. Place your left hand there. Under your thumb is a button. Press that button."

Devin did and immediately saw three icons appear on his window like a heads-up display. Text appeared beside them. "This is Lead, I have Pharma 1, Lab 1, and Grapple in sight."

"Use the controller by your right hand to rotate the vehicle. You should be able to find everyone. Do this now."

Devin did and quickly found the remaining two vehicles. "I have a visual on all team members, Mary-Ellen."

"Understand, and let's stick to call signs, please." CAPCOM replied. "We're introducing you to the PICC line now. Remove your hands from the controls. You may want to close your eyes. You'll be on autopilot through the pulmonary system and down the arterial network to the victim's right leg. You may get separated—don't panic. The autopilot will get you there. The infection is halfway up her thigh and spreading quickly. Perform a reconnaissance and try to prepare a plan of attack. Disengage your inertial sensors and tactile systems now. The intense acceleration through the heart could black you out, otherwise. Understood?"

"Pharma 1, roger."

"Lab 1, roger."

"Grapple, roger."

"Comms, roger."

"Weapons, roger."

Devin keyed his microphone. "Lead, roger. We're standing by for injection."

"Injection in three, two, one, zero." The whitish-grey blur turned to darkness as the capsule accelerated through the superior vena cava and through the heart. Devin didn't watch. With his eyes clenched tightly closed, the only thing he could do was pray.

Please don't let us be too late.

"Ingress complete," CAPCOM said. "Do you copy, Lead?"

Devin opened his eyes and the vehicle's heads-up display came to life on the screen in front of him. Red blood cells jostled around him as they careened through the victim's body like a 360-degree traffic highway at dizzying speeds. At a two-micrometer size, his vehicle would be roughly the size of the bacteria they were chasing. The red blood cells seemed like immense tractor trailers zooming through the plasma by comparison. "Roger, CAPCOM. I'm through the pulmonary system. Dampeners up and guidance is locked to target."

The HUD showed a diverging artery ahead and as it passed, the next targeted vessel was smaller and less constrained against the flow of blood. Devin activated the vehicle's tracking system and locked onto the other vehicles.

"Does anyone have a visual on Grapple?"

"Lead, CAPCOM. He's behind you a bit. Got caught in the right upper ventricle. He should be with you soon."

"Copy." Devin looked up. "Closing in on the site."

As the nano vehicle rocketed down the femoral artery, the guidance program identified and maneuvered the vehicle to branch off at a small junction called the arteria femoral profundal. Inside the smaller artery, the red blood cells thinned out with plasma and for the first time Devin could clearly see white blood cells converging. Larger than their red brothers and sisters, they were hard to miss. "CAPCOM, Lead. What's the patient's white count?"

"Latest lab was a little over 20,000."

Damn. Devin jostled to the right as a white cell he recognized as a neutrophil bumped the vehicle. The amoebic cell flexed and pulsed in a dozen directions at once and slowly moved to the capillary wall. The dark walls were full of them in various states of pushing through to fight the infection. "Copy, I've got visuals on neutrophils in the vicinity of the wound. Approaching capillary boundaries."

"Lead, Weapons. Recommend we anchor to the capillary wall before breaching the infection site."

Devin nodded. The battle against the bacteria would be chaotic. More neutrophils approached the site and pressed through the capillary wall into the infection site. White cells normally grab infected cells and devour them. If the team could stay protected inside the cellular wall of a neutrophil, they had a much better chance of isolating a single bacterium for capture. Outside of a neutrophil, too many bad things could happen and waiting for one to push though might be too late for their patient. "Copy that. CAPCOM, did you hear that?"

"Roger, Lead. Our patient has asked to listen in. Are you okay with that?"

Devin checked the display and finally saw Grapple appear behind them in the capillary tunnel. "Sure, what's her name?"

There was a crack in the transmission and a small, scared voice replied in English. "My name is Chiyo. You are in my leg?"

"We are, Chiyo." Devin smiled. "We're just about to go after this bug."

"You don't sound like you're in my leg." Chiyo said, her voice tired and soft. "Are you sure?"

"I promise, sweetie." Devin replied. He hoped the term of

endearment, one he used for his own daughter, wasn't lost in translation. "CAPCOM, we're breaching the capillary wall now."

"Roger, Lead. Good luck."

"Weapons? You're up. Get us through."

Devin released one manipulator arm and swung his vehicle to the left. He saw Joanna in a capsule unlike anything he'd ever seen. A long, rotating blade stuck out in front of the capsule like some freakish chainsaw.

"Copy, Lead. Everyone, single file line grabbed on to me. Pharma 2 will stay in the rear to close the entrance site. We can't afford to let even one of those things through," Joanna said.

Devin pushed his transmit button. "Grapple, you're number two through the hole. Pharma 1, you're next in line with Comms behind you. I'll be number five with Pharma 2 on me. Any questions?"

There was no response. Grapple appeared in line behind Weapons with what looked like three small cranes for hands. Pharma 1 and Comms attached themselves next. From an external view, their vehicles were similar to his. Devin released the capillary wall and pivoted behind the line of vehicles and latched on with the forward arms. He realized that with Pharma 2 attached behind them, the attached spheroid vehicles looked like a small centipede and because of their size, almost exactly like bacterium.

Devin pressed his radio transmit button. "Once we're inside, break apart. Weapons, you've got security—keep away anything that tries to come after us. Grapple, you're with me. We'll isolate a bug and grab it. Pharma 1 and 2, you'll move in. Comms, keep in line of sight. We're going to need you to relay uninterrupted data."

"Roger, Lead." Comms replied. "I will maintain lock on you."

"Perfect." Devin said. "Weapons? Once we're through, get into the nearest neutrophil. We'll select our targets from there."

"Copy, Lead. Standing by."

Devin took a deep breath. "Okay, Chiyo. Here we come."

Warning klaxons rang out as the line of nanovehicles broke violently apart. A bacterium swarmed them and ripped Pharma 1 into two pieces before Grapple could defend. Devin was thrown clear, spinning out of control. Neutrophils converged toward the infected tissue as bacteria swarmed over the thick white cells like millions of neon green worms. Devin stabbed the radio button. "Seal the breach! Seal the breach!"

"Pharma 2, breach is sealed. I have Comms with me." Siobhan called.

"Stay there!" Devin nulled out his spin and sighted on Grapple and Weapons. The big forcep arms of the nano-vehicle had the first bacterium secure. Weapons floated nearby firing the antibiotic microballs into the thrashing bug. The bacterium shuddered and blanched. "Weapons?"

"First salvo complete." Joanna replied. "Data transmitted to Mission Control. Positive identity on the majority bacteria."

Siobhan's voice shattered the connection. "Help! Pharma 2! We're under attack—"

Devin swung around and saw another bacterium swarm the stay behind vehicles. He pulsed his thrusters and deployed the port weapons array in one smooth motion. "Rounds out," he said as he fired small antibiotic rounds. The bug spasmed and quivered, but did not die. Losing color, the bacterium swam away like a drunkard. Behind it, Devin saw the shattered remains of both nano vehicles.

Three down.

"CAPCOM, we've lost both Pharma vehicles and Comms. I

have the main relay engaged." Devin fingered the controls and collected data from the remaining vehicles for upload.

"Understood. Weapons must finish the antibiotic deployment for mission success." CAPCOM replied.

"We can't breach a neutrophil. There's no time."

"You're going to have to go deeper, Lead." CAPCOM replied.

Shit.

Devin scowled and turned back. Grapple was in serious trouble. "Copy. Moving to engage. Weapons, fire as soon as you can."

"New target identified," Joanna replied. "Grapple! Move in and grab it!"

Grapple swung around and hit the bacterium in the midsection. The bacterium reared and coiled around Grapple. Devin vectored his vehicle to see Weapons square to the bug.

"Firing!" Joanna called.

The rounds penetrated the bacterium's hard shell and Devin watched expectantly for a spasm or blanching of its color. Instead, the bug coiled and snapped around on Grapple.

"It's twisting on me! I can't hang on!" Grapple shouted.

"Don't let it go!" Devin screamed. He pushed forward and slammed the forward manipulator arms into the bacterium.

Not this time, you sonovabitch! Using his hands, he squeezed down on his internal controls and grabbed the thing as firmly as he could. In the corner of his eye, Grapple's telemetry winked out. "Move in, Joanna! Get its DNA!"

"Moving now!"

Devin tried to watch, but couldn't. He trained his antibiotic rounds at the thrashing bacterium to at least distract it. "Ready to fire."

Devin watched the bacterium contort again in slow motion. His hands cramped on the arm controls but he did not let go. "Hurry, Weapons!"

"Capture!" Joanna called. "Package deployed."

Devin reached for the trigger and held it down, sending a dozen rounds into the bacterium as it bucked. Data streamed in to his console. Straining forward, he pressed the transmit button with his chin to upload everything to Mission Control.

Warning klaxons rang in his ears, but Devin hung on to the controls with all his might as the hull of the nano vehicle buckled. In a microsecond, the connection went black and the cold avatar room surrounded him. He disengaged the connection and quickly peeled out of the haptic gear and down to his almost dry swimsuit. Devin raced down quiet hospital halls toward his office, completely oblivious of the rain hammering the windows.

Once he told her, his daughter wanted to make the trip. As they touched down at Chitose International Spaceport, Jenny looked up at him. "Is she going to make it?"

Devin shrugged. There was no easy way to lie to a child. "I don't know. Before we took off, the reports were good."

"The medicine was working?"

Devin looked at her wide, brown eyes. Jenny was a perfect mixture of her parents. He could see so much of his wife in the growing little girl. "They think so."

"Because of what you did, right?" She said and mimed shooting a pistol with her fingers.

The antibiotic microballs had worked and if the sample of DNA Joanna gathered could be reverse engineered, Chiyo would live. Joanna's vehicle had made it another twelve seconds before the bacterium ripped it apart. She'd even had time to retransmit what she'd collected.

They stopped at customs and found their bags next to a small Japanese woman who looked familiar. As they got closer, Devin smiled.

"Doctor Matsuyama?"

She grinned and stepped forward with her arms outstretched. They embraced. "Ryoko, Devin. Is it wonderful to meet you in person."

"Thank you," he said. They released each other and she smiled at him and then squatted down.

"And you must be Jenny," Ryoko smiled. "Chiyo is going to love playing with you."

Jenny looked up to Devin's face again before turning back to Ryoko. "Is she going to make it?"

"Yes," Ryoko beamed and stood. She reached out a hand to Jenny and looked up at Devin. "Why don't you come see for yourselves?"

Aboard the maglev, Jenny pressed her face to the window and gawked at going three hundred miles per hour. Once Jenny was settled, Devin turned to Ryoko. "So, what's her condition?"

"Stable." Ryoko said. "Doctor Imdiche completed a battery of tests an hour ago and is analyzing the results. By the time we arrive at the hospital, we should know more."

"The infection? Has it spread any farther?"

Ryoko shook her head. "The majority bacteria continued to attack the fascial areas in Chiyo's thigh, but it did not proceed toward the hip area. The effects are localized and there's still significant damage, but her renal system is functioning properly and her heart appears to be normalizing. The next 48 hours are the most critical. Chiyo was lucky her parents realized something was very wrong and sought medical attention. She was on the verge of septic shock."

Devin turned to the window. His daughter giggled at something flashing by as they sped to Sapporo. He touched her curly black hair lightly and she smiled at him. For a split second, the smile was Sharron's and it broke his heart. The train slowed to arrive at Sapporo and they disembarked to find a waiting autocar. The hospital was only a few minutes away and they goggled like the tourists they were. Devin couldn't remember seeing a cleaner, more beautiful city anywhere else in the world.

"Is the rest of the team here?" Devin asked.

"Just you and I, so far," Ryoko replied. "Doctor Imdiche wanted to see you first. The rest of the team will fly in for mission review and lessons learned tomorrow. You'll be back in Hawaii by the weekend."

"A whole week out of school!" Jenny bounced in her seat. "Awesome!"

As the car decelerated under the hospital's awning, Devin saw Doctor Imdiche waiting. Her green eyes glittered against her dark skin. She turned to Ryoko. "Will you take Jenny up to see Chiyo? She is very excited to meet a new friend."

Jenny waved and they were gone, leaving him and Mary-Ellen facing each other.

"It is good of you to come, Devin. Chiyo has asked to meet everyone on the team because you all saved her life."

Devin blinked. "The DNA sample? We found a way in?"

Mary-Ellen grinned. "Yes. We're duplicating the customized bacteriophages now. We'll have enough for direct injection in twelve hours via PCR." Polymerase chain reaction amplified a specific region of DNA by several orders of magnitude. In a short amount of time, they'd have enough to directly overwhelm both strains of bacteria in the infection. "It will be a long, slow process. There will need to be peer review and such, but it appears we stopped R2021-X, Devin."

He nodded and felt sudden tears sting his eyes. The relief of Chiyo's recovery washed over him. He snorted and dabbed at his eyes. "Marines aren't supposed to cry."

Mary-Ellen nodded. "And yet you are, but not for Chiyo."

"My wife," he started and looked away. A fresh cool breeze blew in from the harbor and steeled him. He turned to Mary-Ellen and the words so many asked him to share came out of their own volition. "My wife was on vacation with friends in Costa Rica a few years ago. What she thought was a mosquito bite inflamed into necrotizing fasciitis. By the time they got her to an actual hospital, it was too late. Sharron's kidneys had failed and septic shock killed her. I was in Nepal helping with the earthquake response and unable to connect to her, even to say goodbye."

"I'm so sorry, Devin." Mary-Ellen said. "Thank you for sharing. There was nothing more you could have done."

Devin nodded. "I guess." The irony of being an infectious disease specialist and losing his wife to one felt like an albatross around his neck. One he needed to cast off.

"You were willing to do anything to save Chiyo's life for a reason. Even sacrificing your nano vehicle and avatar for milliseconds of precious data. And while you could not save Sharron's life, you continue to save others, including a little girl you've never met. I think we should at least go say hello."

Devin nodded and wiped his cheeks. He looked at Mary-Ellen for a moment and started to say something, but the words stopped on his tongue. He held out his arms and they embraced for a long moment. As they separated, Mary-Ellen looked up at him and smiled. "You are a good man, Devin Morris. You have a beautiful daughter who is making a new friend nine floors above us right now. Would you care to do the same with me? How about a cup of coffee before we go upstairs? There will be time for business and mission review soon enough, but not just yet."

Mary-Ellen was intelligent and captivating. Being able to be anywhere in the world via avatar had some disadvantages, but not many. A casual cup of coffee really wouldn't have been the same via connection. "I hear Japanese coffee is delicious."

Mary-Ellen grinned and took his hand in hers. "You have no idea."

THE GHOST OF THE MOUNTAIN

BY ANDREA G. STEWART

THE GHOST OF THE MOUNTAIN

BY ANDREA G. STEWART

L ilia peered at the tracks in the dusty ground, her muzzle twitching. Scents were richer in the animal avatar; she could smell the loam of the earth, the sweetness of grass, the musky scent of some creature's urine, long since dried up.

There. Buried beneath everything else—the sharp scent of a snow leopard. She placed a cloven hoof in one of the paw prints, a little thrill running through her. She'd smelled this before, but only as a part of the avatar tutorial, so she knew it when it hit her. Never here, in the wild.

She was close.

And then a wave of the scent washed over her, hitting her like a cloud of her grandfather's cigar smoke, overwhelming her. All four of Lilia's legs stiffened. Somewhere, distantly, she felt her actual body back in her apartment, her teeth clenched so tightly that her jaw hurt.

Her reflexes were too slow, too hindered by the excitement that had brewed within her only a moment before. She gathered herself to run; all the mechanisms and gears inside the avatar tightening in preparation for release.

Something heavy dropped onto her back. Fire raked across her skin, the hot breath of some other animal at the back of her neck. Briefly, the sensation of claws tearing through her hide. The pain sensors cut out automatically. Still, Lilia felt the crushing, the pressure, as the snow leopard closed its jaws around her throat.

One blink, two, and her connection dropped.

She came back to herself in her apartment, her neck tingling. The haptic suit, zipped up to her chin, suddenly felt constricting. Lilia tore off her goggles and mask, and fumbled at the zipper. Her room seemed too bright after the cloud-encased Himalayas.

"Damn it!" she said. She slipped the cap from her head and breathed in deep.

"Did you fall off a cliff again?" Melanie, her roommate, leaned against the doorframe, her arms crossed. She looked like a crane at rest, all lithe legs and neck. "If you keep this up, you're going to burn through your grandfather's inheritance."

The avatar would have to be repaired and they'd debit her account for the cost. It was the second time she'd incurred such damages. The first time, she'd slipped on a loose rock, her avatar tumbling into the ravine below. "No. A leopard. I was close this time," Lilia said. "I was right on top of it." She shook her head. "And then it was right on top of me."

"Maybe you shouldn't use an avatar that looks and acts like something the leopard eats," Melanie said. "Don't they have others you can use?"

Lilia ran a hand through her hair. She needed a shower. "Snow leopards aren't wary of ibexes. They'll get close, and I need the cat to get close so I can tag it. And I can cover more ground as an ibex. If I get that prize money, it'll more than make up for the rental fees and the damages."

Melanie shrugged and turned away. "Hey, good luck. But it seems like a scam to me."

An angry retort burned in Lilia's throat and she bit it back as she watched her roommate retreat. Melanie didn't mean anything by it. She just didn't understand. Lilia's gaze went to the framed butterfly on the wall, above her desk. The Xerces blue, now extinct. A gift from her grandfather when she'd been a teenager.

She studied the curve of the wings, the fade of periwinkle into brown. Every detail carried with it memories. The scent of cigars, the soft feel of her grandfather's favorite corduroy jacket, the gravelly rumble of his voice. He hadn't spoken the last time she'd seen him, only four months ago, and the hospital gown had been crisp beneath her fingertips. He'd smelled of antiseptic and the faint floral scent of hospital soap. She hadn't been ready for him to go.

But he'd been ready, and that's all that really mattered.

"When these creatures are gone," he'd liked to say to her as they sat together in his living room, "they're gone forever. There are pieces of them left behind, but there's no breath of life in pieces. There's no soul." And her gaze would follow his sweeping arm across the prizewinning photographs he'd taken of animals both extinct and endangered, past the specimens of species long since gone.

Lilia hadn't understood what he'd meant until the funeral, three days later, when she'd looked at his unmoving body in the casket. There was something irretrievable now missing from the world.

She leaned back in her chair, the creak of the cushions somehow reassuring. Despite the bravado she'd shown her roommate, she really did need that prize money. The inheritance her grandfather had left her was still in probate, and renting out the avatars wasn't cheap. Her parents sent her money for school, but she'd quit her job a few months before her grandfather passed away. The money in her account wouldn't last through the end of the month, and when rent was due ...

Lilia gritted her teeth. "It's not about the money," she said as she pulled the cap back on, zipped up the suit, and reached for the goggles.

It was Saturday, so she had the time. She'd been close, and how many of her fellow ounce hunters could say that with any honesty?

Ounce Club met on Saturday evenings, in the community room of the local Round Table Pizza. Snow leopards were most active during dusk and dawn, and with the fourteen-hour time difference, Saturday evening was poor hunting time.

She'd been coming here for over six months, though more regularly since Grandpa had passed away. The idea of crowd-sourcing a search for an endangered species had excited him, and then he'd gotten sicker and sicker, until nothing could excite him at all. The pizza tasted like cardboard; Lilia washed it down with some beer and listened to the other ounce hunters exchange tips and tricks. Snow leopards were referred to in medieval heraldry as the "ounce," and the nickname had been quickly adopted by avatar hunters as shorthand over online chats and forums.

"I almost tagged an ounce the other day," Nathan said to her right. He gesticulated wildly as he spoke, so she had to lean a little away to avoid being struck. "It was right in front of me, so close I could see the color of its eyes. But when I tried to shoot my tagging gun, it jammed. I filed a complaint. They'd better refund me my rental fees for that session."

Lilia rolled her eyes. Nathan told nearly the same story at every meeting, with slight variations on the theme. He'd always almost tagged a leopard. There never seemed to be a session he spent wandering the mountains, alone but for the sound of his footsteps. And, as Lilia knew all too well, this was how the vast majority of sessions turned out, for everyone.

Grandpa would have laughed at Nathan's stories, a cigar clutched between his teeth. "Snow leopards are some of the most elusive creatures on this earth," he would have said. "If you've seen one every session you've gone out, that would mean they weren't endangered at all."

Lilia held the words at the back of her throat. To speak her grandfather's words would be like admitting he was gone, that someone else had to say the things he couldn't. And she was just a wannabe, a college kid who couldn't even manage to tag an ounce—not an award-winning photographer. So she just listened to Nathan as he went on about the size of the leopard's paws, about what he would do with the prize money. He'd pay for a trip to Europe, of course, and rent out a mansion on New Year's Eve for all his friends to party in.

"How about you?" Nathan said, turning to Lilia. "You get close at all lately?"

She thought about the feel of jaws around her neck, the sharp scent in her ibex nose and the paw prints in the dusty ground. She picked up her beer, tracing the wet circle it left behind on the table with one finger. "Besides the prize money," she said slowly, "do you ever think about what happens if there are no more snow leopards to tag? If the few they've already relocated to the sanctuary aren't enough for a breeding population?"

He stared at her. "Well, yeah, of course. I mean, they'd go extinct. That would suck."

That would suck. She thought of Grandpa's hand on hers, putting a pangolin scale into her palm, explaining how they'd been hunted until they didn't exist anymore. The scale was all that was left of an animal that had once wandered the forests of Cambodia, its wet nose to the ground. Her throat tightened.

"Yep," was all she said as she took another sip of her beer.

She set her alarm for 4:00 AM, about an hour and a half before dusk in the Himalayas—prime ounce hunting time. Her room was dark when she woke up. She switched on her desk lamp before slipping out of her pajamas and into the haptic suit.

When she logged in, her avatar choices popped up before her.

All the Himalayan wolves had been taken, which Lilia thought was a poor choice to begin with, anyways. The ibexes were all rented as well. She needed to get up earlier. So she selected a blue sheep, checked it out for three hours, and entered the avatar.

Her senses jumped from her dark, cluttered room and into a shed, streams of light falling through gaps in the wall. The wind whistled through those very same gaps, rattling the loose boards. It smelled like livestock in the shed—they really did try for authentic avatars, to lessen any disruption on the local environment. And there were always moderators checking in to make sure no one was abusing their privileges.

She trotted toward the door just as another avatar returned. Lilia hovered her gaze over the wolf, but no username popped up. It was on remote return.

Outside, the sun hung low over the mountains, the sky crisp and clear. The rocky ground was nearly barren, broken by patches of gray-green grass and scrub.

"Snow leopards move in large circles," her grandfather had told her. "They have a territory, and they pace around the perimeter, like a soldier on the parapets. It's never a small area, but if you see signs of a snow leopard somewhere, they'll likely be back around at some point."

Lilia took the long way around, circling once to make sure

no other ounce hunters were following her. Once you found signs of a leopard, it was best to keep the location a secret. Slopes were easier to navigate as a sheep than as a person. Her hooves gripped the rocks, her body adjusting as she picked her way across a landscape that she would have broken her neck on without the avatar. Walking on four legs had been difficult for Lilia to become accustomed to. And then there were the sounds and the smells. They flooded her senses, so much sharper and more well-defined than in her own body. She'd spent her first two sessions wandering in circles, dizzy with the effort it took to filter everything she was sensing. She could have dialed down her avatar's receptors, and some ounce hunters did that, but Lilia always felt that would be limiting. Instead, she'd kept the receptors at their maximum levels and had learned how to focus, and on the third session she hadn't vomited when she returned back to her body.

She leapt over a gap between the rocks, the shuffle of her hooves sending marmots scattering and back into their burrows. Fat little babies lingered near the entrances, and Lilia felt the haptic suit crinkle as her lips curved in an involuntary smile. She'd have to tell Grandpa—

Her smile faltered. Grief was stronger than all her animal senses. Sometimes she forgot, and the remembering came with its own fresh pain.

It took her another hour to reach the place where the leopard had attacked her. A repair bot had wiped the area clean, the gravel brushed back into place, all stray pieces of the damaged avatar collected for later reassembly. The snow leopard scent was gone. Hopefully this hadn't spooked the leopard off of its territory.

This time, she stood in the open, her ears pricked, her head swiveling.

The day waned, painting the sky in streaks of pink and orange. Lilia's heart sank with the sun. Snow leopards were active at dawn and dusk; the later it got, the less chance she'd have of tagging one.

It could have been the repair bot, raking the rocks back into place. It could have been the ibex avatar, with its metal and silicon flesh. It could have just been the wrong day or the wrong time. So many factors and no way to know which ones truly had an effect.

No wonder only a few leopards had been tagged and relocated since the program had begun seven months ago. A similar program had worked well for the Amur leopard, two years ago. Land being encroached upon by human occupants? Move the endangered animals to a preserve before people destroyed the local species—whether for their body parts or to protect their livestock.

Lilia checked the clock superimposed in the upper right of her vision. She'd have to log out in five more minutes or incur a charge for the next hour.

She stamped the ground with one hoof. She'd begun the session filled with hope and elation, and these had drained away with each step into the mountains. Lilia clung to the stories her grandfather had told her of waiting in blinds with his camera and his journal, long hours spent to capture that one moment.

This was her own sort of photography, capturing not just a moment, but a life.

One minute. She folded her legs beneath her and started the logoff process, a green progress bar lighting up next to the clock. Frustration clawed at her chest, her ears flattening against her skull.

Maybe this was why she didn't hear the leopard.

She did see it—two flashes in the darkness, the *tapetum lucidum* of a predatory creature reflecting the last light of the setting sun. It crept through the brush and rocks, its spotted coat blending with its surroundings; its large, soft paws touching the ground, a kiss of velvet only briefly felt.

Lilia couldn't think. She shook with excitement, blinking three times in rapid succession to bring the tagging gun to bear. A slight click sounded in the darkness as the muzzle emerged from her avatar's neck.

The green logoff bar was halfway full; there was no way to reverse the process.

She aimed the crosshairs at the leopard. It moved like mercury, liquid and graceful, filling the spaces between the rocks even as it slid past them. She'd seen the photos, the videos, but seeing one this close—she could see why some people referred to them as "ghosts of the mountains." Lilia's palms grew sweaty in the haptic suit.

Maybe it was this splitting of her awareness that distracted her.

Everything seemed to happen at once. She fired the tagging gun. The dart clinked uselessly off the rocks. The snow leopard rushed toward her just as the green logoff bar stalled and then rushed to the finish line.

Lilia jolted back to her body in her apartment, sweat sticking her hair to the back of her neck. She pulled off the goggles, the mask, the cap and the gloves.

All her muscles ached. "So close, and you choked. You choked." Her throat tightened, her eyes itched. If she started crying now, she wouldn't stop. So she clenched her hands into fists, bringing them down on her desk, trying to stay angry. Everything on her desk clattered.

"Hey," Melanie said from behind her, quietly at first, and then, "Hey! Some people in this apartment are trying to study."

"Go to the library," Lilia said without thinking. What would she do now? She didn't have the money to pay for next month's rent, and she couldn't ask for it from her parents without explaining what she'd been doing. They wouldn't approve.

Grandpa had been good enough to look after her while they'd both been working at the hospital, but following in his footsteps, in however sideways a manner, wasn't to be borne.

"I live here too, you know," Melanie said, her voice hurt and plaintive.

"I'm sorry," Lilia said, unclenching her fists. "I'll keep it down."

The silence between them stretched, their breathing matching in the still air. Melanie broke the quiet first, crossing and then uncrossing her arms. "Why does this mean so much to you? Why spend your inheritance this way? Is this really what your grandfather would have wanted?"

"He would have wanted me to do what I wanted with it," Lilia said. "Whatever made me happy."

Melanie sighed. "You don't seem happy."

She wasn't happy. There weren't many snow leopards left, and they needed to be moved to the sanctuary if they were to have a chance of living on at all. If they were to be anything more than just photographs on a page or unmoving pieces. She stared at the extinct butterfly on her wall. Arms crossed in a casket, chest still. "I need this," Lilia said.

She could feel Melanie's eyes on the back of her head. "Look, do you want to go grab breakfast or something?" she said. "You've been cooped up in your room all night."

Lilia pushed the goggles and mask to the far side of her desk. She felt as though she were still returning to the world. "Yeah, sure."

The figure on her phone had to be wrong. Lilia's stomach sank. The screen was too bright in the dark of her apartment, making her eyes water. She blinked and squinted, hoping she'd misread, but the numbers didn't change. She'd opened her email as soon as she'd woken up and had found the bill from Bioethos in her inbox. But the final amount was more, much more than she'd spent on rentals. She clicked over to the line item invoice. Her rental fees were clear, listed by the hour. Plus, damage fees for the ibex. She'd expected those damage fees.

And then, damage fees for the blue sheep.

She hadn't incurred any damage to the sheep avatar. She remembered signing out, the black of the screen. Nothing had happened!

Lilia shuffled through the company pages, searching for the help line, and then their billing department.

The wait was short, thank goodness. She hated the music they played for calls on hold.

A man picked up on the other end, his voice smooth and supercilious. "Hi, thank you for calling Bioethos Corporation. I'm Michael and I'll be helping you today. What issue were you calling for?"

"I've been charged for damage to an avatar that occurred after I signed out," Lilia said. "The blue sheep. Invoice number three-five-two-six-eight."

"Hold on while I look that up." A pause, the sound of breathing, in-out-in. "Yes, I have that right here. It seems the avatar was badly damaged. Looks like it was leopard damage." He whistled. "You got close, huh?"

She would have basked in his admiration another time, but not this time. Rent was due in a week, and she wasn't going to have the cash if they debited her account. She wouldn't even have enough to rent an ibex again. She remembered the shine of the snow leopard's eyes, flashing like a bicycle's reflectors in the dark. "If a leopard attacked my avatar, it happened after I signed out. I'm not responsible for that damage."

"If it happened after you signed out," Michael said, "it happened right after you signed out, before one of our techs could log in for retrieval." Again a pause, his breath sounding in her ears. "If you refer to clause 2.4 of your contract, you'll see that users are not to leave avatars in precarious positions at the end of their sessions. It states: 'Users who leave their avatars in precarious positions upon logout will be responsible for damage that occurs as a result of the location in which the user left them.'"

Lilia wanted to chuck her phone across the room. She clutched her bed sheets, her fingers aching. "That refers to leaving avatars on the edges of cliffs or in ravines. Not to leaving an avatar in an open area with no foreseeable danger. How was I supposed to know the leopard was going to attack? I was already signing out."

"So you *did* see the leopard."

Lilia hung up. Goddamned corporations were all the same, no matter if they were trying to save an endangered species. It all came down to the bottom line.

She sat there on the bed, the rising sun bleeding red through her curtains. What now? Melanie was her friend—she'd understand if Lilia didn't have the money for rent, but she wasn't rich either. She couldn't cover the cost.

The only option she had was to call her parents—ask them to front her the money until her inheritance was out of probate. They'd lecture her, they'd confiscate her haptic suit, they'd tell her she wouldn't make anything of herself if she kept down this path. And maybe they were right. But they'd cover the rent. She pulled up her parents' number, her finger hovering over the call button.

"Sometimes," Grandpa's voice said in her head, "I'd be ready to give up. Ready to just tear down the blind and walk away from wilderness. There were times I would have killed for a hot bath, for a night in my own bed. But then I'd push on a little farther.

"And I'd get the shot. I'd always get the shot. Nature—she doesn't make it easy on us, Lilia. She never does."

Lilia bit her lip, running figures in her head. There was still a little money left in her account. She checked the time. Dusk in the Himalayas.

Screw it.

She found her haptic suit on the floor, her goggles and mask shoved to the side of her desk where she'd left them yesterday.

The suit fit her like a second skin, though her scalp itched a little as she shoved her hair beneath the cap. She could shower another time.

When she logged into her account and got to the avatar selection screen, she paused. The last bit of cash she had would only cover the ibex rental for an hour. It would cover the blue sheep rental for an hour and a half. But it would cover a marmot rental for a full four hours.

She thought of her grandfather, hunkered down in his blind. Maybe she'd been going about this the wrong way. She couldn't cover a lot of ground with a marmot, but it was smaller, more maneuverable. And easy to hide among the rocks.

The smells washed over her first. Dried grass and dung.

Her avatar was in the depths of a burrow. She shuffled her way out, passing another user who was clearly still learning how to control an avatar. The marmot turned in circles, scratched absently at a spot in the ground and sniffed.

The sun was already half-hidden by a mountaintop, a few stray clouds drifting across a vermilion sky. Lilia checked her map. She was several miles out from the path she'd marked for the snow leopard. If she hurried, she could still make it before nightfall.

Her avatar's mechanical body was thankfully more durable than a real Himalayan marmot's body would be. She scurried over rocks, keeping an eye out for predators from above. The avatar never tired, never needed to stop to catch its breath. The ground blurred beneath her feet. She checked her map again, looking at the places she'd marked. If she saw it there yesterday, then it might be ...

Lilia chose a spot she hoped was right.

She still remembered the first time her grandfather had shown her his photograph of a snow leopard. "I used a tele-photo lens," he said as he handed it to her. Her fingerprints marked the glossy paper, and it smelled faintly of tobacco. The gray-green eyes of a snow leopard stared out of the photograph, its fur ruffled by a slight wind. Lilia had never seen anything so magnificent. It belonged among those rocky mountains, the snow, the clouds so close they looked like fog. "Best photo I ever took," he said, his voice a little gruff.

And then he took it back from her, gently, wiping her sticky child's fingerprints from the surface with the edge of his sleeve. He could have shown it to her on the big screen upstairs, in her parents' living room. But the basement, where Grandpa lived, was a place out of the past—everything a little more tangible, a little more real.

Her breath quickened back in her apartment. She stopped, the faint smell of snow leopard in her nostrils. Here. This was the right place. She found a spot between two rocks, where she could easily retreat to, and waited.

The clock ticked forward in the corner of her vision. There just wasn't enough time. There had to have been moments during Grandpa's career where his clock ran out, where he returned home empty-handed and without the photographs he'd wanted.

Not this time, please, not this time. She was an ounce hunter, and she'd gotten closer than anyone in her club, no matter what Nathan told himself.

The rocks in the distance seemed to move.

The snow leopard emerged from the fog like a ghost, its heavy paws passing silently over the ground. It took Lilia a moment to remember to breathe. This was her grandfather's photograph come to life, and the photo could not do the living animal justice.

It took her a moment to realize she was holding her breath in her apartment. She let it out in a *whoosh*, thankful her sigh couldn't be heard here in the Himalayas. It wasn't until she'd let out her breath and had begun readying her tagging gun that she saw the ibex behind the leopard.

Her eye hovered over it for just a moment, but that was long enough for a username to flash in her vision: ouncearama5284. Nathan. He must have followed her out here. She'd looked for predators above, but she hadn't done her customary circling to check for other avatars.

A low *click* sounded as Nathan's tagging gun slid from its hiding spot in the ibex's neck. The snow leopard froze, its body crouching low to the ground.

Lilia's targeting crosshairs popped up in her vision. "Please, Grandpa, help me out here," she whispered.

She fired almost without thinking, the photograph vivid in her mind, her grandfather's rough fingertips against her hand as he laid the pangolin scale in her palm, his voice rumbling in his chest and the softness of corduroy.

The leopard dashed off into the darkness, as silently as it had arrived, and Nathan's dart clinked useless against the rocks.

Her heartbeat pounded in her ears, her head feeling as though it had floated away from her neck. Had she done it? Or had she missed?

Her vision exploded in superimposed fireworks. *Successful tagging! Thank you for helping Bioethos preserve our planet. Someone will be in contact with you shortly.*

"Thank you," she mouthed. She knew, back in her apartment, no one could hear her. Just her and Grandpa, like they used to be, together in his living room. The prize money would cover what she'd spent and then some. And there was space on her wall next to the Xerces blue for the tagging certificate. The start of her own collection. Already, her mind was racing forward, to other hunts she could partake in. The pangolin was gone, but there were always other species in need of relocation.

A chime sounded—Nathan pinging her. Lilia accepted the call, still halfway numb with disbelief.

"I almost had it," he complained into her ear. "You got lucky."

For a moment, anger surged within her breast. And then her grandfather's voice sounded in her mind.

This time, she spoke his words aloud. "Luck is just the byproduct of patience, persistence, and preparation. Better luck to you next time, Nathan."

She hit the logout button and smiled.

ACTION FIGURES

BY MARTIN L. SHOEMAKER

ACTION FIGURES

BY MARTIN L. SHOEMAKER

I stare intently at the pale green serpent blocking my way —or I'm blocking his, it could be either way. Despite myself, I make the mistake of staring into his eyes. Avatar eyes are mechanical. It's one way that you can tell that they're not alive, even if they're humaniform. Human eyes reveal so much more.

But this serpent, the eyes merely stare, optics taking in my image. My own avatar is humaniform, in fact it looks almost exactly like my real self. I want my patients to recognize me. So the only nonhuman touch is my bright gold eyes and hair.

A surprisingly deep male voice comes from the serpent's mechanical body. "Well, which is it lady, left or right? I'm trying to get through here."

The voice is all wrong, but I take a chance anyway. "Timmy, is that you?" He might be using a voice synthesizer.

But no. "I don't know who Timmy is lady, but it ain't me. Now please, I'm still getting used to this thing. It's hard for me to walk through the park. Could I get around you please?"

I step aside as the serpent wriggles past. I should have

known better. I've heard of these new serpent avatars. Even with all the autonomic algorithms, it takes real work to travel as one of them. You don't have feet, you've got coils, and you have to learn new instincts to drive them around. This was Timmy's first day ever at Avatar Park. Prior to this, all he'd done was play with some of my therapy avatars back in the home. No way he could master a serpent like that. If he'd tried, he'd still be back in the changing room, trying to figure out how to move.

Damn, if only I'd kept an eye on the changing room. But Rafe had gotten into a fight with Phil, and I had to break them up or our field trips from the group home would get cancelled for sure.

And Nia ... I shouldn't have counted on Nia to keep an eye on Timmy. She doesn't hate him. She's a teenage girl with troubles of her own. They *all* have troubles of their own, that's why they're in the group home. Nia's got no patience with a young boy clinging to her like she's some sort of surrogate mother or sister. She tries to be patient but here in the freedom of Avatar Park, she'd simply forgotten him and so had I. And I was the responsible adult in charge, so I can't blame her. I did worse than she did.

And now Timmy's lost. He changed out of the avatar I selected for him—a winged monkey, I knew he liked Wizard of Oz—and into something else.

As the serpent passes, I look around at all the avatars, trying to figure out which one is my lost patient. There are dozens in the area, hundreds or thousands across the park. Scattered in among them are plenty of "Norms," people who aren't in avatars themselves, they're just here to watch the fun, see the shows, and ride the rides. Is Timmy the giant robot? Is he the astronaut? The frog in the baseball cap? The swamp creature? I'm sure he's not one of the flyers. You need a special license to run those, they're much trickier than serpents. The park wouldn't dare let a Norm get hurt, and a falling flyer could be dangerous.

I can't guess who Timmy might be, but maybe he'll give me a clue. "Timmy," I call across the avatar net, "are you an animal?" No answer. But my voice relay shows that he's listening. "Come on, Timmy. Give me at least a little help. Tell me if you're an animal ... Or a human ... Or an insect ... Or a monster ..."

"Not a monster," Timmy says, his voice low and sullen. That was a mistake. As a therapist, I should have known better. "Monster" was a trouble word for him. That's what his latest foster parents had called him when they had brought him back to the home.

I'd lost Timmy. He'd trusted me, and I'd lost him, and I feel the beginnings of panic.

Or *had* he trusted me? Maybe this is some sort of a test. He's always withdrawn, even after all our sessions. He still flinches if I touch him. He doesn't like to be touched by anybody except Nia. Somehow, she'd gotten through his defenses. Too bad Nia often wants nothing to do with him.

And then Nia's in my other earpiece. "Dr. Kim, can't you just have the park tell you who he is? You're responsible. Or just go back to the home and unplug him. It's not like he's in any danger. He's just lost here. His body's still fine."

I can't answer. I'm their therapist, ethically bound to keep their private lives private. If this had come up in group therapy, we could've addressed it as a group, but I can't discuss it with Nia this way. I can't tell her about Timmy's dead parents and the string of foster parents who had given up on him one after another. And the abandonment issues, attachment issues, and trust issues that those temporary homes had led to. If I violate that trust now, I'll push him farther away, so far he might never come back.

I can't explain all that, but maybe I can make her understand. "Nia, how would you feel if I disconnected you, or if I had the park lock you down so I could follow you?"

"Well, that ain't right, Dr. Kim. But he's just a kid."

"He is, but we're supposed to be having fun here in the park. And like you say, he's safe. So please just help me chase him down."

Nia pauses before answering. "I will. I promise."

Nia's a good kid. She feels bad about losing track of Timmy even if she resents him most of the time. And I feel bad about using her guilty conscience against her, but she'll recover.

Timmy though ... Is this an act of rebellion, or an attempt to escape? Rebellion could be good. It would mean he's trying to take some control of his own life. But running away would mean hiding from a world which has already hurt him too much.

I turn back to Timmy's channel. "You're right, Timmy, you're not a monster. I'm so sorry. You're a little boy having fun in a park. Tell us what we can do, so we can all have fun."

"I'm having fun," Timmy answers. What does that mean? Does it mean this game is fun for him? Hiding from me?

Just at that moment, a circus strong man plants himself in front of me. Is that Timmy wanting to be big and strong to scare off the world?

Then I realize, no, there's a big smile on that avatar's face. Timmy never smiles.

"Hello, Dr. Kim," says the voice of the strong man, booming. So, it's one of my patients. Many of them enjoy this game: *Let's see if Dr. Kim can guess who I am.* All right, if it's not Timmy, it's somebody who wants to be strong. Or maybe somebody who likes to play tricks to fool me.

I want to keep after Timmy, but I have a responsibility to *all* of my patients. I have to play the game. "Wow, you are a big strong man."

"Am I? Heh, heh, heh. Or am I a dog who thinks he's a man? Am I an elephant who thinks he's a dog who thinks he's a man? Am I?"

From the pattern of riddles and jokes, I suspect that it's Lacey. Some of the kids like it when I finally figure out who their avatar is, but Lacey likes secrets. She likes mysteries and fooling people. If I guess too easily, she'll be disappointed. So I guess wrong. "Well, hello, Monroe, have you seen Timmy?"

And Lacey's avatar laughs. "Maybe I *am* Timmy."

"Well if you are, I'm pretty impressed. But I don't think you are. I think you're Monroe or Leon or, oh, I don't know who." Let her keep her secret for a little while longer. "But if you see Timmy, please tell me right away. I need to know. Call me on the avatar net."

"I will, Dr. Kim," Lacey's voice comes across the avatar network, and then she giggles. "I fooled you."

"You did," I smile, "very clever. Timmy has fooled me, too."

"Timmy? The little guy?" The strong man frowns. The avatar has an amazingly flexible expression. "He scares easy, Dr. Kim."

"I know. But I also want him to have fun. So, if you see him, please tell me, so I can check on him."

"I will!" And the strong man ambles off, watching the crowd.

It's a fine line sometimes in therapy. I never want to deceive my patients, but I don't tell them everything I know either. Sometimes there're things about them that I've figured out but they're not ready for. I guide them into making the discovery themselves. It's one of the benefits of avatar role playing, both in the group home and here at the park. I can help them to pick shapes that will help them think through a problem. And when they get healthier, I let them choose their own shapes, and I observe to see what that says about them and how they feel about themselves.

Nia, for example, joins up with me again in the avatar of a tall, strong knight, armored head to toe in silver so polished it's practically radiant. This is Nia as I know her from our therapy sessions. Her troubles are all too typical for a teen girl developing too fast with too much pressure on her. Knight armor is her protection. In therapy, I've been helping her to develop armor beneath that: self-confidence, willingness to say "no" to people. Especially boys, who tried to talk her into things she didn't want. She acts tough, but I know that in private she's given in far too many times. So, we've been working on her strengths and her resistance, and that one vital word: *no*.

"What about that, Dr. Kim?" Nia says, pointing at a kid-high puppy dog that's running through the park. "He always chases me around like a puppy."

"It could be, but I couldn't get him to answer if he was an animal. Why don't you show your face to see if he comes up to you?"

"Okay, I'll give it a try." A holographic display appears on the knight's helmet: Nia's face, dark and warm and smiling. "Hey, buckaroo," she says, "do I know you?"

The pup walks up, bows its head so she can scratch behind its ears, and then looks up at her. "My name is Wayne. I've never met you before. Thank you for the scratch." And then the pup gallops off. Four legs aren't as difficult to manage as snake crawling, but it still takes more skill than two legs. We should have realized that whatever Timmy is here, he's a biped.

I try again. "Timmy, I'm with Nia. We're both worried about you."

"No you're not," he answers. "She doesn't care."

I speak out loud to Nia, cutting out Timmy's channel. "Nia, did you say something to him?"

"Dr. Kim, he's such a pain."

I wince; but then I remember that we're on a private channel. Timmy can't hear. From Nia's tone, I know: she said something, and now she's afraid she caused this. "I know, but did you say something?"

"It wasn't mean. I just ... I told him I wanted to get lost, and he shouldn't follow me."

"You did?"

"And ... Ummm ... I told him maybe he should get lost, too."

"Nia ..."

"It was a joke, Dr. Kim. I didn't know." And that's why she feels so guilty. She didn't just lose track of him, she chased him away.

She doesn't need that kind of guilt. I have to talk her through it. "Nia, I know he's annoying."

"Dr. Kim!" Nia's holographic face shows her shock.

"I'm being honest with you, and I need you to be honest with me. I promised I'd always be honest, right? There might be some things that I *can't* tell you; but I've never lied to you, and I won't now. Yes, he's annoying. Have you ever had a little brother?"

The look on Nia's face jolts my memory. Nia *does* have a baby brother, but I'd forgotten that was one of the reasons she'd run away from home. She didn't feel appreciated with a new baby in the house. It was my day to step in it with my patients.

All right, time to change my tactics. "Look, I had a baby brother just like Timmy, he tagged along with me everywhere I went. This was back before avatars. We actually *went* places. He always wanted to follow. He'd throw a tantrum when he couldn't."

"At least Timmy don't throw no tantrums."

"So, I know you feel frustrated when he follows you around. I get it." Timmy doesn't throw tantrums because of the punishment he'd gotten at the last foster home, but I can't explain that to Nia. "But it's because he looks up to you, he trusts you. You're like a big sister for him. He just wants some of your time."

"I know, but he's a kid, you know? When he's around, I can't talk about things like I do with my friends. About ... stuff ..."

I smile. "Well, that's very responsible of you. You're wise to not bring up some 'stuff' around him." She smiles back, and I continue. "Look, when we get back to the group home, let's set up some time for you and me and Timmy to talk through this. He sees you as strong and brave, a protector. But you never asked for that. You don't need that sort of pressure." Actually, Nia needs to be seen that way, but I don't tell her that. She'll figure it out someday.

"Me, a protector?" Nia's face brightens.

"Is he wrong? If he were in trouble?"

"I would beat the shit out of whoever hurt him. Oh, sorry, Dr. Kim."

"I've heard worse, Nia, you can't shock me."

"But that's just the right thing to do. Doesn't mean I want him following me all day."

"That's what we'll talk about. I promise." I create a reminder in my calendar: *Nia and Timmy.* "All right, now let's go find the little kid. We don't want him alone here. In a place like this, all this fun, he shouldn't be alone. He should be sharing it with somebody." That's the problem with Timmy. Deep inside he's a very social, needy kid who wants not to be alone. But all his life, people around him have let him down or hurt him. Hurt him badly. So, is he hiding in the park, trying to be alone? Or is he trying to cross that gap? "Timmy, you don't have to be alone. Unless you want to be."

"Not saying."

"That kid," Nia says. But I don't hear rebellion in his voice, and I don't hear timidity. He doesn't sound exactly happy, but adventurous. He's taking a chance. He couldn't feel like that if he were alone. "Nia, keep an eye on groups. I think he's playing with someone, or at least near them."

"Okay." We start watching different groups at play. It's a challenge to my psychological training. There are lots of groups running through the park, some lining up for games like Gladiatron and the Marble Race, while others simply play in large open fields. One group plays a game of catch. With no one wearing their regular bodies, it's hard for me to tell which groups might be adults, teens, or kids. I can only judge by their behavior.

This group struts around, preening, showing off their elaborate avatars. Well-muscled humans with adaptations, horns, wings or an extra head. Teens, I guess, showing off for each other.

That group over there, the ones playing catch, they seem very organized. Probably adults.

I look for groups who're acting more childlike, and then among those I look for someone hanging on the fringes, ready to run away if he gets scared. So many avatars, so many shapes, so many games; and mixed in among them, of course, all the Norms, watching and laughing, joining in.

Then I think ... "The Norms," I say.

"What, Dr. Kim?" Nia asks, and I realize that I said it on our open channel. I start watching the Norms and the mixed groups, kids playing. That would draw Timmy, regular kids. "Nia, watch for Norm kids and avatars playing together. That's where he'll be."

"You sure?"

I can't lie. "No, it's a hunch, but we don't have anything else."

Now that I know in general what I'm looking for, I can move more quickly. I ignore crowds that are only avatars or older Norms, and instead I concentrate on the kid groups. Here a group plays with a small blue horse giving pony rides. There another group plays baseball. A winged fairy tosses the ball, and a Norm child swings, hits the ball, and knocks it across the field. That wouldn't appeal to Timmy. He isn't into sports.

"Timmy," I ask, "what are you doing?"

"We're just playing."

We're! "Playing what?"

Then Timmy screams in my ear—a happy scream, not a frightened scream—while at the same time my avatar hears screams right nearby. I look to my left in another field, and I see children chased by monsters. Not scary monsters, funny monsters: big bug eyes, long wavy fingers, tentacles that jingle as they run, and stumbling gaits the children can easily outrun. It's a pretend chase, and the kids are having fun.

"He's got to be one of those, Dr. Kim," Nia says. "I'll go get him."

I stop. "Wait. He doesn't want you to go get him. He'll come to us when he's ready. Now we know he's in there somewhere, but for now we'll just watch." Another monster joins in, this one a tall green spider with giant googly eyes behind large pink sunglasses. This one moves faster, and the children run away shrieking, Norms and avatars alike. Then one Norm child falls, and suddenly I hear a loud shriek in my ear.

"Zoom in," I say to my avatar, and my mechanical eyes telescope. That's not a Norm, it's an avatar: a plain, unadorned little boy, just an ordinary kid playing with other ordinary kids behind the safety of an avatar.

Now I hear Timmy's fear. The spider has woken something in him. He's terrified, and it's time to get him out.

Or ... I look at Nia. "Silver Knight."

"Yes, Dr. Kim?"

"Yon lad on the green could use your protection." The Knight nods, draws a holographic sword, and charges into the fray, leaping, tumbling like no human armored knight could possibly do, but an avatar can. She interposes herself between the spider and the fallen boy and cries out, "Hold, varlet! I am the Silver Knight. This boy is in my care and you shall not touch him!"

The spider answers, "Oh, a wise guy eh?"

"Wise *girl!*" Nina shouts. "Defend yourself, beast," and she swings and chops with the holographic sword. Each time the blade hits a leg, holographic sparks fly, and the spider reacts as if injured. "Ouch! Oh, good shot. Oh brave knight, you have wounded me." And they circle around, thrust and blow and parry. Once the spider surprises Nia, swinging a back leg to hit her and knock her to the ground; and the spider looms over her, two legs raised to drop. "Oho, brave knight, I have you now!"

But then Timmy's avatar runs in and kicks one of spider's legs. "You leave her alone!" The spider lifts that leg, cradling it in two others. "Ow, ow, ow, ow, ow." Whoever's inside is a good actor. All the kids nearby are cheering the show.

Timmy's kick leaves the spider with only three legs on the ground, and Nia sees her chance. She rolls to a crouch, dives at one of the remaining legs, and knocks it out from under the spider. The monster falls to the ground. "Come, lad," Nia says to Timmy, "let's dispatch this beast!" They grab three legs and bend them into a ball with the spider's head in the middle.

Other children run up and tie the remaining legs into the knot. One of them says, "It's a giant medicine ball!" All the children laugh, and the spider laughs as well.

"Woe is me!" the spider cries. "What's a poor spider to do? Trapped here, trapped!"

"We'll get rid of him," the Silver Knight says. "Come on kids, let's push him away!" They begin rolling the spider around the field. Soon all the kids and monsters are playing an impromptu game, rolling the spider back and forth while he jeers at them.

When I think Timmy is fully engaged, I join in, and we roll

the spider around for nearly an hour. Avatars don't get tired, so we could keep this up all day; but eventually the kids get bored. Nia asks, "Have you learned your lesson, spider?"

"I have, brave knight. Now I leave you in peace." He unrolls his legs and walks away.

With that game over, the kids—Norms and avatars—run to swings and monkey bars. Timmy heads for a sandbox; and led by the knight, I follow. We all sit, and I can see it's no ordinary sand. It's more like clay, and the kids start molding it into shapes. Nia starts sculpting a large boxy shape, and Timmy's avatar sits next to her. "What are you doing?"

"Building a castle," Nia says.

"A castle? Can I help?"

"Sure."

"What about me?" I ask.

"Okay," Nia said. We built elaborate clay castles, as well as clay horses and knights.

Then Nia builds a dragon and sets it outside the castle gate. "Argh! I am the dragon who breaks down castles," she says.

"No," Timmy says. "You shall not touch this castle!" He grabs one of the knights, then uses some more clay to forge a sword. "I am the Silver Knight, protector of this castle."

"I am a mighty terrible dragon," Nia answers. "No knight shall stand before me!"

Then I have a thought. I grab another small figure and set it down next to Timmy's knight. "She does not stand alone. Together, we are strong!"

Timmy's avatar nods. "Together we are stronger than any monster. Prepare for battle, dragon!" We lift our figures and drop them on the dragon's back, Timmy repeatedly chopping with the sword. "Take that, and that!"

I swing the smaller figure and kick the dragon as Timmy had kicked the spider. "And that! You shall not hurt my friend, the Protector!"

Nia lifts the dragon. "I cannot defeat you. I must flee!" And with a flapping motion, she lifts the dragon into the air.

"But I have a surprise," Timmy says. "I can fly!" With his knight in hand, Timmy stands and reaches for the dragon. Nia's avatar falls over, giggling, and Timmy lands on top of her, giggling as well. They wrestle. At last, with a high laugh, Nia says, "Enough! I yield. I yield to the Silver Knight!"

"And to Brave Boy!" I say.

Timmy's avatar rolls off Nia, comes over, and wraps his arms around my neck. "You did it! You did it!"

"*We* did it," I answer. "We did it." I hug him close. "We did, Timmy, we did."

Too late, I remember that I wasn't planning to use his name. And, just like that, Timmy's avatar goes limp. It backs away and starts walking towards the dressing rooms. The blinking blue light on top of its head indicates that it's unoccupied, available for rent. Nooooo ... Have I scared Timmy away?

And yet, I still feel his arms wrapped around me. That could only mean ... I pull off my VR helmet.

I'm sitting on the low couch in the group home, and Timmy's wrapped around me, face buried in my neck. "We did it," he says. "We did it. We did it." I hold him, afraid to say another word.

Then I feel another pair of arms around me. Nia has joined us. "That was fun, Timmy!" she says.

Timmy lifts his head and looks at her. "It was?"

"Lots of fun." She grins.

Timmy's eyes grow wide. "That was you, the Silver Knight?"

"Uh-huh."

"But I thought you were too grown up to play games like that."

Nia smiles at me, and then at Timmy. "I figured if Dr. Kim can, well, you're never too grown up to play with a friend."

Timmy lets go of me and hugs Nia. "Thank you, Nia. That was the best day ever."

"It sure was, kid. It sure was." I pat Nia's shoulder, and she looks at me. "Can we do it again, Dr. Kim?"

I nod. "Not today, but real soon, we'll all go back to the park." I put my helmet back on to check on the other patients while Timmy and Nia discuss what avatars they'll play next time.

COVERING THE GAMES

BY RON COLLINS

COVERING THE GAMES

BY RON COLLINS

M aggie was dreaming of a real job when her boss, Allyson, stopped by.

As always, her cube was a disaster area.

Four months as the junior food editor for *Repozy*, one of the hundreds of pseudo elite netzines that sprung up every year, and already she was loathing it. At least it was telling stories—which was better than nursing or anything else she might have gotten in the healthcare biz if she listened to her dad.

"You can't go," Allyson said in her always direct fashion.

"We need to be there," Maggie said, coming out punching because the alternative was just too depressing to deal with. "The AvaGames are already becoming, well, like the biggest thing ever—bigger than Burning Man, bigger than the whole ComicCon thing."

The Games were already defining the world in ways nothing else could. Robot vs. robot, with people in the background, was the perfect merging of AI and human. Maggie wanted to go so bad it made her teeth hurt, but she was worried her eagerness was now officially too much for her boss. Despite being barely thirty herself, Allyson was old-school. She expected "kids" to pay dues before they got to do anything real. But Maggie could write the hell out of the AvaGames. She knew she could. Sure, she could patch in on the net like the rest of the world, but her equipment was phase 3, at least five years off the best; not much more immersive than watching a vid. And this was the future. *Her* future.

She would do just about anything to get to San Diego.

"It's just a huge tech-mash," Allyson replied. "We've already got Kenji on it."

Maggie grimaced.

Kenji Jones was a metal head with all the skills of her sophomore journalism professor. The only qualifications he had for the assignment were that he covered Tech Beat and that he had been here for two years—which really meant he wasn't good enough for anyone to hire away.

"I've got a better slant than Kenji," she replied. "One with a wider demographic. More clicks, more bits, right?"

That got Allyson's attention. Maggie may still be a fresh-out but she hadn't needed orientation to learn that if she waved a hundred thousand clicks under Allyson's nose she was liable to see drooling like the world had never seen before.

"Tell me about it," Allyson replied.

"I've got a meeting with Harvey Kloor."

"The head honcho?"

"The one and only."

"President of the Games Committee? Originator of the whole thing?"

"And," Maggie said, sitting back and trying to find the right amount of coy while pushing a nonexistent, but supremely elegant, strand of hair off the side of her face, "as it turns out, connoisseur of all things gourmet."

"I'm impressed."

"I've got an inside game," Maggie said. "He invited me to a private gathering if I could make it out there."

"Sounds like a stalker."

"A private gathering of people on his various boards," Maggie replied. "He said he liked my piece on the fondue place."

"That *was* a good bit."

"The headline could be something like *Dine Like a RoBrainiac.*"

"All right," Allyson finally bit. "Two days per diem. Two-star hotel."

"Not a problem," Maggie said, unable to hide her smile.

Allyson left her alone. Maggie gave a sigh, then pumped a clenched fist in victory.

Freakin-A-yes! She was going to the Avatar Games.

Now, all she had to do was to find a way to get an actual meeting with Dr. Kloor.

"Welcome to Yancey's," the greeter said as Maggie stepped into the foyer.

Its grip was firm and warm as it shook her hand and scanned her pass. It was a Claude model, a copy of the version that won the Avatar XPRIZE back in '24. Probably upgraded several times, but a nice touch, nonetheless. She assumed it scanned her fingerprints, took biometric readings, and any one of a hundred other things such bouncers were capable of.

"Thanks," Maggie replied. "Where are you right now?"

Claude's eyes blinked and the corner of his lip crinkled into an almost human smile. "Cleveland," he said. "Two feet of snow."

"Sucks to be you, man."

"At least the pay's worse."

She laughed. "Oh, I doubt that."

Chances were the operator behind Claude was a middle

manager or a marketing hotshot pulling down ten times the cash she could scrounge, but at least Maggie was here in San Diego the night before the AvaGames were slated to begin, where it was seventy-two degrees with the wind out of the south and sunshine forecasted into forever.

"Whoever had the idea to use Claude as a greeter is probably in line for a big ol' bonus," she said.

"Oh, perchance to dream," Claude replied, moving her toward the glass and steel doorway with the gentle pressure of its hand. "Enjoy yourself."

She stepped into the club and picked her way to the bar.

Yancey's was an upscale place that Endomel, the Games' original sponsor, had nicked for probably several thousand an hour. It's a place you read about in interviews of celebrities, as in "Jennifer Lawrence sat at a table, looking regal in a comfortable Capri suit and a pair of custom Ray-Bans as we chatted about her role in this year's remake of *The Hunger Games*."

Maggie heard that both MacKenzie Ward and Kevin Kajitani were going to make appearances here, and that Dr. Kloor himself might come with them.

Thank God for press credentials.

She needed to finagle dinner with Kloor, of course, but the truth was that the mere idea of meeting MacKenzie Ward in the flesh was enough to make her squee like a fangirl from way back. She had been trying to downplay the idea for the last few hours lest she get her heart broken, but now that she was here, Maggie couldn't help but power-scan the crowd for the trademark cascade of brown-blond hair that Maggie had not-so-shamelessly mimicked throughout most of her high school years.

She had friends who got all squishy about singers, and she could spin up a wicked crush for anyone related to *Dr. Who* or the original cast of *Shenzi*, which was clearly the best of the show's ten years, but MacKenzie Ward and a few others had always been more important for Maggie. They were doers, not dreamers. They weren't afraid to take the world on their own terms. When Maggie was a kid, MacKenzie was in her early twenties—like Maggie was now. Back then, Maggie didn't really understand what a kick-ass deal learning about consciousness and decision making was, but she understood MacKenzie Ward was young, smart, a girl, and pushing the world to be better for everyone.

What was not to like?

The fact that Maggie looked like MacKenzie didn't hurt— they shared thin features and that hair color. Maggie had first come across MacKenzie when she and a friend watched one of the original XPRIZE videos from the Teens and her friend joked about them being time clones. After that, she did a selfie mock-up that made herself look even more like MacKenzie. It wasn't perfect, but if she smudged things a bit she could pretend. Maggie liked to think her brain worked like MacKenzie's, too, but she wasn't kidding herself: Maggie Lynch was no MacKenzie Ward. Yes, she liked weird complexities, but rather than being technically minded, Maggie took those nuances and threw them into making stories she thought were interesting.

Not that any of that mattered now. None of the XPRIZE winners were here.

The place smelled of hors d'oeuvres and sweet cocktails.

The floor plan was open. The tables were tall, octagonal-shaped surfaces of white composite held up by chrome rods bolted directly to the floor. The room was perfectly crowded, filled by groups of youngish people making busy-talk, all nursing tall drinks that were appropriate for the time of day, all with bright, round eyes and that aura of chic geek that made it feel like the room might start growing brains any minute. The tall ceiling came complete with a steampunky mishmash of pipes and rotating ceiling fans, all painted white or silver. A mix of techno jazz was being piped through the Net. The buzz was energized, but not so overbearing you couldn't hear anything.

The opening to her article formed as Maggie arrived at the bar and slid into a space between a woman with dark auburn hair and a guy with dark blue G-shades.

"Mimosa," she said to the bartender, trying to decide if he was an avatar, too, and coming to the conclusion that he was all human. You couldn't always tell these days. That was one of the PR problems the games had. Some people were always going to be afraid. But as far as she was concerned, people were people. Good or bad, life in the future was going to be whatever the whole of the people made it. No different from any other time.

"You've got to be shitting me!" the guy beside her said, putting his hand on Maggie's shoulder and forcibly turning her his way. "I didn't think anyone else from *Repozy* was coming."

It took a minute to recognize him with the glasses. The fact that he was wearing a sport coat and a stylish open collar shirt rather than a relic-grunge T-shirt hadn't helped.

"Hey, Kenji," Maggie said.

He was sipping a martini that his grin said wasn't his first.

"Hey, it's Ma-GAG-ie!" he cried out, using her least-favorite nickname in the entire world. His voice carried enough it turned a head or two. Then he leaned in. "How did you get vacation so soon? Is Allyson a softie under that cold-bones exterior?"

"I'm not on vacation," Maggie said.

"What?" Kenji's expression grew bemused. "Are you saying you got a gig?"

Maggie used the bartender's return to avoid responding, taking the mimosa from him and dropping a 20 percent tip.

"I'm going to mingle," she said, sipping and leaving Kenji at the bar.

Asshole.

She spent the next ten minutes casing the place, going

upstairs, then down to get the lay of the land. Endomel had put displays in every nook—so she got glimpses of everything from the newest wearables to something called a dream catcher, which was a device that monitored thought emissions in your sleep to help people optimize their down time. Some kids had turned it into art by plugging several emission streams into a display that weaved about in gorgeous waves of amazing colors. As Maggie strolled from table to table, she kept her eye out for XPRIZE royalty. It was probably too early for them, especially Dr. Kloor, who had a thousand details to pay attention to, but she kept scanning, anyway.

When she finished the tour, Maggie found an unobtrusive spot next to a real plant, leaned back against a wall, and took in the whole of the room.

No MacKenzie Ward.

Sigh.

She looked at a holographic clock and checked her stomach. She needed to eat something. As she raised her half-full glass, a woman on her way to the restroom bumped her elbow. Orange liquid spilled down Maggie's shirt.

"Damnit!" she said. "That's my best top!"

Actually, it was the only top she had brought, a white short-sleeved shirt with a purple flower print falling over one shoulder. Now, it was blotted with orange mimosa.

"Sorry," the woman said. She was wearing a pair of golden pants and a blouse. "Let me help you."

She took Maggie by the elbow and led her down the hall toward the restroom. Maggie was in such shock that it took three steps before she even tried to twist out of the grip. The woman's hand clamped down harder and the other pushed the small of her back toward the door at the end of the hallway.

"What are you doing—"

The woman hit the handle with her hip. The door swung open.

Maggie started to scream, but a cloth wrapped around her mouth and a meaty arm closed tight around her waist. A chemical smell burned her throat and made her eyes water. She kicked backward and got full shin, but received only a solid *thunking* sound for her effort. Her vision watered more, but she saw a dark car with its trunk gaping open.

The man carried her to the car.

No, she thought. It wasn't a man. It was an avatar.

Her brain got fuzzy then. Grayness closed in from the edges of her vision. The thing dumped her into the trunk, and everything got dark.

She never even heard the sound of the lid closing.

"That's not MacKenzie Ward," the voice said.

"Of course it is." It was the woman's voice—Ms. Golden Pants. "I heard a guy call her MacKenzie, and she looks ..."

"This woman is barely out of school!"

"But the guy ..." The woman's voice trailed away.

As Maggie's consciousness returned, she recalled Kenji yelling her name, *"Ma-GAG-ie"* at the top of his lungs. The woman had misheard him in the din of the crowd, and mistaken her for MacKenzie.

Maggie pried her eyes open.

She was seated in a hard-backed chair. Her head leaned back against a wall.

They were in some kind of technical lab—something like the electronics classrooms at school when she was dating Kendra, who had been an engineering major. Maggie's hands were tied and in her lap—actually wrapped in duct tape. Her ankles were also taped together. Her captors had perched her there with her legs straight out. Tables were filled with circuit boards and wiring. Soldering irons sat in nooks between an array of monitors and control boxes. Two people stood there: Ms. Golden Pants and the man who had been speaking. A few others were sitting at tables, wearing headsets with sleek wraparound helmets, and moving their hands this way and that. Second-seat monitors that allowed onlookers to follow along displayed their situations.

Avatar runners, she thought.

Those people were connected to the net, operating remote robots.

She rolled her head forward.

What was happening? Why was she here?

"She's awake," the woman said.

The man loomed over her. His eyes were hooded and questioning, his lips curled in a curious smile. The whiskers of a three-day-old goatee crinkled around his face.

"Who are you?" he said, his face near hers.

Maggie edged up in the chair, looked at him, then screamed as loud as she could.

The man jumped back like he about wet his pants.

"What the hell was that for?" he said.

"Don't play with her, John," Golden Pants said. "If that's not Ward, we need to get rid of her."

"What are you suggesting?"

"I don't know, but no one's going to give us E-Tech if that's not her."

Give us E-Tech? Maggie thought. *Not her?*

"The first thing we have to do is keep her quiet," the man said. "Where's the tape?"

Maggie's mind raced.

She could stand, but her hands and ankles were tied, so unless she could hop like a kangaroo she wasn't going anywhere. Then she stopped. There was another way to get her hands free—she had never done it, but she had seen it on a show—but the problem remained that she didn't know if she had time to free her feet, and she wasn't sure what to do even if she did get loose.

The room had three doors: one to her right, the other two on the opposite side of the room.

"I've got her on-screen," one of the others suddenly barked.

Both John and Golden Pants turned to take in the image that played on a large roll-up screen that hung on the far wall: MacKenzie Ward entering Yancey's.

A flash of disappointment hurt. She had been so close.

"Send in Rover-1," the man said, leaning over the table to adjust the screen resolution. "Get the car out back again. We need to take her as soon as possible."

One of the controllers got to work, and Maggie could see a monitor with a different view of Yancey's. The man's Rover-1 avatar was a long way from MacKenzie, but clearly making his way toward her.

Maggie froze, pieces suddenly coming together.

E-Tech ... Entanglement Tech ... the next amazing step forward.

It was built off advances that engineers in Norway had developed using quantum entanglement to allow immediate communication between two remote points. E-Tech placed into avatars would change everything—again—because it would remove the greatest impediment to avatar use there was: the lag time for precise control that was inherent in the speed information could travel. Remove the time lag, and a surgeon, for example, could do surgery literally any place in the universe. Remove the time lag, and interstellar space exploration would get a total kick in the excitement meter.

E-Tech's development was being managed by Foundation for the Future, which was a multinational scientific and engineering organization that had among its founders one MacKenzie Ward.

Suddenly, it all made sense.

These people were planning to kidnap MacKenzie Ward and ransom her for the plans to E-Tech.

Maggie gritted her teeth, suddenly mad.

Her captor's backs were turned as they all focused on the screen.

She moved without thinking.

She bent over, brought her knees to her chest, and grabbed the duct tape around her ankles—there were five or six loops, enough to keep her feet together but still thin enough she could rip it along its cross section.

Her feet came loose with a tearing sound that brought attention.

She stood, raised her hands over her head like the video had shown, remembered to keep her elbows tucked in like the admittedly hunky guy had done, and brought her wrists down in a violent plunge toward her hips. The restraint tore, and she was running toward the door to her right before she even had time to be thankful.

"Get her!" John yelled.

She yanked the door open, stepped in, and slammed it shut. Her fingers found a lock, which she slammed down just as one of her pursuers got to the handle on the other side.

The door held.

Panting, Maggie ripped the rest of the tape from her wrists and turned to find she was in a rectangular room, maybe fifteen meters to the long sides, each of which were lined with rounded VR stations that had shell-shaped second-seat monitors on the wall before each.

Pounding came to the door, so Maggie slipped down the row of machines.

The VR stages made the center feel like an aisle.

The stations were familiar. Basic systems at their core, but obviously more advanced than any she had seen before. Each included sensor-laden floor pads, mechanical gloves and head visors, as well as full-haptic drive strips that Velcroed onto arms, legs, and torsos to give a user sensory control of the avatar they suited into.

The room reminded her of an ExTreme center—places her friends had held parties to play in shared-world environments like ExTreme Rescue or ExTreme Adventure. She had been particularly taken by a white-river rafting experience.

Maggie scanned the room. There was no way out. No doors other than the one she had come through.

The pounding intensified into booming.

She looked for a weapon and saw nothing beyond power cables and VR boxes. Maybe she could rip down a monitor to use as a club. No, they were too big. She doubted she could actually lift one if she were able to pry it off the wall. At best, it would be a shield rather than a weapon.

An idea hit then—if she couldn't get herself physically outside ...

She flipped the power switch of the closest station.

An image of a locker room snapped onto the second-seat monitor. Actually, it wasn't a locker room. The area was well lit, and there were figures there, but they were not people. They were robots, rows of robots that stood at some form of attention beside equipment cabinets.

She recognized two.

They were avaletes, controllable avatars slated to compete in tomorrow's games.

Holy crap.

These people had hacked into the avalete system. Whoever was doing this planned to mess with the Games. Made sense, she supposed. Install QE, win the Games. She wondered what lines the oddsmakers were laying, and how big this could be.

A deep thump came from the door. The walls shook.

She slipped into sensor footies and legging strips that had

been looped over a nearby rail. The gloves went on easily, as did the arm sensors.

Another huge thump rattled the floor.

No time to find torso sensors.

Maggie jumped on the sensor pad and wrapped the VR set onto her head.

It automatically adjusted to her skull, and a screen snapped down over her face. Her vision sharpened. With a glance, she toggled full haptics. When she moved her arm next she felt the weight of the movement and saw the robot's hand wave in front of her face. Totally awesome.

She scanned the area in front of her avalete and confirmed she was in a storage room, not a locker. No humans were there. She jumped her avalete off its battery charger and ran to the door.

Tools rattled at her side. Cool. She had a utility belt complete with rope, gloves, and a few other doodads. A tiny drill, even. As her avalete made it to the storage room door, an eye movement brought a series of icons onto Maggie's upper vision—they were separate controllers, she realized, toggles for accessing body modifications that would make it easier to climb, electromagnetics to deal with other unique situations. A first aid compartment that was probably inside the avatar's torso listed everything from bandages to EpiPen to antiseptic swabs. That meant she was running an avalete that was part of the Search and Rescue Games—awesome. It made her feel like some combination of Bruce Wayne and Diana Prince.

It also made her think of Rover-1 closing in on MacKenzie.

Maggie had no idea where her physical body was, but if she was right, her avalete was at the Endomel Coliseum. That would mean Yancey's was just down the street. She had to get there if she was going to save MacKenzie.

The door was locked from the outside, but it opened to her avalete's touch.

She found herself in a hallway, and she ran, both feeling and hearing the *clickity* sounds of her progress.

Another banging sound boomed from behind her physical self, this time accompanied by a crackling that said either the wall or the door was breaking.

She was at full speed when she got her avalete to the security center.

"Hold it there," one of the guards said, putting his hand on his hip.

"Come with me," Maggie said as she blew past him.

Two other guards tried to block her, but they hadn't expecting problems from *inside* the storage area, so her advantage of surprise was enough to help her avoid them. Her feet pounded on the expansive tile floor. The exit was a revolving glass door. The jangle of pursuing cops came as she slipped through it.

Yancey's was at the corner, its classic marquee rolling with news of the Games.

The sound of a wall crumbling came from behind her.

She ran her avalete harder, her chest burning with the exertion.

Yes, she needed to work out more. She knew that now. She would give anything for a rocket booster. But it was what it was.

She ran through crowds that were suddenly gasping at the sight of an avalete racing through their midst.

People cheered.

One boy called out a name and applauded for her.

The security police raced along behind her as she ran into Yancey's, pushed past Claude, and crashed into the pack of warm bodies who were now crammed into the place.

"Find MacKenzie Ward," she said to her controller.

Face recognition software returned a blue dot.

Upper floor, against the rail, speaking with a reporter.

Kenji Jones, for Christ's sake.

She was giving freaking Kenji Jones an interview.

The clamor caused by her appearance turned everyone's heads—everyone's except for the Rover-1 avatar that was moments from reaching MacKenzie.

A final crash came from behind her real self. The door burst open, and Maggie could feel John and Golden Pants entering the room.

Maggie grabbed the grappling cord from her avalete's belt as she raced it farther into Yancey's.

Screams rang out.

"Stop it!" one woman said, but Maggie kept her focus.

She released cord from her belt in a rapid-fire loop, then swung the hook up over the deck's railing to loop around Rover-1's wrist. Once she had him, Maggie pulled it tight. The thing fought back, but Maggie set herself, and her avalete was strong. The unit lurched toward the railing as Maggie reeled in line, playing Rover-1 like it was a game fish.

A moment later, the thing was stretched over the rail, and the room went silent.

"Get away, MacKenzie!" Maggie yelled. "It's trying to kidnap you!"

Then everything went dark, and Maggie fell backward. The back of her head thumped on the ground, and pain bloomed in her elbow. Two sets of hands held her down, and someone stripped the VR helmet from her face.

"I think you're going to be a very sorry girl," John said, standing at Maggie's feet.

"We've got to bug out!" Golden Pants called from the doorway. She was wearing an ear clip. Her skin had paled, and her lips thinned. "Orders," she said. "Total abort."

"Take her out back," John called out, motioning to Maggie. "Then get this place under total lockdown."

The men yanked Maggie up. She yelled and screamed, and tried to bite, but there was nothing to do. They dragged her out of the room, down the hallway, and into a vacant parking lot—where she was reacquainted with the trunk of a car.

She pounded the lid.

She yelled some more.

She kicked and pushed and dug to get out, but there was nothing to do.

Maggie groaned. She was probably going to die, she thought. They couldn't let her live, could they?

Then ...

In the distance, a sound ... sirens ... growing nearer ... the squeal of wheels arriving ... the crunch of tires on gravel. Doors opening. Voices calling out: "On the ground! Get on the ground!"

She pounded on the trunk again.

"Hold on," a voice came. Then the sound of the lid being pried open.

Maggie took in the view of darkening sky, and the face of the most magnificent police officer she had ever seen.

Only then did she break into tears.

It was late when the police brought Maggie to Yancey's, but MacKenzie Ward was still there, sitting in a private booth. A waiter brought them drinks.

"I need to thank you," MacKenzie said. "I think you saved my life."

"I understand you returned the favor," Maggie replied.

"I helped, but a few other folks did the real work."

The cops told Maggie a different story, but she wasn't going to argue with her hero doing the humble thing. MacKenzie had understood what was happening the minute things went down. She used the Rover-1 system to trace the location of its controller. Others helped, but MacKenzie had shown them the way.

"I've got a present for you," MacKenzie said, handing Maggie a package.

It was a long-sleeve jersey with MacKenzie's "Squishy Robot" logo.

"I understand you were in need of a new shirt."

"I love it," Maggie said. "I adore it."

"I'm sorry you had to go through that."

"It's all right." Maggie shrugged. "I just hope this doesn't cause you problems."

"Like what?"

"People worry about criminals getting ahead."

"They do, but that's good, too. Powerful technology has to be dealt with responsibly."

"You mean like there's no Force without the Dark Side?"

MacKenzie chuckled. "Kind of. The press are already calling you AvaGirl the superhero, after all. So that's pretty cool, right?"

Maggie blushed. Yes, that was pretty cool.

"I understand you're a writer, too."

"Yeah," Maggie said, "just a food editor, though."

"Oh, I think you're more than that."

"What do you mean?"

"I did some background work while I was waiting. I loved that piece you did on the fondue place. Never seen a foodie use information from biotech, agriculture, and petroleum engineering in a way that made me actually want to have fondue."

Maggie smiled. "Thanks, I think."

"And you're right about people being afraid of the future. No one can stop the few bad apples we have from making a mess now and again, but you're the kind of person who can help other folks understand that the world has more good people in it than selfish ones."

Maggie smiled.

"Have you ever thought about writing for the technology field?"

"Only every day."

"You want a job?"

"What?"

"We have several groups working on new things. I love working with people who have your kind of passion and attention to detail. If you're interested, I would love to have AvaGirl writing about them."

Maggie's smile was wide enough it hurt. She crushed the jersey in her fists and held it to her chest. "This is too much."

"Is that a no?"

"Of course not. It's a full bore yes." She hesitated, thinking about Allyson. "I have one request, though."

"What's that?"

"I owe my old boss an article. Do you think I could get a dinner with Dr. Kloor?"

"I think we can manage that," MacKenzie said, sitting back with a grin.

"That would be awesome," Maggie said, sipping her drink, remembering how it felt to power AvaGirl through the streets, and dreaming about her real job. "Totally amazing."

AVATAR SYNDROME

BY HARRY DOC KLOOR

AVATAR SYNDROME

BY HARRY DOC KLOOR

T he cacophony from the torrential rain sounded like a thousand cymbal-banging monkeys. The noise irritated Mike, grated on his already frayed nerves. It was one of the reasons he hated coming to Rio de Janeiro. He was a California boy, and had an innate dislike of overindulgent storm clouds. Whenever it rained like this in Southern "Cal," homes went mud surfing down the Malibu hills. Anything over a light sprinkle made him feel uneasy.

He looked up into the sky. The dark mocha clouds reminded him of a bad vacation he once took when he was six, but he couldn't recall quite where he'd gone. It was one of his favorite memories, he knew that much—but the details eluded him. In fact, these days much of his past seemed to be a forgotten dream, a sign that he needed to take a break, or perhaps use less Avatars. He heard that some rare individuals who spent too much time in them could have memory issues. It was why he decided to come here in person. (Well, that was a lie. He came in person because he needed to be here in the flesh.) He pushed away the thought that he might be suffering

AMFS—Avatar Memory Loss Syndrome. He just needed to rest, but that wasn't going to happen till he caught the Roman.

He scanned the sky again and let out a sigh of relief as he spotted a small formation of bees flying toward the large warehouse. Only they weren't bees, but surveillance drones. Mike activated a matrix of mixed-reality screens (MRS) with a simple touch on the frame of his Buddy Holly replica-style eyeglasses. He loved Holly's music, a classic musician from the last century, whose life had been cut short by a plane crash. Almost no one used eyewear anymore, though Mike still did—but at 53 he was set in his ways and not about to get an implant. Besides, he had these MRS glasses 3D printed to his exact specifications. They made him feel cool. Too bad no one else thought so.

He had worried that the rain would delay their raid; that it would interfere with the drones. He was wrong. The screens showed that the twenty or so microdrones were nearing their target, a decaying mega-warehouse, the central building in this long-forgotten complex. *At least the damned things are waterproof,* he thought, *and the rain should cover their hum.* A hum the manufacturer insisted didn't exist, but anyone whose ears had not been blown out at a Holo-Gendev-VR-Concert rave would easily hear them coming.

The antiquated "hummers" slipped through a broken window on the third story. The building once served to process thousands of tons of raw sugar, but that was more than fifteen years ago, before the collapse of the sugar market, a commodity that much of the world in the year 2042 considered to be an addictive poison and the leading cause of preventable diabetes.

Mike scoffed at that thought that sugar was somehow a poison in a country that still served as the key export portal for South American nose candy. If you asked him, the world was focused on the wrong white stuff. Mike thought it was all organic horseshit. Sugar was awesome in his book. The key was not to overindulge. Sugar wasn't poison any more than fat or his favorite holo-programs. He dared his doctor to fine him for the occasional candy bar and ribeye he consumed. (And the doctor did fine him—monthly.)

Mike shifted back and forth, antsy. He looked at the various drone video feeds, which appeared in front of him as augmented overlays. The drones located and labeled twenty-seven human guards positioned throughout the building. They were completely unaware of the drones, or of the thirty ICE agents and Brazilian police that had eyes on them.

Mike turned to Agent Lacy, who was leading the raid. "Let me come in with your team. It's only fair. After all, it was my investigation that discovered this work hive."

"In your meat suit? Don't be ridiculous," she replied. She was right, of course. Mike was in person, whereas Lacy and her fellow ICE agents and the Brazilian special force officers were on location as avatars. Most had taken possession of DC4 AUs (Defense Class 4 Avatar Units), but Lacy inhabited a R4X AU (Regal 4X fully-skinned humanoid Avatar Unit). The RX4 appeared as a six-foot-four Brazilian male officer. These fully-skinned models were reserved normally for dignitary security details, and cost about ten times as much as the DC4s. Mike suspected she was in this avatar model just to screw with him.

"Like I said before, many of these kids will be suffering from Avatar Syndrome. They need to have real humans present to ground them. Those DC4's will terrify them," he explained.

"Not as much as your dead body will. Stay put. You shouldn't even be here. If you get hurt, it's my career, not yours." She jabbed a finger into his chest, hard. "I mean it Mike, stay the fuck *here* ... until I give you the all clear."

"Fine, fine ... but I need to be there before you unplug them." He reached over and gave her avatar hand a loving squeeze. She softened, and gave him an affectionate squeeze back.

One of the Brazilian officers, Sgt. Luiz, in a DC4 spoke up.

"My God! There must be over ten thousand in there!"

"Impossible!" Mike hoped Luiz was wrong, but then he looked at the screens, expanded it with a gesture—and found that Luiz was correct. Displayed clearly on screen now were endless rows, stacked thirty high, of Avatar Control Pods (ACP's). Only these were not ordinary home SOUL (Sensory Operation User Link) pods, these were the kind reserved for severely paralyzed humans; people suffering from late stage Parkinson's disease, ALS, spina bifida, multiple sclerosis, Guillain–Barré syndrome, etc. Most likely, these were knockoff models, built in Russia based on their crude, yet, sturdy construction. Each unit provided for waste removal, muscle stimulation, and intravenous nutrition. The pods provided direct mind interface to Avatar Units, which based on the array of satellite antennas nearby could supply labor anywhere in the world.

"Okay, people, let's move in. Luiz, radio HQ that we are going to need ten times as many busses and medical personal on hand. This is far bigger than Salvador or Bogota."

Lacy powered up her weapon, motioned to her agents, and took off running toward the building, the other agents and officers following at breakneck speed, splitting up so that they could breach the building on all sides. One of the advantages of these Avatar Units was speed. They could cover the 300-yard gap in a third of the time of the world's fastest sprinter. They were also ten times stronger than a normal human, and had a sophisticated targeting system.

Reaching the building, Lacy activated her RF capture vision, enabling her to see through the outer wall. RF vision was rather old, but it was all these particular units had in them. It used Wi-Fi signals, which would bounce off humans and other objects, enabling a crude version of Superman's x-ray vision. More advanced units actually had a form of neutrino detectors that allowed for higher resolution scans, but this was

South America. Seeing no humans, she placed a sonic breach grenade and backed away as it blew a huge hole through the wall. Gun drawn, she leaped inside, with four more agents right behind her.

She and her fellow agents rounded the building, knocked down doors and breached the outer walls. Moments later the zap of high voltage stun bullets could be heard, as well as machine gun fire from the men the agents sought to take down. From afar, Mike watched the raid go down like clockwork. The human thugs were simply no match for the Avatar Units. As the outer hallways were cleared, Lacy and her team moved toward the heart of the building, toward the Avatar SOUL Pods.

About a dozen of the Roman's gang remained. Most took up positions around the Avatar Pods. Lacy and her avatar team readied themselves for a final push. They needed to strike fast, and in such a way as to not endanger the occupants of the pods. Mike spotted two of the Roman's guards moving away from the heart of the building, toward the power generators, led by an Avatar Unit. There were no drones down there; Lacy and her team would have no idea what they were doing.

Mike rewound one of the screens, and spotted an avatar with the guards; an avatar that was clearly not operated by any of the agents. It was a slick model with a holo-projected head screen. The avatar used a rapidly-modulated uplink frequency. It was odd, containing in fact dozens of signals that made it impossible for Mike to block or even trace the avatar's source signal. He would need to get close to the unit and tap into it with a near-field scanner. His heart leapt as his gut told him who was operating this unit.

"Lacy, you need to get some agents into the basement to the power generator," Mike belted into his microphone. "I think the Roman is on-site as an avatar."

"What makes you think it's the Roman?" asked Lacy.

"It's using a heavily shielded signal system and it's a *Benford*

Cosm Avatar model. Those babies cost a fortune. No way it's a guard or an administrator. Whoever is inside is special. We need to get close to it and perform a near-field scan."

The sound of gun fire erupted, followed by people cursing in several languages, then Lacy spoke up. "Let it go! I need to secure these pods, and these assholes seem to have a death wish and don't care who they endanger." She signed off and signaled her men to take up sniper positions. She had no choice but to end this, and to do so fast. And that meant using real bullets. It was against orders, but the Roman's people were firing indiscriminately and several pods had already been hit.

Mike cursed, then took off running. Halfway across the open yard, he stepped into what he thought was a shallow puddle, and ended up knee-deep in water, invoking the names of several deities performing unspeakable deeds. His boots filled up with muddy water, and he was quite literally a sitting duck. He scrambled out of the mini pond, made it to the building without being shot, then moved through the breach created by Lacy. It was dark, but his eyes adjusted almost immediately to the darkness, a gift from his last eye surgery: implanted IR lenses. He would have to thank his doctor if he could ever remember her name.

Moving through the maze of corridors, Mike drew his Colt from his shoulder holster—another relic, a symptom of watching too many old movies like Dick Powell in *Murder My Sweet,* Bogart in *The Big Sleep,* and of course Ralph Meeker in *Kiss Me Deadly.* (He used to watch these nearly century-old classics with his best friend, Nancy. She was one of the few people he could recall from his childhood, but in reality, it was really the movies he mostly remembered.)

Reaching the bottom of the stairs, he pushed open a heavy wooden door, and moved down a service corridor. Rusting pipes overhead had dripped water for decades, creating red rust vein lines in the concrete walls. It gave the place an eerie and forbidding feeling that caused him to pause. The hallway was long and cramped. If he was spotted before he made it to the door at the end of the hallway he was dead meat.

He decided to creep to the door. Each step felt like an eternity, but he made it unseen. Peeking inside, he saw two armed men in their twenties, clearly well paid based on their grooming, shoes, and advanced firepower. The third figure was the Roman's avatar, with a perfectly projected holographic display of the user's head—except that it displayed the image of a green animated skull with piercing blue eyes. On the skull's head was a gold laurel wreath crown. This was the Roman, and he was calmly issuing orders to the men on how to arm the charges. The men had already attached the charges around the power generator, intending to blow it up. The sudden power drop could be deadly to the occupants inside the Avatar Pods above.

There was no time to waste. Mike stepped inside and aimed his gun at the two men, who had placed their machine guns on the floor as they planted the charges. "Hands up, move away from the generator," he grated, gesturing with his gun.

One of the men decided to dive for his weapon. Mike placed a well-aimed shot in the man's head—an extraordinary shot for a man of his age, but his adrenaline was pumping and he felt superhuman.

The other man, seeing his companion's fate, dutifully put up his arms. The avatar, however, moved to the control panel. Mike pulled out a second weapon that looked like a small baton, pressed a button that sent out a plasma bolt, and put a hole in the avatar's back, taking out its motor functions. It was a perfectly placed shot—not at all an accident. The Roman avatar spun around by the impact, then dropped to the ground. Its secondary power unit was still operational, and the operator —via the animated eyes in the holo-projected skull—looked up at him, grinning in a way that a real skull couldn't. It gave Mike the creeps.

"Mike Anderson, I can't say that I am glad to see you here."

Mike reacted with surprise. "How do you know my name?"

"We know a lot about you, as well as your girlfriend, Agent Lacy. She is annoying, but you're the one that's really becoming a problem. We thought Bogota was a fluke, but clearly, we underestimated you. How did you locate us? This installation should have been completely invisible." The Roman avatar seemed honestly amazed.

"The same way I figured out that you're the Roman. I simply followed the clues. Your team is good, but I'm better." Mike glanced down at his scanner—it was running a trace to locate where the Roman was broadcasting from, but the damned thing seemed to be malfunctioning as it was still detecting over forty, no make that sixty, locations—and even these were constantly shifting. He fingered a reset while trying to keep the Roman talking.

"Why are you doing this?" he asked. "There has to be a better way to make a living."

"I am providing a much needed service: cheap labor. With labor democratized, its cost has risen globally."

"To the benefit of all," Mike countered.

"To the benefit of the workers. But my clients prefer to pay less, a lot less, so they can make more—and so do I!" he concluded with a laugh.

"You won't be laughing much longer. This had to hurt, and soon, I plan on making you hurt in a more personal way." Mike reset the scanner again.

"Now, now ... don't let emotions cloud your thinking. This is business, so let me make you a business proposal. Walk away, and I am willing to forgive this sizable loss, provided that you stop this crusade of yours. If you don't, we will find you and your family, and when we do—it won't be pretty. I will kill them —but you will be kept alive as my personal plaything, and I will have you relive their deaths over and over again."

The third reset didn't work, the trace scanner still showed multiple operator locations for the Roman's avatar. Somehow, he was masking his location, or the tech genius who sold him this device was not so clever after all.

"A personal plaything? Thanks. That gives me an idea of what to do with you once we get our hands on you." Mike aimed his pistol at the Roman avatar.

"That's never going to happen. That toy you're trying to use is not going to work, but my men will be seeing you real soon. Ta-ta for now." The Roman's avatar holo image froze, a sign that he had signed off. Mike put three rounds from his Colt into the head, shattering the screen. The holographic image persisted on the shattered pieces, creating a jigsaw puzzle of the skull all over the floor, one fragment containing a blue eye. Mike shuddered briefly, then stepped on it.

Lacy had entered the room with three agents just as he fired. One of the men rushed over to the man who was standing with his hands still raised high. His hands were roughly pulled behind his back and cuffed.

Lacy's avatar's face went from furious to relieved. "I'd yell at you, but there's no time." She gave him a quick kiss, and he kissed her bearded male avatar back, despite the scratchy beard.

Mike stood near the next batch of thirty avatar pods. Next to him were a group of healthcare workers, half of them in an odd array of Avatar Units. In time of crisis, such as natural disasters, governments were able to co-op any avatar in operation in a city. This "emergency use" was an extension of the *One-In-Seven Rule* created by the *UN Kloor Global Impact Accords of 2028*, which created a globally-reserved bandwidth for the operation of avatars anywhere in the world, in exchange for the shared charity use of avatars by each country that signed the accord. This rule essentially required all operators of avatars to provide their Avatar Units one day each for social benefit. This initiative ensured that volunteers around the world could provide their assistance as teachers, doctors, engineers, and agriculturalists to all the world's underserved populations.

With over a billion and half avatars in use around the world, there were now always at least a hundred million or so available any day of the year. The collection of avatars assisting today enabled medical and psychological personal from around the globe to essentially teleport in and give the necessary care. The collection of avatars ranged from executive models to waiters, from animated characters to historical figures. Human volunteers rotated in every few hours, as there was always plenty of available labor willing to give their time now that it was as simple as stepping into a SOUL pod. It was the driving force for Kloor when he created the XPRIZE back in 2016, a means to solve most of the UN's sustainable challenges by creating a means for people to instantly get where they were needed. Since the winning of that prize in 2022, the world of 2042 had vastly improved.

Unlike the rotating volunteers, Mike refused to rest. He'd been at this for over 18 hours, overseeing the release of each group of teenagers and young adults out of the pods. He tapped his foot impatiently as the next phase of volunteers took control of the avatars. "Is everyone ready? Hey, Einstein!" He pointed to an education Avatar Unit that looked exactly like Einstein did at 45, wild hair and all. "Pay attention!"

"Sorry sir … It's my first time taking possession of a male avatar. Back home, it's against the rules to change sex via avataring." A high-pitched woman's voice came out of the Einstein model. It was actually not her voice, as her native tongue was unlikely to be English, but most avatars translated audio in and out depending on who they were speaking to—and since Mike spoke English, the unit translated her voice into English. The operator must have selected the option to keep her vocal range that of a woman.

"That sounds like a stupid rule," answered Mike. "Now, all of you focus. From the logs we pulled up, the kids in these next thirty pods have been inside for over two years. Most are under ten years old. They will be suffering from Avatar Syndrome and will probably have forgotten they are children. They will be completely disoriented and may react violently. Imagine discovering that everything you think about yourself is a lie and multiply that by a thousand. Make sure they don't harm themselves and move them gently into the ambulances. Make sure you strap each one to the gurney, even if they act as if they are fine. Believe me—they are not."

"Sir ... shouldn't their parents be here or something? Wouldn't that make it easier?" asked the Einstein model.

"What's your name?" Mike replied, trying to remain calm. This woman was a medical student and volunteering her time, and he appreciated her even if his tone indicated otherwise.

"Marinette," she answered. "I live in Croatia, but I was born in Italy."

"Well, Marinette, many of these kids may not have parents, others were kidnapped, and some were probably sold by their parents. Although that is becoming rare these days, we still find cases. It's going take us a while to locate relatives, and we don't have that time. In fact, we don't have time for any more questions. Understood?"

"Yes sir." Einstein took her position.

Mike signaled to an ICE agent avatar, who with a few key strokes powered down the Avatar Control Pods. As the doors on each unit opened and the children inside each one awakened, the medical personnel, via their avatars, ushered them out of each pod. Some freaked out, some cried or screamed, one pleaded, "Put me back, put me back!", another asked, "Is this heaven?" The children were carefully moved onto gurneys and into the ambulances.

The moment the links were cut around the world, the

avatars operated by these children froze. Most were construction, factory, maintenance, or mining avatars used by small illegal operations around the globe. When the link was broken, they became lifeless robots. Most had simple assistive AI that prevented them from tumbling off buildings or hurting people around them, so that that the avatars simply sat down and turned off or balanced in standing positions.

A little more than three weeks had passed since the Rio operation, but Mike couldn't put the Roman out of his mind. Even though he was in bed with his lover, his mind was elsewhere. Lacy moved. He looked at her, curled next to him, nestled between his left arm and chest. Her long red hair cascaded down her back. Lacy weighed perhaps 48 kilos, was only one and two-thirds meters tall, and had a martial artist's muscular physique that he both admired and envied. He looked down at his own belly. How did it get so fat? He needed to do something about that soon, otherwise Lacy would leave him for sure. Time to stop drinking. *No*, he thought, *that's not going to happen*. But how about drink less, and stop eating so many late-night cookies and hoagies? He pocked his belly, watched it sink in. *Damn, I'm fat*, he thought. How the hell did it get so bad? He tried to think back, but found that he could only remember being super-fit and then like this. For a moment, he considered seeing a doctor or cutting back on avataring round the globe ... but his investigations required it, and he couldn't afford the time to move his physical body everywhere.

Lacy looked up at him, "Morning honey. What's wrong? You look perplexed." She gave him a kiss and touched his face gently, giving him a sweet smile.

Mike was strangely honest. "Sorry, just trying to recall how I got so out of shape. It was just last year that I used to run marathons and barely had an extra ounce on me."

Lacy laughed at the thought, "A marathon? I'd love to see that."

"No really, I did, like three or four times a year. Even did an Ironman."

Lacy said, "I think that it's been a lot longer than a year, honey. We met perhaps a year ago on the Paris case, remember?"

He did remember. *Damn! My memory sucks!* "Perhaps it was three years," he admitted. "But a year ago ... was I this out of shape?"

Lacy read the worry in his face. Should she lie and say he was thinner—and if she did, would that just make him feel worse about how he looked now?

"I'll take that as a no," said Mike as she was still considering her answer.

Lacy kissed him again. "You look great, honey. You've always looked great. You just need to get busy. You always get this way when you're idle."

She was right. He needed to get on a case, any case. In the meantime, Lacy had a short-term solution. She climbed on top of him and he was instantly at attention—for an older man he had the stamina of a young buck, and this was one of the reasons Lacy stayed with him. As he pleasured her, his mood lightened and thoughts of the Roman were driven from his mind.

The following day, Mike arrived at his office and was surprised to find a woman, in her fifties, dressed in a long flowing dress with a fitted designer jacket, standing outside his door. She was smoking, and no one smoked these days, not even those stupid electronic cigarettes. She looked completely out of place in the dilapidated halls of his North Hollywood office. She recognized him as he approached. "Mr. Anderson."

Reading his expression of disgust, she dropped the cig and stepped on it.

"Perhaps," he replied. "Who's asking?" He assessed her. She didn't look like a threat, but these days he couldn't be too careful. He reflexively moved his hand down to his chest for quick access to his revolver, which was concealed beneath his jacket.

"I'm Ms. Georgia Benford. I've been leaving you messages all week." She offered her hand. He relaxed and shook it. It felt like real flesh and blood. In fact, she looked completely real. If she was in an avatar she was a damn good one.

He spent a bit too much time holding her hand and examining it. "Oh, I assure you, I am quite real. I've come a long way to see you. You see, my daughter is missing—and no one will do anything about it."

"I'm sorry to hear that. Please come in." He grabbed the door knob—it activated a dozen biometric sensors reading everything from his fingerprints and DNA to trace biochemicals on his skin and clothing that lined up with his profile. The door opened with barely a delay.

He guided her to a coach and sat in a chair across from her. A cup of coffee was waiting for him, provided by his office bot.

"Here is a menu of beverages we have available. Would you like something?" it asked, displaying a range of cold and hot beverages via an augmented reality projection which she could see floating in front of her. She selected a cup of tea.

While the bot distracted his guest, Mike ran a scan on her. She was real, and he relaxed somewhat. He then surreptitiously looked up Georgia Benford, discovered that her brother was Dr. Harry Conway, the deep machine learning computer genius who had created the latest generation of near zero lag time avatars. She indeed had a daughter, Elle, who was a brilliant software and engineering hacker, who—at the age of eighteen —won the Kurzweil-Resnick Hardware Hackathon. A review of the records indicated that a missing person report was filed two years ago, shortly after Elle's twenty-second birthday, and then again a year ago. Mike speed-read through the rest of the report and found what he was looking for.

"Ms. Benford, I see that you have filed two missing person reports and each time your daughter was located by the police, she indicated that she just wanted to be left alone." Mike gestured so that the report become visible to them both.

"Yes, I knew you were going to say that. But this time is different. Usually, I get a message from her, but it's been over nine months and not a single word. This time it's different because she found who took her friend Lacy ..." Georgia gestured and pulled up a 3D holographic image they both could see of a young girl.

Mike's heart leapt as he recognized the girl. It was Lacy Sawyer, who was taken at the age of thirteen, put into a work hive—kidnapped while she and her parents were on vacation in Venezuela. It was a rare case, as the human traffickers generally stayed away from anyone but the poor, taking those who were quickly forgotten. But her family worked for a rich couple that sent them on the trip, the rich couple's name had been kept private, but Mike quickly surmised it was the Conways.

"The Sawyers, they worked for you?" he asked, leaning in, for suddenly the case was far more interesting to him.

"Yes, and Lacy was like an older sister to Elle. The two were inseparable." She pulled up images of the girls playing together.

The images created a mix of emotions in Mike. The girls seemed so happy. They delighted him. But then the happy images juxtaposed with the knowledge that this little girl died made him feel sick to his stomach, and he spilled his coffee.

"Are you OK? You look like you're going be sick." Georgia caught his hand before he dropped the cup.

"Yes ... yes, I'm fine. The Lacy case—she was found dead. It reminds me of some other cases—the rare ones where I've found work hives too late, and where some of the children have died or become permanently damaged. The Lacy case is the one that motivated me to focus all my attention on avatar abuse cases." Mike looked at the image of Elle, and was certain he'd seen her somewhere. "What does your daughter do these days?"

"She takes after her father, obsessed with designing avatars —or at least she was until recently. Now I think she has become obsessed with finding the Roman."

"The Roman?" asked Mike harshly. "How does she know that name? What does she know about him?"

"Is that important?" asked Georgia in concerned tones.

"Very," insisted Mike. "Tell me everything she told you."

"Well, in our last call, she said she had determined that the Roman was the one behind it all, that he was the kingpin of the hives as you call them. She was certain that it was his fault Lacy was taken, that tens of thousands of kids have been taken ... and that she was going to stop him." Georgia became tearful, "My God—he has her, doesn't he? The Roman has my little girl!"

Mike felt for this woman, more than he normally did. He moved to her side, took her hands in his. "Take it easy. Elle sounds like a sharp cookie. We don't know if the Roman has her, she's certainly not his normal target."

"But if he felt threatened, he could have taken her? He has her, I know he does! Mr. Anderson, please—you have to save her! You have to save my baby!" The dam breaks. Tears and grief she had been holding back for months came flowing out.

Mike took her in his arms and hugged her, rocking her like a baby. "It's going to be all right, I promise. She'll be fine," he said, then thinks, *Why the hell did I just make that promise?* Then he followed with, "I'll find her, and I'll make the Roman pay for all he has done. I'll make him pay for Lacy."

Nine days after making his absurd promise, Mike found himself no closer to finding Elle. He had avatared into 84 Avatar Units on five continents, in 48 cities. *Great,* he thought as he ran the tally. *Soon I won't even be able to remember where I live.*

He had spoken to every prominent Avatar hacker, hobbyist, and expert, had followed a dozen rumors to her location, only to hit a dead end. During his quest, he discovered that Elle was a legend in the avatar hacker community. She was a wizard at making upgrades to avatar software and hardware systems, all before the age of twelve. She was truly the Mozart of avatar engineering, having inherited her uncle's genius and then improved upon it.

Tonight, would hopefully be the time he finally located her, for tonight he gained entry into Haven, a pop-up underground hackers avatar club that moved around the globe weekly. This one was located in the outdoor Shakespearian Theater of Ashland, Oregon, a little town at the southern end of the state. At 3:00 AM a parade of avatars began entering the backstage door. Mike's avatar was *Ink Spot,* an avatar apparently config-ured after a character in a Steranko-Kloor miniseries called *The Seekers.* Mike looked at his face in the mirror. The face of this avatar was a mask of shifting ink blots, hence the name. He'd rented it from More Fun Comics. It was normally not for rent, but the owner recognized Mike from a news story and made an exception.

At the door, Mike gave the appropriate passwords and the Big Gorilla—an actual twelve-foot-tall Red Ape avatar—allowed him entry. He thought to himself that those passwords had cost him all the favors he had garnered over the last few years, so this place better be worth it.

A little more than a hundred avatars moved about inside the outdoor theater. The stage was set for a *Mid-Summer Night's*

Dream, which was perfect for this gathering of mythical and pop culture characters. Mike scanned the theater looking for Voloor, a character from the VR-TV series *The Reluctant Wizard*. Rumor had it that Voloor knew Elle's location.

He spotted what he thought was Voloor, but when he talked to him, he turned out to be a Winged Ogre Chieftain. The Ogre sent him over to talk to a group that included two Amazonian Warriors, a green-haired, purple-skinned female super hero called Smasher, a Monkey King God, a French super hero girl named Lady Spider, and an Asian female Doctor Faustus avatar.

All the avatars were rented from More Fun Comics or the Theater, which apparently offered the most colorful avatar characters in town. Lady Spider took a fancy to his avatar.

"Cool Ink Spot, have you watched the new Seeker series?" Lady Spider asked earnestly.

"To be honest, I thought this was a character from the Merlin Gang's reboot," Mike answered, his ink blots for a moment formed into the shape of a King Arthur, before dissolving into a squashed raccoon. At least Lady Spider thought that was what it resembled, but she was stoned on a cocktail of vodka and TLC infused olives.

"Why are you looking for Voloor?" she asked.

"I hear he may know how I can contact Elle."

Excited, she jumped up and looked around. "Is she here?"

"That's what I am trying to find out," he answered. "I need to warn her that she's in danger."

"Danger from who?" She started swinging her yo-yo, a habit or perhaps a triggered preprogrammed action by her avatar's assisted AI.

"From the Roman," Mike replied.

The Smash avatar scoffed. "The Roman is a puny myth, made up by fleshers who think avatars should be outlawed."

Doctor Faustus disagreed. "No, he's real. There's always

some asshole who can find a way to make a bad use of something that was designed to do good."

The conversation rapidly took on a life of its own, as the King Henry avatar spoke up. "This whole flesher movement is ridiculous. Do you know that before avatars there were over a billion people on Earth without any medical care? Now, everyone can see a good doctor. Hell, I treat patients from Africa to New Zealand on a weekly basis. Try doing that without avatars! Fleshers want to go back to the dark ages when it took a day or more to travel around the world instead of seconds."

Belcher, a humanoid frog character, jumped in. "Exactly—and now everyone has proper education, plenty of food, and work opportunities. Avatars have equalized opportunity around the world. Fleshers suck."

Doctor Faustus interjected, "So do you, Belcher—but in a good way."

He laughed. "That's true DF—but seriously, the UN last year announced that fourteen of the seventeen sustainable goals have been achieved in great part due to the billion plus avatars in use around the globe. Many of the fleshers have benefited. They're just too blind to see it."

Voloor stepped into the gathering. "Fleshers are just like Flat Earthers or those idiots who wanted everyone to walk instead of drive in cars or fly in planes because it was unnatural. Tools for good can always be misused."

The Smasher slapped Voloor on the back in agreement. "Exactly! There's always someone who abuses technology. Before they could clone organs, there was an underground market for hearts and livers because you had to wait in line for them."

Doctor Faustus piled on. "Right ... and no politician ever called for making transplants illegal!" She got in Mike's face, having forgotten completely in her high state of mind his original question. "So if you think we should outlaw avatars just because some sewer rat like the Roman is using them for illegal work hives, then you're just as bad as he is!"

Mike gestured for her to calm down, and decided to speak up before his avatar was stomped into an ink blot. "Back it up! I'm with you! I'm trying to stop the Roman before he hurts any more people—and especially before he hurts one of your own."

Voloor pulled Doctor Faustus away from Ink Spot. "So, you're the one looking for Elle?"

"Yes," answered Mike. "She's in grave danger."

"Follow me." Voloor led him away from the crowd, which continued its rant against fleshers who had gained some momentum in the media ever since Mike's big Rio bust. Like most enthusiasts, they were over-reacting to the stupidity of the drive-by media that was playing up the danger of illegal work hives. The truth was that out of the billion and a half avatars in use around the world, perhaps a few hundred thousand were used for illegal activities. It was horrible for those victims of work hives, but it didn't negate the good the vast majority of them did. Mike and his allies were working to stomp out the abuses.

"You're the one who tracked down the Rio hive, the one they call Mr. Anderson?" Voloor asked.

For a moment, Mike's ink blots started dripping like the Matrix logo—programmed to react to the conversation the avatar is engaged in. "Yes, I'm Mr. Anderson. You can call me Mike. Elle's mother, Georgia, hired me to find her daughter. She's worried that the Roman is after her. And from what I have been able to determine, she has good reason to worry. I've gathered enough clues to indicate that the Roman has a keen interest in her."

Voloor was quiet for a moment, then opened his hand to display a small holographic image of Georgia in his hand. "This is Georgia, Elle's mom. Are you sure it was her?"

Mike zoomed in on the image. "Yes, that's her."

"And she wasn't an avatar?"

"No way," replied Mike. "I scanned her, and she was human. I touched her, as well, and she was real flesh and blood."

Voloor became very concerned. "That's not good. Not good at all."

"Why?" asked Mike.

"Because Georgia has been in a coma for over a year," explained Voloor.

"Impossible!" Mike insisted. "I tell you she's not an avatar."

"You're mistaken," replied Voloor. "She's the next stage in avatars. I know, because I created them with Elle. It's a top secret project—or at least it was, until someone hacked into our network. Elle vanished shortly thereafter."

"Do you think she was kidnapped? Taken by whoever hacked in?" asked Mike.

"Perhaps. Though it's just as likely that she went underground." He paused. "That's the problem with Elle. Never been much of a team player. Always rushing in without thinking."

"What exactly is this new avatar?" inquired Mike.

"It's designed with cloned flesh and a nano-neuronet—a kind of cyborg. It's built with a range of countermeasures so that sensors designed to detect avatars are auto-hacked by the avatar's defenses and given a false data signature, so that it reads all the nonorganic materials beneath the flesh as simple human upgrades."

By his voice and expression, Mike could tell that Voloor was very proud of the design that he and Elle had crafted. He projected schematics as he spoke and manipulated them with his hands, showing how the system was able to fool even the most sophisticated sensors. It was true brilliance, a giant leap forward in avatar technology.

"Why would you create such a thing?" queried Mike. "It

seems like it would provide criminals with a lot of opportunities."

"I understand your concerns," replied Voloor. "But we created this system so that people whose bodies no longer worked, like late-stage ALS victims or the elderly, could have a second lease on life. A lot of people are prejudiced against long-term avatar users—not just fleshers. We wanted to give them back a normal life, a normal body."

"I understand," said Mike. "Believe me, I do. But I think people will find it unsettling that someday we won't be able to tell who is human and who is not."

"Not if you're someone who has to use one twenty-four hours a day," answered Voloor. "But I understand your concerns—we shared them, which was why we were keeping it a secret until we could determine the right balance of protections. The Georgia situation is exactly what we wanted to avoid."

"So, who do you think is operating this Georgia?" asked Mike.

"I think the answer is obvious," replied Voloor.

Mike nodded in agreement. "Then he's finally made a critical mistake." He paused. "Will you help me?"

Voloor nodded his head. "Yes ... I will. We *all* will."

The following day a drone delivered a new tracking device to Mike's office. This one had been modified so that Voloor and his associates could backtrace an avatar's link signals, regardless of the number. In Rio, Mike had not been prepared for the Roman to have had multiple passive users inside his avatar with him. It was rare these days for passive riders to be inside a single avatar, but when avatars first emerged into the market, it was not uncommon for a dozen friends to enter the same avatar. Only one person at a time could control the Avatar Unit, but the others could passively ride along to experience what that AU was seeing, touching, hearing, etc. These days, with a billion plus avatars in use around the world, passive riding was rarely done and most systems didn't even allow for it. This time, Mike was prepared, and with the help of Voloor and his network of hardware and software geniuses, they could do parallel tracing, so that even if several hundred passive riders were in an avatar, they would be able to trace each to their SOUL pods.

Mike contacted Georgia and told her that he had made contact with one of Elle's friends who knew where Elle was hiding. He concluded that the Roman must not actually have Elle, otherwise why would he use Georgia to hire him to find her? He told Georgia that Elle's friend would only share the information with Georgia face-to-face.

They agreed to meet at Neptune's Deep Sea Bar, which was literally a restaurant located a mile off the Santa Monica coast, on the ocean floor. Mike took the Hyperloop train from the old SM pier to the restaurant. Sarah and about a hundred agents were at the L.A. ICE operations base, waiting for him to give them the location of the Roman and his associates. They could access Agent avatar units anywhere on the globe, enabling them to perform a raid with local law enforcement in thirty minutes or less.

Mike spotted Georgia sitting alone at the bar. She was drinking a Sazerac, a drink most considered to be the first original American cocktail. It had evolved into a drink with American rye whiskey and a dash of absinthe, though the original was actually made with Sazerac-de-Forge *et fils* brandy.

She spotted Mike and waved for him to join her. The bar circled the saucer-shaped building. The entire thing was like being in a fish bowl, made from self-cleaning plastic that afforded a gorgeous view of a brilliantly-colored coral reef, with an abundance of sea life visible from every seat in the restaurant. Among the true aquatic life swam various fantastic avatars in the form of sea dragons, green gilled sea monsters, pirates, zombies, and of course, a wide range of mermaids and undersea characters. All these exotic avatars could be rented on the spot or accessed from almost anywhere on Earth. It was one of the first man-made—yet, natural— coral reefs, part of the Resurrection Sea Life Projects of the late 2020's.

Mike recalled from his historical studies that the twenty-five million dollar Conway Reef XPRIZE, which was won in 2028, not only saved the world's dying reefs, but led to an entire reef industry that revived reefs around the globe, and led to the creation of thousands of new living reefs. Early undersea avatars had played a big role in the building of these reefs.

Mike ordered a Monkey gin and tonic from the drone bar bot and it created one on the spot.

"I thought you said you had a friend who was going to join us?" asked Georgia.

"I do," explained Mike. "He's a bit nervous, afraid the Roman is watching us."

Georgia nodded her understanding. "I expect he is. It's all the more reason we need to find Elle before he does. The man is a monster."

Mike took Georgia's hand, pretended to comfort her. He found it hard to believe that this woman was actually an avatar when all his senses told him she was real. The well scans he is running and sending to his mixed reality screens also can't tell that she's an avatar. "He is worse than a monster, but don't worry, we'll soon find Elle. Her friend is right there." He pointed outside to a merman with a trident, and the man motioned for them to join him.

Georgia and Mike each strapped into old-fashioned SOUL systems—antiquated systems which still used VR glasses, sonic haptic generators, haptic gloves, and motion capture sensors—

throwbacks to the first systems of the 2020s. But they did provide a flotation system that enabled natural control of aquatic avatars. These SOUL systems were nowhere near as sophisticated as the latest direct brain interface systems, but more than adequate for operating the exotic aquatic avatars. Mike noticed that at first Georgia was reluctant to use the avatar system—and for good reason, he thought, because if they had to use a DBI system, it would likely fail, as he doubted the Georgia avatar was equipped to plug into a DBI.

A few minutes later, Mike found himself in the avatar form of a half man and half seahorse. He practiced swimming around for a minute and was surprised at how quickly he adapted to the motion. He noticed that Georgia had entered the youthful body of a young bare- breasted mermaid. Soft pink sparkling scales covered her lower fish body. Georgia swam up to him and smiled. "This is quite remarkable, I don't know why I have not tried these exotics till now. I had no idea how liberating and natural it would feel. The floatation tank is a nice touch."

"I agree, it's not at all what I expected." Mike pointed toward the merman, who had moved deeper into the reef. The restaurant was nowhere in sight now.

They joined him in a reef valley, full of a wide variety of fish, with no other avatars around. He looked behind him. The reef seemed to go on in all directions. They had entered their avatar sea bodies in the reef, which was part of the intended immersive experience.

"Are you Elle's mother?" the merman asked.

"I am," replied Georgia. "And you are?"

"Your daughter knew me as Keith, but most people call me Voloor," the merman replied.

"Keith Miner? From Grants Pass?" she asked, still suspicious, or at least acting the part of the concerned mother.

"From Ashland, actually. She's the one who grew up in GP."

"Are you both satisfied?" interjected Mike.

The mermaid Georgia relaxed. "Yes ... but where is my daughter? I need to find her. Have you heard from her? Do you know where she is?"

"I haven't spoken to her, but I have managed to trace a line of purchases that she made, and through those I have determined her location." He displayed a range of purchase and delivery traces, but the final destinations were all blocked out. "You understand that this took a lot of time and favors to unlock?"

Georgia's breasts literally seemed to be perking up. Mike suspected they were programmed to react to the operator's adrenaline or heartbeat rate. The Roman must be getting excited at finding Elle. And as Mike suspected, asking for payment from the mother would fit his sick worldview. Why else would someone try and help the distraught mother of a friend? Mike hid his disgust by smiling warmly.

"Of course, of course. I can pay. How much do you want?" Georgia asked as she pulled up a bank transfer app that they could all see and interact with.

Mike shifted to a new voice channel—one preprogrammed to reach Lacy.

"We are a Go, Mike," said Lacy. "The switch worked. When Georgia used the SOUL to enter the mermaid we were able to send the passive riders into another identical mermaid on the opposite side of the sea station."

"Who's operating the other avatars?" Mike asked.

"You all have been. We mirrored the avatars—but when Voloor pulled up the product shipments, we switched over to the prerecorded script on you and Voloor and an agent is now operating the other mermaid. As far as the passive riders know, he has entered a long complex negotiation."

"How many did you detect?"

"The Roman is super paranoid," answered Lacy. "We have

58 distinct signals. Some are on rotating nodes, but we are isolating and agents are already deploying to half the locations. We should have them all located and will move in simultaneously in about five to ten minutes."

"Perfect, I can't wait to see his face when he finds himself in a rat's cage," said Mike.

Lacy laughed, "Mike, I had no idea you had such a sick mind! I love it!"

"Well, I love you," he replied.

"Thanks. Now get back to work." She cut off the signal.

Mike found himself back to hearing Voloor and the Roman —as Georgia the mermaid—concluded their negotiations. Having agreed to terms, Georgia transferred twenty million dollars into Voloor's accounts.

"Thanks," said Voloor. "That will go a long way in helping the victims of illegal work hives recover." He then chuckled and added, "You piece of shit."

For a moment, Georgia was caught off guard, "What, how dare you ..." Then she just shrugged, and caressed herself in a rude way. "If you wanted a donation you just had to ask, Mike. What gave me away?"

"Elle's mother is in a coma," explained Mike. "It was kept private, but still someone with your sources should have found out."

"Thanks. I'll make sure the idiot who missed that pays the price. Still it was worth the ride, and the confirmation that Keith here is a friend of Elle's brings us one step closer to finding her. By now, my people have traced his accounts—and soon we will locate him and then her."

"True," replied Mike. "Voloor and his friends are exposed. That couldn't be helped." He shot her a triumphant smile. "You never would have stayed here if we hadn't brought her real friends here."

"Friends?" repeated the Roman with a concerned frown.

"Oh, didn't I explain?" said Mike with a grin. "It's not just Voloor, but his entire network—we've backtracked everyone— all your passive riders were peeled away and agents are taking them into custody even as we speak. And one more thing. By now you've probably noticed that you can't disconnect from Georgia. That's because Agent Lacy is standing next to your real body—would you like to see?" Mike displayed a full holo of the Roman's room as a dozen agents could be seen taking his men into custody. Lacy—in an ICE agent avatar unit—was standing near a cutting edge Avatar Pod covered in black and gold leaf inlays. There was a crude-looking device connected to it—an override created by the Roman himself, that was used in his hives, but this one had been attached to his fancy avatar brain interface pod.

"You can't do that!" screamed the Roman. "It's—it's not legal!"

"Well, let's say it's a gray area," replied Mike. "And one more thing: Voloor's people modified your attachment for better sensory feedback."

With that, he delivered two kicks from his horse feet. The blows struck the most sensitive parts of the mermaid's anatomy and the Roman screamed in agony.

"If it were up to me, you would stay locked in your pod for the next thousand years, but I imagine your lawyers will get you into a nice, dark, dank cell in a few weeks. Extradition from your country to ours is likely to come up with complications."

Mike turned to Voloor. "You ready?"

"Yes."

Voloor activated a final surprise for the Roman, breaking the link to Georgia and connecting the Roman into a new avatar. The Roman screamed again, only this time, it came out as a squeak, for he indeed had been transferred into a rat cage, and inside an avatar rat body. It was a rather small rat avatar— but at least he was not alone. The Roman looked around and found that he was surrounded by twelve real rats. They seemed to like him, which was when he realized he was the only female rat in the cage. Mike watched all this via a video feed and laughed out loud. It seemed totally fitting that the Roman should get a good measure of pain and punishment before his barrage of lawyers worked their way through the nest of procedural delays that Lacy and her many sympathetic allies had put in place.

Mike looked at the empty rat cage. He had cleaned it out a week ago. The Roman had been confined there for a good six weeks prior to that, and during that time, all the Roman's accounts had been confiscated. The confiscated funds would go to help all those hurt by the Roman, he'd made sure of that.

The Roman had rolled on all his people and everyone else even remotely connected to his abhorrent trade. His lawyers had cut a deal for the Roman—life in solitary confinement in a federal prison in exchange for not facing the death penalty. He had caused the death of over thirty children during the decade his illegal work hives were in operation, damaged the lives of over sixty thousand others. His plea deal led to the arrest of everyone in his network, as well as dozens of other men like him, known competitors. Illegal work hive operations around the world had come to an end, and would remain so for the foreseeable future, because they all used similar cloaking technology—and with the source code and hardware confiscated, it would be easy to locate any new scumbags who tried to abuse the use of avatars and set up work hives or any other type of operation.

A knock at the door startled him. It was past midnight, and he wasn't expecting anyone. He reflexively pulled out his gun, but concealed it below the table. "It's open."

Lacy entered the room along with a plump older woman in her seventies, though these days, she might be over a hundred and fifty with the advancement of gene reprogramming and stem cell rejuvenation regimes. "Relax, Mike. Put it away."

Lacy knew him all too well. He pocketed the gun, then got up to greet her and her friend. "Sorry," he apologized. "Still getting used to the idea that it's all over. Who's your friend?"

"Mike, it's me, Voloor—but you can call me by my birth name, Mary." She gave him a long, endearing hug. He enjoyed it, rather surprised at Voloor's identity. He'd extrapolated Voloor was in his or her twenties.

"What the hell!" exclaimed Mike. "I thought your name was Keith and that you were a school friend of Elle's. Speaking of which, where are we on locating her?"

"That was all a cover story that Elle and I crafted to keep our research secret. And we are still looking for her. The good news is that we're certain she was not kidnapped by the Roman or anyone else for that matter."

"Where are my manners? It's so good to finally meet you— in the flesh, I mean." Mike gave her another hug. "What brings you to L.A.?"

"I was in the area, a rare physical trip, and thought I'd come on by to show you this." Mary pulled up a 3D terrain map that the two women could see with their ocular MA implants. Mike was old-school, donning his Buddy Holly glasses. Through them, he saw a map of greater Los Angeles, with a few hundred areas highlighted, each area covering several blocks.

"Enlighten me," he inquired. "What am I looking at?"

"I took a look at the data from your first scan, the encounter you had with the Roman in Rio," explained Mary, "and after eliminating all the known geo points from the Roman's men, I came up with this."

"It still looks like noise to me," said Mike. "You're not saying these are all associates of the Roman's at these locations, are you?"

"That was my thought at first, too," interjected Lacy. "But Mary explained that these don't match any of the signatures of his avatars."

"That's right," said Mary. "What you are looking at is actually a single avatar signal, but it's been ghosted to hide the operator's real location and in a very sophisticated way."

"So we missed someone?" Mike's face reflected his concern, because he'd been certain this was over.

"Perhaps," answered Mary. "That's why we came to you. Whoever is behind this has a level of tech far above what we thought the Roman possessed. It could mean the threat is not over, but just gone deeper."

"Damn!" muttered Mike. "So what are we waiting for? We should be narrowing this down."

"Way ahead of you," replied Mary. "I've been working on this for a month, and located the actual broadcast point." The ghost signatures began to fade away, leaving one red glowing area—a single home overlooking the ocean in Malibu. They zoomed in on it. Mike frowned. The place looked a bit familiar, but he just couldn't place it.

"Are you okay?" asked Lacy.

"This place," he said, frowning. "I'm sure I've come across it before in some research. I just can't place it." He grabbed his gun, checked to make sure it was loaded, and holstered it. "Come on, let's go! It's a long shot that they're still there, but they may have left some clues."

It took twenty minutes by human carry drones, an eternity for Mike as he tried to recall where he had seen this place before. He decided that it was a damned good thing he had an appointment next week to see Dr. Babak, a leading edge brain doctor and founder of the Brain Mapping and Therapeutics

Society. Dr. Babak had assured him they will be able to treat his memory issues.

By the time they arrived, twenty-three other agents were already on scene, most in human form, with an elite SWAT avatar crash entry team. The avatar SWAT team had already surveyed the place, which was empty except for a single avatar SOUL unit; a very sophisticated one. There was a single occupant inside, but it was impossible to tell who was in it, as it was highly shielded. Mike insisted on being there when they opened it. "Who knows how long the person has been held captive inside here? We've got to be careful."

Mary agreed, "Mike is right." Then: "Can I come with you?"

Lacy answered for him, "Certainly, and I'll come as well."

They entered with an escort of a half dozen human agents and two medics who had come in avatar form, their union not allowing them to come in human form.

As Mike approached the chamber, it looked familiar to him. "I *know* I've seen this before. Lacy, do you recognize it?"

Lacy held his hand, "No, Mike, no one here has seen anything like it before."

Mary corrected her. "*I* have." She went over and in short order entered the codes to shut it down and release its occupant.

"Mike, I'll let you do the honors. Just hit this button." Mary pointed to a purple button.

Mike looked at Mary, then at Lacy, who gave him a loving smile. His finger floated over the button and a sudden dread filled him. The life scans came up blank. What if it wasn't a shielded life force, but a dead child inside? He started to panic, images of Lacy's dead body coming to mind, as well as those of so many others he has seen. His thoughts come back to her, such a sweet young girl. She reminds him of his childhood friend ... Nancy ... his best friend.

Tears running down his face, the world a mass of confusion

to him now, he stabs the button with his finger, the system reacts, system checks suddenly run, a series of injections are applied to the occupant as the pod opens and the link between SOUL and avatar are severed. A young woman was inside, in her twenties. Mike stared at her. She was so familiar ... Then he placed her—it's ELLE!

He smiled. *She is alive!* Suddenly, he began to feel ill, the world started fading to black and he passed out—but instead of falling, he froze like a mannequin.

Elle opened her eyes and stared at them all. She was completely disoriented, especially when she saw Mike's frozen form. And then she saw Lacy and she was flooded with emotions.

Lacy came over to her. "Take it easy, Elle. You've been linked to him for over a year according to your system logs."

Elle looked at Lacy, then pulled her in for a deep kiss. It was the first time she had actually kissed Lacy in the flesh, so to speak. Lacy welcomed it, she loved Mike, and the fact that he was actually a girl is perfectly fine by her, she's always swung both ways. Mary had tipped her off before they came to Mike's place, though it had taken her all this time to figure out that Mike was actually Elle, and she knew that she needed to be there in person when they woke her up.

"I did it again, didn't I? Went in too deep." Elle asked Mary, but it was not really a question. She looked at the Mike avatar, the most sophisticated avatar on the planet.

"Yes ... it would have been nice if you gave me a heads up," said Mary, giving Elle one of her patented love hugs.

"Sorry ... but it works ... works so perfectly that I fooled even you." The two exchanged a smile and then another huge hug.

"Yes, yes it did ... your uncle Harry would be so proud."

THE GATHERING

BY KAY KENYON

THE GATHERING

BY KAY KENYON

L ee Ji-min entered the excellent Unified Republic motor car and managed to sit down without slopping the goldfish out of the bowl he held. He closed the door, but it was not a tight fit, and as the driver pulled away from the apartment tower, a draught of frigid air crawled up Ji-min's thigh. He turned to the stranger who shared the back seat with him.

"Who are you? Where is Ro Tae-joon?"

"A thousand apologies, Manager, but I am Ro Tae-joon's replacement," she said. "I am Nam Ha-yun, Interface Specialist."

"I do not need a new Interface Specialist. Ro Tae-joon has served me for a decade."

She dropped her gaze to her lap. "Unfortunately, Ro Tae-joon has fallen from favor."

As the motor car swung around a corner, Ji-min adjusted the goldfish bowl so that it did not splash out water—or goldfish. He kept his face sternly passive, despite his dismay for Ro Tae-joon.

"If I am permitted to say, Manager Lee Ji-min, yesterday's Gathering was a triumph."

They drove through the crowded city center. Even though the gallows were empty at this early hour, Ji-min darkened the windows so that he did not have to look.

"Thanks to the wonders of avatar technology," he responded. Ro Tae-joon had never seemed political or verbally indiscreet. And now he was jailed, or worse.

This new Specialist, who seemed so young—they all seemed so young once one passed age fifty—chattered on. "Oh yes, and with your innovations! The improved haptics allow us all to shake the hand of the Chairman, to experience the utmost refined presence of our Flawless Leader. It was an exceptionally immersive experience, thanks to your delivery software."

As always, the surrogate who shook the Chairman's hand was one of his trusted generals. Not all avatars need be a robotic telepresence unit. The general wore special gear with optic, auditory and temperature sensors as well as haptic gloves. These transmitted a vivid and realistic experience to the nation.

"The Workers were all deeply moved during the ceremony."

Ji-min dutifully added, "The masses of the People are placed in the center of everything, and our Leader is the center of the masses."

The driver halted the car at an intersection clogged with solar powered skateboards. Ji-min sighed. Respectable bicycles were now just for the old.

She was still talking. He wondered if he could get by with denouncing her and then getting a new, quieter assistant. One older than twenty. "I am pleased to report to you, Manager, that yesterday we completed installation of telepresence units in thirteen more sectors. Soon, through your brilliant PY6 interface, all may be in Flawless Leader's presence at the Gatherings."

Specialist Nam Ha-yun went on, "Everyone acknowledges our work is a great calling."

Ji-min kept his hands flattened around the goldfish bowl to make sure the water stayed warm. Chrysanthemum, the female goldfish, huddled close to Thistle, her flashy mate.

His assistant's voice dropped lower. "Except for the old women of Sunchon."

"Who?"

"The shameful aunties of Sunchon." She glanced at him to see if he reacted, which he did not, having never heard of them. She babbled on: "They asked permission to listen to foreign radio, including the Imperialist propaganda of the Mheeramhir first contact." Now *that* he had heard of. The whole world knew of the first communications from an intelligent alien species. Except certain corners of the globe, including his, but one did not work in the Directorate of Free Information—monitoring enemy broadcasts—without learning a few forbidden things. She went on, "Of course, the meeting with these new beings, even if true, is irrelevant to the People and distracts us from our collective purpose. Naturally, the aunties of Sunchon have erred."

"Sometimes age has wisdom," he murmured, as though speaking to the goldfish. A quick glance in her direction. "I do not speak of these aunties, of course."

They pulled up in front of the vast and solid Directorate of Free Information. As the driver held the car door open, Specialist Nam Ha-yun followed the Manager out, asking the thing she was bursting to know. "Why do you have goldfish with you?"

"My apartment is too cold." He looked fondly at the mated pair of goldfish. "Goldfish like it warm."

As they entered their section of the Directorate, the Office of Interface Control, everyone stood at their work stations in honor of the great success of yesterday's Gathering. Their clapping followed Ji-min as he walked through their midst to his office, to place Chrysanthemum and Thistle in their new home.

"Bring me the long way, by the river."

The driver nodded and they took a fresh approach to the People's Palace. With new snow furring the hills, Manager Lee Ji-min darkened the windows against the blinding whiteness and also the disturbing views of the food lines.

The darkness of the car suited his mood. Ro Tae-joon had now been executed for the disloyalty of his cousin whom he had not seen fit to denounce, though he hadn't seen his cousin in years. One must be careful to choose the right family. An orphan, Ji-min considered himself lucky he had no relatives. If he should fail in his duty, no loved ones would fail with him.

Inside the great palace, his footfalls echoed on the polished marble floors. After a very long walk, he was ushered into the Chairman's presence.

Ko Yeung-su, the Great Unifier, High Commander, Respected Comrade and so forth stood with his arms outstretched as a tailor fitted a new suit to accommodate his expanding girth. An attendant led Ji-min to one side to wait.

Ji-min stood next to a giant glass-fronted receptacle. Inside were tropical plants and artfully placed branches. Among them were moving things. He caught a flash of iridescent blue as a giant butterfly flew into a thicket and disappeared. Now he saw that the case housed many butterflies, their fragile wings afire in gold, emerald, orange, indigo and patterns of breathtaking beauty. One he especially liked was turquoise, with scalloped black wings, edged with rose. It slowly fanned its wings, revealing tiny green scales in the shifting light.

"Ah, I see that you admire my lepidopterarium."

Ji-min turned to find Ko Yeung-su had joined him.

He bowed to the leader. "A great privilege to see such a thing, Chairman."

Ko Yeung-su nodded and pointed to the butterfly Ji-min had been admiring. "That one is the Luzon Peacock Swallowtail. It lives only in the cloud forests of a mountain range on an island in the Pacific. There are seven left in the world."

"Such rare beauty. One is speechless."

Ko Yeung-su regarded the Manager. A smile was trying to come into his face, but it struggled against his padded cheeks. "I summoned you here to convey my commendation for the performance of the People's Interface on Friday. My generals tell me that, across the country, Workers wept with joy at the experience."

"My staff has worked diligently, Chairman."

Ko Yeung-su tapped the glass of the lepidopterarium, causing the Swallowtail to flit to another branch. He straightened. "We will have an even finer Gathering in two weeks for the Worker Loyalty Day Gathering. I am pleased with your leadership, Lee Ji-min. Very pleased."

The Manager bowed.

"Except for one thing."

Ji-min waited as the world slowed. The butterflies settled. Distant footfalls from the palace reached his ears like muffled screams.

"Your housing is not without heat. My Workers do not live in such conditions."

With a stab of dismay, Ji-min remembered his comment in the car about his apartment being cold. "Of course not, Chairman. I am quite warm at all times."

"I thought so." As a tiny smile managed to bore into Ko Yeung-Su's cheeks. He lifted a hand in dismissal.

Ji-min walked back through the palace with two gifts: the

Chairman's commendation and the knowledge that his new assistant was his enemy.

———

The Manager sat at his desk, looking out the door of his private office into his staff's collective workspace. He had never noticed before how ugly his work surroundings were. He thought of the Luzon Swallowtail in its soft iridescence, its living delicacy, and sighed. The world was a deep and mysterious place to hold such beauty.

At her desk, Specialist Nam Ha-yun, the foolish little spy, peered at her holo display. On the main display just outside his door, a map of the Unified Republic glared with pricks of light signifying delivery and activation of the interfaces. As a new sector acquired a Gathering set for every citizen, another light winked on.

Someone moved into the doorway, obscuring his view. It was the Director of Free Information.

Ji-min stood. "Welcome, Director Cho Sang-won."

"Good morning, Manager." As his gaze caught the goldfish bowl, his brow lowered. Perhaps the Director was not fond of pets. "I am concerned about your performance, Lee Ji-min."

"How may I improve, Director?"

"What is said cannot be unsaid. You are reported to have complained that your apartment was too cold."

"A thousand pardons, but I did not say such a thing." A sincere lie was the best defense.

"There were two witnesses, unfortunately." The Director went to the door and with a flick of his hand summoned Specialist Nam Ha-yun into the office.

The Director demanded that she repeat what she had heard Lee Ji-min say in the car.

The Specialist replied, "He said that his unit was very cold, too cold for even a fish to live."

The Manager gathered his courage. If he was to be denounced, he would keep his dignity. He would teach the younger generation how to face downfall. Their turn was coming.

Specialist Nam Ha-yun continued, "He also said that he had carelessly left his window open."

It was then that the Manager realized who had reported him. Not Nam Ha-yun, but his driver.

The Director frowned. "I see." He had embarrassed himself, but perhaps he had not wished to upbraid his employee, but had been ordered to do so. It was very difficult to discern who believed what or who cared about what.

As the Director left the office, he turned back to say, "If you have remembered to shut your apartment window, you can now bring the goldfish back."

That evening, Ji-min worked late. When he finished testing the software delivery code, he put on his coat and wool hat, picked up Chrysanthemum and Thistle's bowl, and made his way through the maze of office cubicles. One station's holo display was still bright.

He stopped at Specialist Nam Ha-yun's desk. She was viewing an enemy broadcast about the alien first contact event.

When she spun around to find the Manager standing there, it was too late to change the display.

"The whole world will be watching," Ji-min murmured low.

Her face lost its alarm. "Indeed, Manager." She glanced around the office. "It is irresponsible to meet with a new intelligent species, of course."

"Quite irresponsible." He walked closer to her display and watched the real-time space capsule view of the avatar that would greet the Mheeramhir at the rendezvous point. With medium dark skin and black hair in a buzz cut, the robot looked quite human. Its advantage was that it would not be affected by passing through the radiation belt on the approach to asteroid Prometheus. The Mheeramhir had accepted the idea of a surrogate, as long as it was under control by a human being, as of course it was, through telemetrics.

"They call the avatar Surro," Ji-min said, thus revealing that he, too, had been following news of the expedition.

"Surro, for surrogate." Nam Ha-yun gazed in rapt attention at the feed from the capsule. "The aliens are smaller in stature than we are. The pictures that have been sent to Earth show a creature—"

"—A being," the Manager corrected.

"A being, who is very broadly built, but short. Bipedal. Some think, because its arms are covered in fur—"

"Hair, I believe they have decided."

"Yes, as I should have said—hair. Some people think they look like panda bears. Without such markings, of course. But that is surely an insult."

"But if it makes the beings seem friendly to some of the skeptics of our world, perhaps it is a description the Mheeramhir could forgive."

"They must already be aware of what Earth's broadcasts have been saying."

Ji-min savored this unusual and dangerous conversation. It thrilled him to speak his mind. They watched the interior scene of the space capsule, though the avatar had little to do at the moment, and remained immobile, standing before a control console.

The capsule had set out ten months ago for an asteroid that was locked into Earth's orbit around the sun. This was the meeting place designated by the Mheeramhir, who had worked with a UN task force to arrange the first encounter. The Mir Mir, as they had been universally nicknamed, were greatly advanced. And not just technically. They also appeared to understand that a meeting off planet would calm the fears in some quarters that all aliens might not be friendly. A gift of technology from the Mir Mir would be part of the meeting ceremony. Rumor was that it would be fusion technology.

"When they meet," Lee Ha-yun said, "it will be a global, shared experience." She looked around the office, watchful. "Fortunately, our nation is spared this reprehensible activity."

"It is for our protection," Ji-min said.

"Of course. And as well, we are protected from experiencing other cultures: their festivals and false triumphs."

Ji-min agreed. "And our fellow Workers are not subjected to the use of avatars for universal sharing of corrupting influences. Such as, for example, an expedition to a volcano in Antarctica."

"So frivolous," Lee Ha-yun said, smirking. "Or watching the World Soccer Cup from the viewpoint of a referee."

"Hollow indeed," Ji-min said, beginning to enjoy the charade. "As would be cave spelunking in a forgotten underground cavern of Central America."

"Shockingly superficial."

"Entirely without value to our great Republic," Ji-min said, managing to keep his expression neutral.

Lee Ha-yun was openly smiling: "The Workers do not have a desire for such limitless experience. They feel joy through our Leader."

"May his reign prosper," the Manager replied. His thoughts returned to what had happened earlier in his office. "Thank you, Ha-yun, for accurately reporting that I left my window open."

She blushed that he had used her given name by itself. "You are welcome, Manager. Thank you for saying that old ones are wise." His offhand comment when he had first met her. Why had it mattered?

Ha-yun whispered, "The village I was raised in is Sunchon.

One of the aunties is a dear neighbor who nursed my mother in her last illness." Her eyes glistened at the edges.

He bowed his head. "I am very sorry."

"It is my dishonor, of course."

"True dishonor is a choice, Ha-yun, not an accident of birth." He looked down at his goldfish. Then he walked to the exit where his car would be waiting with its too-attentive driver.

Three mornings later in Ji-min's apartment, Chrysanthemum and Thistle were dead.

In the Office of Interface Control, the holo board was bursting with lights. Ha-yun reported that the supreme goal had been reached, all citizens of the Unified Republic now had interface units, and all old units had the PY6 haptic upgrade. All was in readiness for the Worker Loyalty Day Gathering in three days.

The Director stood in Ji-min's doorway. This time he was smiling. People crowded behind him.

"You have the honor, Manager Lee Ji-min, of receiving a gift from our Chairman." The crowd parted, and a messenger came forward bearing a box wrapped in silk. Murmurs followed the messenger. A few hands reached out to touch the gift that the Chairman himself had touched.

When the box was placed in Ji-min's hands, he felt he must open it immediately as everyone was watching expectantly. The wrapping fell away.

He stood holding a book-sized display case with a clear glass top. Inside was the Luzon Peacock Swallowtail, dead, a mounting pin through its thorax.

As he stared at it, people began to clap though they didn't yet know what it was.

The Director reached out, taking the box, and held it up for all to see.

The clapping sounded like breaking glass, like frozen promises falling to earth, like fragments of beauty, too heavy to carry. On and on they clapped, smiling.

All but Ha-yun. Her expression reminded him of when she had spoken of the aunties.

Was all grief the same? A shared dark room that one must return to again and again? And yet in the dark, the sorrow must always be particular, one's own to bear. He received the display case back from the Director and bowed to his coworkers in honor of the things that they could not express, and perhaps had forgotten how to feel.

"There is a technical difficulty, Chairman. We may need a few more days to be sure the next Gathering takes full advantage of PY6 enhancements."

Ji-min sat in the Interface Operations Control Center, surrounded by the read out decks and telepresence panels. He and the Chairman stared at each other by simple augmented reality interface.

In Ji-min's field of view, Ko Yeung-su began to frown, but the creases could only go so far. "It is distressing to hear that we are not ready for Worker Loyalty Day. It was to be a new triumph."

"I am deeply and personally ashamed to disappoint you, Chairman. But there is another auspicious day in two weeks: The Freedom from the Constitution Day Festival on February 3rd. It is an even larger celebration and may suffice, if you approve."

"Very well. But I do not wish to have another delay, Manager. You understand."

"I will see that no further delays happen, Chairman."

Ko Yeung-su leaned forward. "Did you like your gift?"

"Words cannot express how I felt when I opened it, Chairman. A powerful gift, of which I am not worthy."

"True. But I was happy to give you a token of my esteem. Make sure you have earned it, Manager." He cut the connection.

Removing his interface set, Ji-min walked into the common room to announce the revised date for the next Gathering. When he had done this, he walked to Ha-yun's desk.

Making sure his voice carried, he said, "I relied on you to make sure all was in readiness for the Gathering. Unfortunately, I have found flaws in some of the telemetrics. Please recheck all pathways." He frowned down at her. "And do not embarrass me in this manner again."

Ha-yun could not hide her stricken expression. She bowed her acknowledgement of the criticism.

That night, Ji-min stayed late repairing the network. But when he walked through the darkened office to find Ha-yun still at work, he walked by her desk without noticing her.

The last days of January fled by. The first of the aunties of Sunchon was executed. The space capsule carrying Surro sped into the darkness. Ji-min worked hard and slept little.

On February 3rd he had his driver take him to the river. Along the route, lanterns were set out in readiness for the celebrations that would follow the Gathering for the Chairman's speech. Through the undarkened window of the car, he saw a breeze lift a wisp of snow off the gallows, scattering it as a delicate net, bright in the sun.

Along the riverbank. Ji-min's boots crunched through the snow's surface, leaving his tracks behind. At the river's edge, he placed the Luzon Swallowtail in a balsawood box filled with paper strips. He lit them. He set the little box adrift in the river and watched as the flames grew into a deeper fire, consuming the butterfly and its fragile raft. As it sank from view, Ji-min felt acutely aware that beauty cannot last. But that was no excuse for killing it.

His driver held the car door open, impudently staring at him. He did not mind. Ji-min would have a little gift for him later in the day, and he did not begrudge him it. Nor did he begrudge himself the opportunity to reclaim his honor.

Back at the Directorate of Free Information, in the Office for Interface Control, Ji-min stood outside the door of the common room, gathering his intention. He checked his phone for the exact time.

At the correct moment, he burst through the door. He stopped, taking in his startled employees. He remembered from the example of his Director how to assume a stance of dignified outrage.

"The Chairman demands that you all attend him immediately in the atrium on the ground floor. He wishes to announce an unthinkable act of a traitor."

No one moved.

"Immediately! The Chairman will be here any moment and you must all be waiting for him!"

They began to leave, first in ones and twos, and then in a frantic crowd, surging into the corridor, rushing so as not to be seen straggling in when the Chairman arrived. Specialist Nam Ha-yun was the last to leave. She stood in the door and bowed to him. Then she softly closed the door.

Ji-min locked it behind her. Then he dragged the nearest desk in front of the door and snugged it close.

Once he was inside the Operations Control Center, he locked that door as well, using all his strength to drag a stack of backup servers in front of it.

He checked the time again. Then he called up the real-time display of Surro leaving the space capsule. It had docked twelve hours before. For twelve hours, the world had not slept, nor cared that they did not. The world waited with Surro for the time agreed upon with the Mir Mir. That time was ten minutes away.

Ji-min went deep into the systems code where he had previously arranged for a short code word to redirect the interface. He typed that word now.

Butterfly.

In an instant, the link for the virtual spectators of his nation switched from the Gathering auditorium to a place far from their small nation, far from the Earth itself. In doing so, he connected the waiting masses of the Unified Republic with the sensory receptors of the avatar Surro.

He pulled on the interface head and hand gear and gave himself to the full sensory reproduction from the avatar. Ji-min, as well as 400 million of his fellow citizens, experienced walking across the uneven, rocky surface of the asteroid Prometheus. In the sub-zero environment, the temperature sensors were not activated. Surro walked toward an arch a short distance away. It appeared to be a doorway with nothing behind it.

Ji-min overrode the commentary from the global feed for a few moments in order to explain to the people of the Unified Republic what they were about to experience. He told them that in the next few minutes, they would share in a great event, one that would live on in the memories of Earth's people for a thousand years. The first meeting with an alien being.

He explained that the Mir Mir had demonstrated their wish for peaceful contact. That they came with a gift that would be distributed to every nation: limitless power from nuclear fusion. But even if there was no gift, no advantage to be gained, all people had a right to participate in this global experience.

Then he introduced Surro, the robotic avatar that was

controlled by an anthropologist assisted by a team of exobiologists and cultural experts.

To Ji-min's surprise, Surro broke into the feed. The UN technicians must have detected Ji-min's override. Surro said, in their nation's language, "Welcome to the esteemed people of the Unified Republic." Ji-min was glad to find that the universal translator function worked perfectly. Then audio control reverted back to him. He said that he would defer to Surro from this point on, and he bid his fellow citizens goodnight.

Of course, it was goodbye.

As Surro entered the arch, Ji-min saw that a modest hall lay before him. With exquisite sound reproduction, he heard a door *whoosh* closed in the arch; he heard Surro's footfalls on some unknown substance that comprised the floor. The temperature sensors now reproduced for the spectators a warm environment. The walls pulsed with the colors of stone and sea. Ji-min had time to wonder if the Mir Mir's natural environment held such things, or if the meeting place had been designed with Earth colors in mind.

A movement from the side of Surro's field of vision. A Mheeramhir was walking into view.

In the control room, the door shook. Ji-min took off his head gear to ascertain how long he had before the Security Police smashed through the door. Not that he could do anything to stop it. He hoped that he would have a few more minutes so that he could meet the Mir Mir. He put the interface gear back on.

Surro had drawn close to the Mir Mir representative and was reaching out a hand. Ji-min thought of Lee Ha-yun, and how she was participating in this historic moment—how the whole world was, even his people.

And though the control room door was now, at last, caving in, he felt at one with them all. The disgrace of his years of inaction fell away, and all grief.

The people of earth touched hands with the Mir Mir. The ultra-sensitive haptics delivered a touch of silken threads, very soft and yet ... more.

The Mheeramhir's filaments were not like normal hair. They were in fact able to augment tactile impression. Therefore, what was conveyed was not mere reproduction of touch, but an enhancement of the touch. It became, though it was just a resting of the avatar's hand on the arm of the Mir Mir, a new level of sensation. A caress. An immersion in a world of emotive touch.

Across the world, that touch pressed against fingertips, and against hearts. Some people laughed out loud and some cried. Others were rapt and silent. It was unlike anything anyone had expected, and they would be talking about that moment of contact for much longer than a thousand years. Or so the commentators claimed. But it was not for them to say what it meant or how long it would seem wondrous. Each person would just remember this: They had been there at that moment.

As they had been in Sunchon. In Danyang and in Haju. In Yuwon, Minpo, and every town and village and isolated farm in the Unified Republic. They had been there to meet the Mheeramhir.

At the end, Ha-yun removed her head gear and the excellent haptics with their PY6 upgrades. Her thoughts were with Surro and the Mir Mir. And also with Ji-min. The authorities had cut off the interface—they must have breached the control room—but not before the First Touch.

She was sad to think of Ji-min's fate. But also very proud of what he had accomplished. In the midst of his great enterprise he had even had time to protect her. When he had upbraided her in front of the entire office, he had assured that she would not be associated with him and his revolutionary act.

A month later, in Sunchon, the aunties brewed tea. Sixteen women sat together and talked about all that had been lost and gained.

Two aunties had been executed. And then, just when they had expected the guards to come for the third woman, and the fourth, they had opened the prison doors and set them free.

Things were changing. Or might change. If not tomorrow, then next summer. And if not next summer, then a year from now. But nothing would be the same. The idea was cause for the brewing of an especially fine tea.

They had decided to call their crusade the Mir Mir Movement. They had missed the First Touch because they had been in prison, but they knew the power it had unleashed. Each woman pledged to speak to three others, and those three must pledge to do the same. It wasn't that the aunties didn't believe in radio and the internet. They very much did. But sometimes you just had to touch someone to make them understand.

One of the aunties turned to the woman sitting next to her and held out her hand, fingers separated. The other woman matched her, fingers to fingers. Then the women were turning to one side and the other, hands raised, touching.

And so it went, one to another, in the old ways and new.

DELIVERING THE PAYLOAD

BY JOSH VOGT

DELIVERING THE PAYLOAD

BY JOSH VOGT

anika wiped sweat from her forehead as she studied the brainframe. She ran fingertips over her now bald head, dreadlocks shaved off just this morning to ensure a perfect synch. Her turn to deliver the payload. Her turn to slip behind enemy lines and finish their mission.

"You ready?" Larimore asked from his perch by the console.

She eyed him, a stick figure of a man in a too-large lab coat and baggy jeans, with wispy white hair. He squinted back at her, spectacles reflecting the glow of his monitor.

The silvery brainframe cradle filled most of the rest of the room, the cramped space contained by whitewashed, cinder block walls and a single steel door. Wires ran out from the back of the brainframe and into a silvery canister—the projection unit that would send Danika's awareness to the unit waiting for her half a country away.

Danika plucked at the brainframe bodysuit that clung tight to her pudgy self, and then crossed thick arms over her chest. Her dark skin stood in stark contrast to the sterile white of the suit and the silver nodes studded across it, allowing the brainframe to tap into her central nervous system.

"I didn't sign up for this part," she said. "This is Tony's job. I'm just going to screw it up."

Larimore blinked like an owl. "You agreed to undergo synch training as a backup, and now you're needed as one. With Tony down with a fever, you're the next best suited for the run. We have to keep to the schedule, otherwise everything could fall apart." He tilted his head slightly. "Besides, the longer Zoe waits, the higher the risk of her being discovered and captured —if not killed."

Danika's hands went clammy even as her blood heated. She tried her best glare, but it might as well have been a slingshot whipping a pebble into bulletproof glass for all the effect it had on the technician.

"She's *my* daughter," she said. "You don't have to tell me what's at stake."

Larimore coughed, a sound like paper tearing. He blinked again, waiting.

"Fine. Let's get this over with," she said.

Stomping over to the brainframe cradle, Danika eased into the seat, making sure the nodes lined up with the I/O sensors. The chill of the metal seeped through her suit, and she clenched her teeth as her scalp pressed against the headrest. Once situated, she glanced at Larimore out of the corners of her eyes.

"Kick me in," she said.

Larimore's fingers writhed over the console like dancing spiders, head bobbing to some unheard tune. The brainframe hummed to life, and Danika drew a sharp breath as her whole body tingled. Not a painful sensation, but one that made her feel like she vibrated down to the bone. To take her mind off the integration, she tried to smooth out her breathing. However, inevitable worries edged into her thoughts.

What if, despite their efforts to hide it during charging cycles, the SIBYL unit had been discovered by enemy soldiers?

What if the payload had been tampered with or corrupted? What if the solar panels had malfunctioned and she got kicked into a chassis with a dead power core?

Danika sighed and imagined all those worries written in chalk on a blackboard. Then she mentally wiped them away.

"Transitioning in ten seconds," Larimore said. "Nine. Eight. Seven. Six ..."

Danika blinked as sweat trickled into her eyes. Her vision blurred and she fought the urge to swipe at her face again.

"Five. Four. Three. Two ..."

She squeezed her eyes shut. And then the whole world tilted. She felt like she'd been chained to a merry-go-round gone mad, being thrown this way and that, spun about, cast high into the air and then dropped with gut-wrenching speed.

She started to call out to Larimore, to tell him to abort the process, that something was wrong. But her mouth remained sealed shut and her limbs refused to move. Thoughts and memories swirled into a kaleidoscope of faces and places until it all blurred together into an infinite tunnel that she soared through, aiming for the black hole at the far end that grew into a void readying to swallow her whole.

Her mind struck that dark expanse—and everything stilled.

After what felt like an eternal heartbeat, Danika tried to move. Her body felt even heavier than usual, and her eyes refused to open. Panic bubbled through her veins and she tried to suck in deep, calming breaths. As she inhaled, a white field filled her vision. Gray text blinked into being at the center.

Synching ...

The whiteness fizzled away, revealing an arid vista. Danika looked out on swaths of rocks and sand broken up by columns of burnt-orange stone. What little vegetation managed to scrabble an existence looked withered and twisted, brown sprouts reaching up like skeletal fingers. Even the sky looked worn out; its cloudless blue faded, practically bleached in spots.

Wind blew dust flurries across the seemingly lifeless landscape, though the unit's multispectrum optical scanners let Danika pick out tracks and trails through the wasteland. Animal routes going to and from remote watering holes. Tire treads that had to be several months old, worn to little more than rivulets of long-dried mud. Overhead, black, winged forms circled in the distance.

Sensation returned to Danika's body—but not her biological one. Four limbs, each triple-jointed and able to flex in multiple directions at once. A sleek torso that could swivel full circle, with a gyroscopic core for the bipedal movement mode. Each limb ended in six articulated fingers that could juggle eggs without cracking a single one or squeeze a basketball until it popped. Temperature and pressure gauges even let her feel the scudding wind and the unrelenting sun.

She raised a chassis arm, its segmented form painted muted tones of brown, black, and red to blend with the landscape. Larimore and his team had designed and built it in their lab, adapting from military blueprints that he still refused to fully explain how he acquired. SIBYL units had primarily been used for espionage and sabotage, slipping past enemy lines to wreak all manner of havoc. When Zoe's emergency call had come in on the outset of the war, followed by a week of silence, Danika had cashed in all her favors to convince her old friend to use the unit for a more direct mission. She still didn't fully understand Zoe's brief request, but they had her coordinates and the payload secured within SIBYL.

A voice filtered into her awareness.

"Danika? Report in."

Danika kept her external audio off, mentally projecting her reply. "Larimore. I'm synched. I'm in control of SIBYL."

"Excellent. Can you orient yourself to the target site?"

"Hang on. Let me get the motors running."

She moved SIBYL's—no, she moved her arms and legs, trying to adapt to the increased mobility. Yet, while her upper limbs shifted freely, her lower body refused to budge.

Alarmed, Danika pulled up a diagnostic routine and status readouts. She scanned the data that popped into her field of vision, highlighting different unit systems and operations.

"Oh no."

"What's wrong?"

Danika double-checked the readout. The numbers stayed the same. "Power core's only half-charged."

"How's that possible? We had SIBYL on a twelve-hour recharge cycle between runs. You should be full up."

Danika raised her upper body as much as she could and then rotated her head in a half circle. The lower half of the unit, where the primary charge panel had been installed, was buried beneath a hefty mound of sand, a miniature dune that swept up her back.

"Must've been a sandstorm," she said. "Main solar panels were covered. Hang a sec."

Digging into the loose sand, she clawed free of the mound pinning. As she shook loose, standing on all fours, she ran a thermal scan on the area. Her scope remained clear except for one lizard sunning itself on a rock a hundred yards off.

"Everything's functional, at least," she said. "Locking in coordinates. How's the payload?"

A few data streams scrolled past faster than she could follow. *"Intact. But the longer you loiter, the more you risk the core draining before you can deliver it."*

"I hear you. I'm moving."

With a mental command, Danika summoned a map of the area. Tony's last run had gotten the unit past southern patrols, but Zoe's coordinates pinpointed an area almost a hundred miles northeast. No known settlements or villages—at least not ones that had survived initial bombardments. If Danika beelined there and didn't have any interruptions, she just might make it before her energy levels flatlined. Keeping herself on all fours, she loped that way, spraying sand behind her as she churned up the distance.

While she'd trained with SIBYL before, the fluidity of its movement and speed left her breathless—though she didn't technically breathe through the unit. It felt odd to think of her body being so far away while her mind operated this fascinating machine.

Her satellite uplink kept her map updating as she moved, leaping ten feet at a time to soar over gullies, dodging through copses of dead trees, and veering around bombed-out craters and rusted shells of tanks and military mechs. Despite not wanting to get a closer look at the carnage, her optical sensors auto-targeted the withered remains of soldiers, analyzing them to determine if any posed potential threats. Yet their gray and black uniforms were tattered from exposure to the harsh environment, and nothing but insects, crows, and skittish reptiles moved in the area.

Danika couldn't tell if the bodies she passed were from recent skirmishes, or if they'd been dead since the first bombs fell and the region was quarantined. A month after the border war had begun, nothing but military forces traversed the area, which had been a deemed a no-man's-land. And no survivors who'd been living there at the time were allowed out, trapped in a fight none of them had started.

They'd just been abandoned. Left to starve or die when caught in the occasional crossfire or air strike. Any civilian relief programs that attempted to help those stuck there were turned back by border patrols—violently, if they persisted. A stalemate enforced by both sides of the war, as neither wanted to "waste" resources helping their fellow human beings if it meant making themselves vulnerable to the enemy.

Fury spurred Danika on. She kept one eye on her energy meters, trying to conserve as much as possible and keep the straightest route to her target.

Zoe would be waiting for her. She had to be.

SIBYL ate up the miles, one by one, sun blazing the whole way. The team had originally tried running these missions during the night, but quickly realized the unit's heat signature was better concealed during the heat of the day. Plus, the direct sunlight let the unit soak up a little extra energy, even when active, which gave Danika the tiniest bit of hope that she wouldn't go dark mere miles away from reaching her daughter.

The wind whistled past as she tried to find the optimal balance between speed and power conservation. Too fast and she'd eat up what little reserves she had. Too slow, and just being powered on would inevitably drain the core, kicking Danika back into her real body. Zoe would move on, and it could be weeks before she found a place secure enough to relay her position again.

As Danika tried to push aside her distracting fears, an alert flashed on her optics. Movement overhead. At first she thought it was a large bird, come to feed on carrion in the area. Then her sensors confirmed the engine noise. A drone—possibly with a pilot's mind kicked in to directly control it.

She veered off her path and lurched to a halt beneath a set of rocky outcroppings along the base of the hill she'd been running along. She tucked herself tight in the opening, but didn't doubt she'd already been detected.

The drone made several passes, buzzing in circles before rocketing into the distance. As its engine noise faded, Danika alerted Larimore.

"I've been spotted. Drone sighted me before my scope picked it up. It's gone now, but I'd bet I'm going to be getting some activity heading my way soon."

"Damn." A few moments passed, and she imagined him

analyzing readouts on his end. *"Must've been a random sweep. Intel said there shouldn't have been any patrols, airborne or otherwise, in your path."*

Danika peeked out from under the overhang, switching through several optical modes to make sure the drone was really gone. "Well, intel's wrong, and if I get tracked to Zoe's location, then I'd be giving her a death sentence."

"Bring the stealth mode online."

"Won't that burn through my power levels even faster?"

"Yes, but better than blowing the whole mission, don't you think?"

"Good point. But if I reach the target without enough power to finish the mission, what will that accomplish?"

"I'll ... think of something."

Danika crept out from her hiding spot. With a thought, she activated SIBYL's stealth mode. The panels comprising the unit's form shimmered and blurred as optical relays mirrored the surrounding landscape, making her extremely difficult to spot and eliminating any shadow she'd cast. Not invisibility by any means, as she'd be seen as a mottled ripple in the air as she moved along, but it would have to do.

Just activating the camouflage dropped her available power by ten percent; Danika eyed the remaining energy meter—dipping from yellow toward red—with trepidation. She needed at least another hour to get to Zoe, and wasn't sure if it was possible. Broadcasting an update to her daughter wasn't possible as any radio communication might be intercepted, giving away both of their locations. The only reason Danika could even communicate with Larimore was because he was tapped in through the brainframe.

Speeding off again, Danika split her attention between the skies and the ground, not wanting to be caught off guard again. If she led the enemy right to her daughter, she'd never forgive herself.

Over the next fifty miles, two more drones zipped overhead, but neither slowed or turned back around. Danika bounded over rocky hills, shot through dried-out gullies, and scrambled over fields of charred earth. She passed a few sets of caves to the west, mouths gaping and empty. Some had signs of prior settlements littered about: shattered and dust-covered solar arrays, blown-up water dredgers, wind-shredded shelters. Even a couple of shells of civilian avatars, designed for manual labor and construction, the units now little more than scrap.

Still, Danika used up a few precious minutes lurking over to inspect the avatars, scanning for energy signatures just in case an old power core might remain within them that she could use to recharge.

As she checked one over, head lowered to peer into its twisted chassis, an explosion rocked the ground right beside her. SIBYL went tumbling, Danika flailing for balance. Her optics screen jittered and fuzzed in one corner; at least one scanner had been damaged or destroyed outright.

"I'm hit," she cried. She got to all fours and scrambled for cover, but one arm hung mangled, making her limp along. Rising to bipedal mode, she hunched as she ran for a row of boulders. She flung herself between these just as another explosion plumed rust-red dust into the air.

"Who's attacking?"

"No clue. At least one scanner malfunctioning and ..." She reviewed her readouts. "Stealth is on the fritz." She shut down the camouflage; no point draining energy for faulty conceal-ment. "And I've got one arm out of order. Power's down to twenty-two percent."

Gunfire roared overhead and Danika's audio input damp-ened the worst of the noise. At the same time, it triangulated where the weapons fire came from. Danika peeked through a space between two boulders. Through the smoke and dust, she picked out a blocky form stamping her way from over a low hill several hundred yards off. Her sensors outlined the figure's mechanical build, plus the flat paneling where its "head" was. One arm appeared to be a machine gun while the other looked to be a rocket or grenade launcher, by her guess.

"Mech," she said. "Small one, but large enough for a single pilot in there. Must be a scout, which means if I don't get out of here fast, there'll be more troops incoming."

"Think you could incapacitate it?"

"I'm not a soldier," she said. "And I'm not here to kill."

"If they destroy SIBYL, then this will have been for nothing."

"I'm already badly damaged and I can't risk taking more hits."

Larimore's silence expanded while Danika's heartbeat thumped in time with the oncoming war machine's steps. At last, the brainframe monitor spoke up.

"I've got an idea. It's desperate. Extremely desperate. But it might be the only chance we've got."

Danika crouched as the mech fired another rocket over the boulders. It exploded a dozen yards behind her. "Lay it out."

"I can trigger a surge in your power core that would effectively act as an EMP blast. If you can get the mech within range, I can remotely activate the surge to knock it offline."

"Uh ... don't EMPs shut down any electrical systems? Wouldn't that affect me, too?"

"Yes. But I should be able to reboot you in less than a minute. Far faster than that beastly thing could recover. It'd give you time to put enough distance between you to avoid being tracked. And hopefully let you retain enough power to reach the coordinates."

Doubt and, yes, a ripple of fear chilled Danika despite the heat waves rising from the stones all around.

"What'll happen to me while SIBYL's rebooting?"

"You'll have to remain synched. It'd take too long to pull you out, reset, and kick you back in."

"And what will I experience if I'm synched with a powered down avatar?"

Larimore coughed. *"In theory? Nothing. You'll just float in a void until external senses are restored."*

"Theory, huh?"

"I didn't say it was an elegant solution. Just the best one I can offer. Have a better idea?"

Danika tried to summon one but came up empty. Knowing every inactive minute was a wasted one, she relented.

"Let's do it. If we don't, it's a guaranteed failure. At least this gives us a chance."

"Give me five seconds to prep. You'll need to get within ten feet of the mech. Get ready to bolt on my mark."

An odd humming filled her metal frame and she assumed it was Larimore tinkering with internal systems. As she waited, she studied the mech, which had halved the distance between them.

Danika reached over with her good arm and tore the damaged one off. Less weight meant she could run that much faster, and her internal gyroscope should compensate. Besides, she needed some sort of distraction if she wanted to close the gap before the mech's targeting system locked on her.

"Ready?" Larimore asked.

"No, but what's it matter?"

"Go."

Danika stepped back and flung the broken arm over the boulders. A microsecond later, she charged through a larger gap and sprinted as fast as the unit could manage for the mech.

The mech had aimed its gun at the arm soaring through the air. A stream of bullets shredded the limb, and the mech's torso began rotating back her way.

But the distraction had let her get in just close enough. The humming at the edge of her hearing rose to a buzzing ... then a crackle ... then a roar. Danika stumbled as a blinding flash swept out through her field of vision. She had a dim sensation of falling, slamming to the earth, and then everything went black.

Danika stretched her awareness out as far as she could and came up empty. Not so much as a flicker of light or blip of noise. The seconds oozed by, and she quickly lost any real track of time. She tried to count her breaths or pulse, but even those sensations had been muted.

The only thing left was the crawling fear of being stuck there forever. What if Larimore couldn't bring her back online? What if the surge had somehow trapped her awareness in an inactive chassis? Was that even possible?

Fear clutched at her again, gripping harder as it rose to panic. She tried to thrash, to feel anything, to move anything, to find an anchor. It must've been at least a minute since she went offline. Why hadn't Larimore done something yet? What had happened to her body back in the brainframe?

She hadn't been trained for anything like this. She hadn't been prepared to enter a battlefield. She just wanted to reach her daughter, stuck on the wrong side of the conflict.

She tried shouting for Larimore, but her voice only echoed inside her mind. Yet she kept it up, increasingly desperate for a response of any—

"Could you keep it down? Yelling ruins my concentration."

A pulse of energy tingled through her and the world reappeared. SIBYL lay sprawled beside the mech, which had frozen in place, right foot forward, weapon-arms pointed above her. The cockpit remained sealed, though Danika glimpsed a shadowed figure inside, fists pummeling the viewport.

"Thank you," she told Larimore, voice breathy with relief.

"Thank me when we finish this. You should move."

Lurching to her feet, she took a moment to assess her avatar's status.

Ten percent power and dropping even quicker than before.

Danika pointedly ignored the warnings flashing before her. No time to count the percentages. She could only run and hope and pray.

Running along on two limbs, now, she didn't bother scanning for enemies. She fixed on the coordinates alone, watching the distance tick down, bit by bit. She tried to stay on hard-packed ground so the avatar would leave less-obvious tracks if anyone tried to pick up her trail. She imagined she could hear SIBYL groaning in protest, rotors whining and chassis plates grinding as she pushed its battered form along.

Eight percent.

Five percent.

The landscape flashed by, a sunburnt blur that might as well have been the surface of Mars. Until, at last ...

There. Her optics zoomed on a low cliffside along a rocky butte. Half a dozen cave entrances dotted the base, and Zoe's coordinates aligned with the nearest. Danika beelined for this, legs whirring.

Three percent.

Two.

No sign of life anywhere. Was she already too late? Had Zoe already moved on?

One.

The cave entrance gaped ahead.

As if she'd struck a wall, Danika's avatar locked up from one step to the next. Joints refused to move as she toppled flat. Her vision field remained fixed on the cave, but she didn't have the power left to run any diagnostics, much less scan for life forms.

Her sight flickered and began to blur. Details faded and color bled away.

Larimore said something in the distance, but his voice stuttered into nothing. As more systems shut down, Danika felt like her consciousness remained in SIBYL by sheer will alone. She needed something, anything, to let her know the mission hadn't been a failure.

Then a figure emerged from the cave. The person was dressed in a dirt-stained white robe and heavy boots, face covered by a head wrapping that left only the eyes exposed. Danika strained to squeeze any last bit of juice out of the power core, to stay synched just a little longer.

Her sensation of being SIBYL continued to seep away. She couldn't feel the wind or heat of the earth any longer. Her remaining three limbs twitched, but she couldn't so much as pluck up a grain of sand.

The robed figure approached cautiously. Once they stood a few yards off, the person undid the headwrap, revealing another woman whose features matched Danika's as they'd been a couple decades ago—though far thinner and etched with weariness. Long black hair fell free, and the woman crouched to peer at her.

"Tony?" Zoe's voice came thin through Danika's failing audio inputs.

Danika barely managed to waggle one of the unit's hands. Her vision flickered black, and she cringed, waiting to lose contact for good.

So close ...

Then Zoe drew a blocky device from under her robe and unraveled a cord from it. She stood and ran over to Danika's side. After another few seconds of wavering on the edge of systems failure, Danika realized her energy drain had halted.

Power funneled back through SIBYL's frame. Vision stabilized, and her other external senses came back online, one at a time. She felt oddly shaky as she rose, but managed to keep her balance.

Zoe stepped back into sight, device in hand, its cord running to a port in SIBYL's side.

"Tony? Still with me?"

Danika brought her external speakers online and fought to keep her voice from quaking. "It's me, Zoe."

Her daughter's eyes widened in shock. "Mom? What happened? Is Tony okay?"

"He's sick, but will be fine. Just too weak to handle the brainframe, so I had to sub for the last leg." Danika nodded at the device her daughter held, the top of which had a solar panel screwed in to electrical nodes. "Solar battery?"

Zoe touched SIBYL's remaining arm as if disbelieving her mother's presence within in. "Yeah," she said distractedly. "We kept it at the school to run the satellite uplink during lessons. One of the few things we managed to salvage before getting out." She stared in wonderment. "You really made it. I had almost lost hope ..." She shook her head, gathering herself. "You have it? The data drive? Is it damaged?"

Larimore piped in to Danika's ears. *"Despite your little adventure, the payload appears intact. We can prep the transfer ASAP."*

Danika pointed to the cave. "Let's get out of sight before we start."

Zoe led her inside. The cave stretched twenty feet into the cliffside before thinning to a tunnel just a few feet wide. Darkness hid everything beyond that point, though Danika thought she picked up on shuffling and whispering back that way.

Ignoring that for the moment, she recited a mental code and a seamless hatch on SIBYL's chest hinged open, revealing a reinforced storage space. She plucked out a holographic data storage cube that shimmered with an inner light.

Hardly seeming to breathe, Zoe retrieved a tablet out of a robe pocket. She powered it on, and Danika placed the cube on the slightly cracked screen. Glyphs flashed as the data in the cube flooded the tablet's memory. The transfer completed in less than a minute; Danika retrieved the cube and stored it back in the chassis.

With shaking hands, Zoe brought up a reading app and began listing off the titles that appeared there.

"*The Earthsea Cycle. The Hobbit* and *Lord of the Rings. Good Omens. Ender's Game.* And the whole *Discworld* series?" Her smile gleamed as she scrolled through the hundreds of novels and story collections the tablet now contained. "Mom, this is perfect."

Danika frowned, despite knowing SYBIL couldn't translate her expression. "I still don't understand. You use your one chance to make contact and ask for this, of all things? I wish we could've brought something more helpful. Fresh food. Water purifiers. Collapsible shelters."

Zoe powered the tablet down and tucked it away. "Mom, this is exactly what we need." She turned and waved to the back of the cave. "It's okay. Come on out. It's safe."

After a few moments, shadowed movement resolved into a small group that filtered out of the tunnel.

Children. At least a dozen children stood there, some shirtless, some in dusty robes, others in torn khakis, many with bare feet. Danika guessed they ranged from five years old up to midteens. Their faces were grave, gazes haunted.

All of them had belonged to the school where Zoe taught before the war broke out. They'd barely evacuated their town before the school had been destroyed by invading forces. Even these innocents had been refused relief so long as the battles raged along the contested borders.

Danika gasped. "It's just you and them?"

"No, thank goodness." Zoe gestured outside. "A few adults are with us and have been out scavenging supplies for a few days while trying to figure safe routes. They should be back tonight, and then we have to move to a new hideout before this one gets discovered. My kids ..." She laughed lightly. "My students, though ... not one of them has made the smallest smile in weeks." Zoe lowered her voice so it wouldn't carry.

"We're surviving. We have to keep moving and we can't carry too much beyond the bare necessities." Her lips thinned in a determined line. "I know we'll find a way past the border patrols. We'll find our path to freedom. But they ... these kids I'm responsible for ... they need hope. They need a reason to keep going."

She smiled up at Danika. "I'm not an engineer or doctor or soldier or anything. But I can still offer a little hope. I remember how, when I was little, you read me these stories." She tapped the tablet. "Ones where the heroes never gave up. Where there was always good in the world worth struggling to hold onto. I remember how much I loved them, how they made me laugh, and could brighten the darkest day. I remember nights when I was scared of the monster in my closet, and I'd finally fall asleep while hearing you read to me, saying 'Once upon a time, there was a very brave little girl ...'"

A nod to the kids, who'd started to withdraw again. "And as long as I'm alive, I want to give them the same experience, no matter how bad things look."

Danika wanted to crush her daughter in a hug but refrained, fearing she might underestimate SIBYL's strength. So she just laid her hand on Zoe's shoulder as gently as she could.

"I love you, Zoe. You can't imagine how proud of you I am."

Her daughter winked. "I've got a pretty good imagination, thanks to you. Maybe next time you can bring us some comic books."

"Problem with that," Larimore said. *"The damage you've taken is causing widespread degradation across all systems. It's unlikely we'll be able to synch with SIBYL again, even if its power core was fully charged."*

Zoe grimaced as Danika relayed the information. "I worried that might happen. Anya is a mechanic. I don't think she knows much about avatars, but maybe once she gets back tonight, she'll be able to scrounge some of the unit's parts and cobble together something useful." She squeezed the unit's arm, and Danika could feel the touch as if standing directly in front of her. "Either way, I need one last thing from you."

"Anything, baby girl."

"I need you to go tell a story, too." Zoe tapped her temple. "I'm guessing everything you've seen and heard is being recorded?"

"Of course," Larimore said.

When Danika confirmed this, Zoe took a deep breath.

"Then use that to tell the outside world about us. Spread the word, show them the evidence of what's happening and don't let them give up on us. Broadcast on every news channel and vid feed."

"You think that will help?"

"Who knows?" Zoe sighed. "Get enough of the right voices screaming in protest, and you could get a cease-fire. Even a temporary one might let us all get out alive."

Danika nodded vigorously. "I promise. We'll do everything we can."

The unit's legs wobbled, and Danika barely caught herself against the cave wall. She slid down until she sat on the ground. Zoe knelt beside her, concerned, clutching SYBIL's metal frame.

"Synch's already breaking down," Larimore said. *"You've got a few seconds left."*

"I can't stay," Danika said. "I'm sorry. But I'll be waiting once you get free. Then you and all your kids can tell the story yourselves. I love you, Zoe. Be strong. Be safe."

As her avatar's vision faded a last time and Danika's awareness of SYBIL drew into the distance, there came a last brush of a hand on the unit's head and her daughter's whisper.

"Once upon a time, there was a very brave little girl ..."

STEDMAN FARRAH'S ILLUSTRIOUS FALL

BY MARINA J. LOSTETTER

STEDMAN FARRAH'S ILLUSTRIOUS FALL

BY MARINA J. LOSTETTER

S tedman always knew he wanted to go into space. He'd wanted to be an astronaut since before he could pronounce it. His room when he was ten was painted all black with little white dots for stars, and big, blue not-so-round-because-his-big-sister-had-painted-them planets. He'd studied hard. Had the top grades in high school despite holding down a burger-joint job to take care of his mother. He'd applied to the Air Force, and then ...

And then he'd discovered he was color blind. You can't fly planes if you can't read the dash properly.

He should have known. All those years, he thought Madeline was messing with him when she pointed to the red sign over the Sips-To-Go mart and asked him to read it.

"There's nothing there," he insisted, and she laughed and pinched him and told him to quit acting stupid.

But it was true—he couldn't see the *Two for one twelve-inch franks!* advert.

Just as the U.S. government couldn't see handing him a plane.

And if they couldn't hand him a plane, they weren't going to hand him a spaceship.

But that didn't mean he'd given up.

"Hey there. Glad to have you with us."

The man at the port authority receiving desk had a long black mustache and a head as close to a cube as a living thing could manage. "Jacks all installed?"

Stedman scratched the back of his head where the little metallic interface nubs resided. They'd just started to heal over. For months, the skin surrounding them had puffed, red and inflamed with infection. Like Madeline's pierced ears. She'd had a lot of piercings and a lot of infections.

"Yep."

"Interface has been verified? I know you're chomping to get in there, but we have to make sure the software has settled or things could go to shit real fast. No one ever takes me seriously when I tell them that."

The scratchy wool covering on the old red chair had split, and the stuffing underneath Stedman's left butt cheek was uncomfortably uneven. He fidgeted, trying to smile, sure he was grimacing. "No, no. I get it."

A fly buzzed near the office's old halogen lamp.

This was not the glamorous life of space travel he'd envisioned. But he'd take what he could get.

"Companies are really counting on us to get lower orbits up to snuff," the mustached man said again, crossing his beefy arms.

"Believe me, I know."

Space debris was a growing problem. Especially now that space tourism was becoming a regular reality. You still needed a pretty penny to get up there—they weren't just serving anyone caviar on the way up and hoping it didn't make a reappearance on the way down. So, even for college-educated Stedman, who had plenty of robotics training, the idea of chartering a space craft was a nonstarter.

But wherever tourists go, they need grounds maintained. Beaches need combing. Museum floors need buffing. Ruins need de-littering. And low-orbit cruise ships need a clear path.

Decades upon decades of junk were flitting around the planet as they spoke. Pieces of satellites, screws off space tele-scopes, torn-to-shreds solar sails. All of it tumbled about, doomed to eventually burn up in the atmosphere.

But it wasn't burning fast enough.

That was where Stedman came in. He was the low-orbit trash man, there to clean up any dangerous space-race era trin-kets floating around.

Not with his hands, of course. Not even in person.

"Are you ready to meet your teammate?" Mustachioed man asked.

Stedman clapped his hands together. "Sure am."

With a skeptical nod, the man led him past the reception desk, down a dimly lit hall with water stains on the ceiling, to a wing marked "Avatar Attachments." The man kicked through a swinging door which led into what looked, and felt, like a doctor's office. The walls were white and frigid, the air tainted with the sour smell of cleaner.

An older woman in a lab coat stood in the doorway of what might have been an exam room. She beckoned them over, a clipboard in her rubber gloved hand. "Stedman Farrah?" she asked.

"That's me."

"Ready to go into space?"

You have no idea.

"Yes, ma'am."

"Well, alright then. This here—" she pushed open the door,

revealing a woman with harshly cropped bangs and a long braid sitting in a strangely shaped chair—"is your partner, Eva. She's been on the job for three years, and is our most senior avatar pilot."

Eva was all business, from her jumpsuit (standard issue, Stedman had on the same), to her focused expression and thin-lined mouth. "How many simulation hours you clock?" she asked him.

"Three hundred."

She frowned. "It'll do."

The lady with the clipboard remained chipper. "No one better to train you," she insisted. "Okay, plug-in time!"

Stedman turned to thank the mustached man, only to find that he was gone.

"Lie down there," the woman gestured with one hand, while shoving an IV into Eva's forearm-port with the other. "I'll get to you in a minute."

The chair she'd indicated was identical to Eva's, all deep-set and funky curves. Almost like one of those ergonomic benches molded into really fancy hot tubs. Boosting himself in was awkward, but he managed. He didn't mind looking a bit unco-ordinated on the ground if he was graceful in space.

Eva closed her eyes and gave a small shiver. He knew that response well—the strange comforting calm that overtook you when the wires connected. It was like being wrapped in a warm blanket in the comfiest of beds.

He laid his head back, letting his body sag into the chair. He was used to the stiff, flat platform of the simulator.

The wires found him before Doc's needle did. They snaked out from the chair and connected to their proper ports of their own accord, as if they were alive.

Instantly, he was transported to another place. Another body. A ship for his mind alone.

Somewhere high above his human form, on the edges of

space, Stedman's avatar woke up. It had triangulated cameras at the fore, which let him see better than with his own eyes, clawed pinchers for grasping and magnets for hauling. Vaguely, he could sense its shape—mostly round, save for the extremities. It was strange to no longer feel his lungs pumping or his pulse running, no matter how many times he went under.

He tested all of the other mechanisms before the cameras. They seemed to be in working order. All he had to do was think and they reacted, like extensions of his natural self.

This his color blindness could not bar him from. He did not need to read dials or charts or readouts. This bypassed the cones and rods of his eyes and projected everything he needed directly into his gray matter.

In this way and this way alone, space was his.

Slowly, he let the cameras' apertures open.

No grainy simulator could prepare him for the sight.

The atmosphere was a deep blue to turquoise band fanning out before him. If he looked directly down, he could see the ocean and clouds, but could not make out waves unless he zoomed in as far as possible. A swift sense of vertigo overtook him and he looked away from the water, clearing his thoughts, banishing all concepts of falling. He could not fall as long as he piloted his avatar sure and true.

And then, he looked up.

It was midday, and so the sun was fully within his view. He could perceive it at its full brilliance because he didn't have delicate human eyes to shield. Its shine was intense, but absent of the usual glare due to lack of atmosphere. It seemed to sit in a dark hole, blacker than the blackest black Stedman could imagine.

And yet, beyond, he knew there were stars. He couldn't wait to pull a night shift.

Another avatar whizzed by him. "Hey, new guy," said what must have been Eva's voice—it sounded very unlike her real voice—in his mind. "No dawdling on my watch. We are here to clean, not gawk. Got it?"

"Uh, yeah."

"Uh, yeah, what?"

"Uh, yeah … boss?"

"It'll do. Follow me. You see that field up there? Busted tele-coms satellite, needs to be redirected and sent on hyper-decay ASAP."

She shot ahead, a shiny black sphere of efficiency. Try as he might, he couldn't catch up. She was just too fast.

"Hey, why—my avatar's not responding like yours. I can't get it to—"

"You'll work out the nuances in time. I've been doing this longer than anyone else. Just try to keep up."

It wasn't long before he reached the debris, but by then she'd already pushed the largest pieces together and was scur-rying after the smaller shards.

Stedman spotted a scrap of metal a few yards away and tried to dash over to it as quickly as he could. But he was a putting tug boat to her speed boat.

"That's it, like the hustle," she said. She gave him a few pointers on arrangement, on how to shape the new pile so that it descended most efficiently, burning up the cleanest. "You know, there's a reason I shoot for speed," she said.

"Oh?" He hadn't expected her to make idle chitchat.

"There's an initiative to get regular space travel going—for your average people, not just the rich. Like, they want to imple-ment field trips for school kids. They think they could get it up and running in the next ten years. People outside of school, it'll be a long time before we get rides. But kids … kids today have a chance."

"So I take it you've got a kid?" he asked, trying not to sound too bored or too interested, feeling her out.

"A kid with a dream," she said. "Really wants to be an astronaut. She loves that she gets to tell her class about my time in space, even if ... you know."

"What?"

"Glorified litter patrol."

"I wouldn't even say *glorified*," he joked.

She laughed. "You know, you're alright."

"Thanks. I was ..." he hesitated, focusing on drawing in a nearby piece with one of his magnets. Maybe she'd think him sappy. "I was your kid once. Wanted to be an astronaut."

"Is space everything you thought it'd be?"

He looked away from their tumbling debris island, letting himself drift, feeling the spin of the Earth like he never had before.

She laughed again. "I'll take that as a yes."

Six months in, Stedman and Eva were the port authority's top team. They could get their space junk burn quota in half the time of any other avatar pair.

Today they were sent to work beneath the scaffolding of the high orbit dock for the Mars cycler. Stedman tried to stay focused, but the beautiful orange and white hull of the ship kept drawing his attention. Its colors looked different here, without the filter of his eyes.

It was set to launch in only a few weeks and had an advanced propulsion system that utilized a newly designed, ultracompact nuclear reactor. Neat stuff.

For a moment, he allowed himself a fantasy: when Eva's cameras were turned, he would jet away, thrusting his avatar into higher and higher altitudes, until he reached the platform. Then he'd find a good hand-hold and settle his avatar in for a ride. He'd mentally stow away on the first round-trip to the red planet, and—

"Yo, space cadet," Eva said, waving a gold-colored scrap panel in front of his cameras. "You with me?"

"Yeah, sorry. But have you seen ...?" He waved all four of his claws emphatically at the ship.

"Believe me, I know that thing like the back of my hand. Kid's got twelve posters of it from all different angles."

"Well, she's got good taste." He admired it again. "I mean, as far as feats of engineering go ... wait."

Speaking of all different angles, it appeared to be at a new one now. Where before he'd been staring at its underbelly, now it had rotated toward the nose. "Are they moving it today, or—?"

The emergency channel opened wide, Doc's voice blaring out in their synthetic ears. "Cover, cover! Meteors detected. Take cover!"

"Cover *where*?" Eva demanded of no one in particular.

Just then, the rocks came streaming past them from the direction of the cycler. Each one large, silent, and pulverizingly quick—they could permanently take out an avatar, no problem. He and Eva huddled together, their avatars grasping one another tightly. But they seemed to be in a dead zone—the stones were falling all around them, but it was as though a giant umbrella had shielded them from directly overhead ...

"Oh, *craaaaap*," Stedman said in realization. He looked up again. The cycler had shifted dramatically, and now he could see that it was tumbling erratically. He and Eva were no longer directly beneath it—their orbits and its no longer synchronized.

"They hit the cycler!" he told her. "It's been knocked out of its moorings. It's *falling*."

"What do we do?" Eva demanded over the emergency channel.

"Evacuate!" Doc said. "Get your AVs out of there. All other AVs, I'm sending you an emergency no-fly-zone grid. We have a major piece of equipment falling out of the sky and I need you to get your avatars safely out of the way."

"No, we can't do that," Stedman said, cameras locked on the dropping vessel above. "No way that thing's going to burn up safely. It might break up, but those chunks are going to cause major damage. I mean *major*. If its nuclear reactor has been activated, *boom*." He made an explosive gesture with his claws. "And even if it hasn't—"

"Shit," Eva cursed. "Nuclear fallout. The materials could eradicate some small town."

"Or big city, or farm land."

"Maybe it'll land in the ocean."

"And if it doesn't? We can't take that chance."

"But what do we do?"

"We need to keep it from falling."

"But our little jets—"

"We just need *more* of them."

He activated his distress beacon, calling to all other Port Authority AVs. "Mayday, mayday. In need of assistance. Mayday, please respond."

Seven of the twelve active AVs indicated they'd heard him. He explained their plight and their plan. No one responded.

"Come on, come on," Eva said, shaking Stedman's avatar as though it were his shirt collar she was manhandling and not a robot. "Closer that thing gets, the stronger gravity's hold, the more jets we'll need—the more *fuel* we'll need.

"Guys, I know you're out there! There's no telling where this thing might land. It could be on your house, or your parent's house—*come on!*"

In the distance, he saw three little dots approaching from different angles.

"On our way," one confirmed.

And still the cycler dropped. It was running away from them, its tumbling visage wide and ominous. Though everything in space appeared to move in slow motion, this threat was quick approaching. It streaked past them. If the others didn't hurry ...

"We can't wait for them," Eva said. "We have to catch it now or it'll be too late. We won't be enough to stabilize it, but we can't wait."

She was right. They ceased with their clinging and shot in the ship's direction.

Now it didn't just swell in Stedman's vision, it ballooned. They chased it with all their mechanical might, pushing their safety controls near breaking. He sprinted at it with claws outstretched, ready to hit it with all the force he could muster, praying he didn't crack his avatar's chassis upon impact.

Hitting the hull was like hitting a brick wall with a sledge-hammer—there was some give, but not nearly enough to stop the wall being a wall. Stedman could sense a heavy ripple sway through the cycler upon contact, but it still fell, pulling their little AVs toward the planet.

With thrusters at full bore, he searched again for their coworkers. They were shiny black marbles now, getting closer, but still so far away.

"We can't keep it from coming down eventually," Eva said, "But maybe we can keep it up long enough for a real rescue team. If we can shoot it out far enough, maybe we won't just save people on the ground."

"Maybe we can save the cycler itself," he said proudly.

"Exactly! Okay, we're going to have to space ourselves evenly around the ship," Eva said, making sure her channel was open to the help on the way.

Stedman shuttered his cameras and listened to her voice. The erratic dive was enough to make his inner ear on Earth revolt. "We've only got so much fuel between the five of us. We probably don't have enough to stop its spinning and get it back up into a steady orbit, so we'll have to settle for a stable spin and slow decay.

"As it tumbles, we're going to take turns being planet-side and out-orbit side. When we're on the bottom—planet-side—we thrust. As soon as we see the edge of the thin blue line, we stop thrusting, got it?"

Stedman gave the affirmative and crawled away, using his claws to grasp various footholds on the uneven surface, and creating some where there were none by digging into the edge of panels. He was sure NASA would forgive him.

As soon as they gauged themselves to be directly opposite one another mass-wise, he and Eva put the theory into practice. They would need to perfectly choreograph their thrusts, be totally in sync with their actions. Everything tumbled, twirled —it was all a blur. There was blue planet—expending fuel— black space—momentary rest—blue planet—expending fuel —black space—momentary rest. Over and over and over.

But Stedman barely felt like they were having any effect on the cycler's fall.

Eva performed the calculations and marked the positions for the new arrivals before sending them to everyone. She gave them all call signs to ensure efficient communications. They were Rescue One through Five.

"Come on, guys," Stedman yelled at his coworkers in encouragement. "You can make it!"

The other AVs finally arrived, slamming into the cycler one by one.

"Okay, everybody, here we go! Rescue Two—" she said to Stedman—"Now! Rescue Three, now!"

As the minutes passed and they kept up with the steps to their strange dance, the ship slowly tilted, its nose lifting up, up, until they were doing a barrel roll across the planet.

"Almost there," Eva said. "Almost!"

A little red light began blinking at the side of Stedman's inner eye. "Eva—I mean, Rescue One?"

"What is it, Two?"

"My fuel gauge is ... it's not looking good."

"No problem, Stedman. When you die off we'll rearrange ourselves."

"And I'll have to let go."

"What? No!"

"Yes," he said firmly. "I'll just be a burden—dead mass. The four of you will have an easier time saving the cycler if I'm not attached."

"Then let go now and save some fuel to reorient yourself."

"You know that's not a good idea."

"Stedman," Eva said quietly after a silent moment, addressing him on a different channel. "If you let go without any fuel, you'll either fall toward the planet and burn up, or you'll be flung out into dead space without hope of retrieval."

He knew what she was getting at. Sure, he'd physically be fine. But there were only so many AVs. If he lost his avatar, the job would go *poof*. They were already disobeying orders by intercepting the cycler. If one of them also lost their multi-billion-dollar equipment in the process ...

She was telling him this was goodbye if he chose to do this. Likely the last time he'd ever be in space.

The dream had been a good one. It was time to wake up.

"I have to do it," he said firmly. "No better way to fall than to fall *up*."

"Okay. If ... if you're sure."

Minutes passed, and the cycler rose. They were doing it—pushing it up, up, up!

His thrusters sputtered. All he had left to do was time his release in his favor.

The spinning was gentle now—he could keep his apertures open. He could watch as he sailed away.

Three, two, one ...

He disengaged.

Steady. Steady.

He rolled away, into a starry sea. It felt calm, peaceful. Though he had no way to turn his avatar's body, he could still pick which way his cameras focused. Which constellation he wanted to stare at. But instead of the stars, he found himself pulled by the heart strings toward the blue marble. It was growing more distant, more ball-like. It almost didn't seem real.

The cycler and the struggling avatars disappeared over the horizon, and he waved farewell with his claws.

Earth was so beautiful. Looked calm and pure from here.

Maybe he could just stay like this until the AV had to power down. Maybe he—

He felt a real-world jolt. Doc was trying to wake him.

No such luck, then.

"Goodbye, little friend," he said to the avatar. "I'm sorry I only got to pilot you for a short while."

And then his distant view of the planet was gone.

He gasped as he was violently thrust back into his true body.

He looked up at the ceiling and tried to breathe steadily, but his heart would not slow and his lungs would not cooperate. He'd just destroyed a multi-billion-dollar piece of space equipment. One man, billions of dollars, down the tube.

It was the red sign all over again. The red sign he couldn't read telling him he'd never go into space. They don't let you fly planes if you can't read the dials, and they don't let you pilot AVs if you fling them into the abyss.

It had to be done, he told himself as Doc removed the IV and gave him water. *You did the right thing.*

He lay there for a long time, not wanting to look at Eva, not knowing what he'd see in her expression.

Fifteen minutes passed. And then, suddenly, there was a gasp in the other chair.

"Stedman?" she shouted immediately.

"I'm here!" he said, holding up his hand weakly, unable to drag himself from the chair just yet—he didn't know when, if ever, he'd be in one again.

Then Eva's face was over his, her usually thin mouth split wide in a smile. "We did it!" she said triumphantly. "We did it! We all let go in the end, just like you, but Doc put me through to NASA before my tumble. They think they can salvage the cycler, and the nuclear reactor is intact!"

She clasped his hand, clutching it tightly it in comradery.

"They'll never let us back out there," he said softly.

Her smile faltered, then became sly. "The Port Authority? You kidding? Now that we're officially heroes they're gonna throw so many pay raises at us you won't know what to do with yourself. But let's say they *do* ground us ... Just between you and me, I bet NASA will happily give us a ride up."

Maybe she was right. Maybe he could dream again—once in a while. "I have one addendum," he said, sitting up. "To your previous assessment of our jobs."

"What?"

"Not only is cleaning up space garbage *not* glamorous—" he put a hand over his rabbit-racing heart—"It's *hell* on the nervous system."

She punched him playfully, and gave him a hug. "Not a bad day on the job," she said. "Not bad at all."

OLD DOGS, NEW TRICKS

BY BRAD R. TORGERSEN

OLD DOGS, NEW TRICKS

BY BRAD R. TORGERSEN

A lice Zankanski savored the feeling of water splashing against her legs as she sprinted along the beach. It was a cloudy, brisk day across Washington State's Olympic coastline, but the weather didn't dampen Alice's enthusiasm. After being confined to her wheelchair for the better part of a decade, she relished the sensation of wet sand beneath her feet, and the bite of the Pacific Northwest wind as it pushed huge combers onto the shore.

Ordinarily, such exertion might have proven fatal. But as Alice continued to race along the water's edge, she realized there was no chance of having a heart attack now. To say nothing of getting winded.

Pumping a fist in the air, Alice picked up her pace. There was a group of other runners not too far ahead. If she pushed herself, she could catch up to them. Maybe even get ahead? Last time Alice had managed such a feat, she'd been forty years younger and easily seventy pounds lighter.

Her legs churned through the foamy surf with the power of a small steam engine. Once or twice, a tall wave threatened to snatch her out to sea, but Alice kept her balance, and charged onward—laughing at the electric sensation of ice-cold water on her skin.

Wish you could see me now, David! Alice shouted in her mind. Her late husband had been her running partner for most of her adult life, right up until the cancer got him. If only he could have been at her side once more, clapping his hands and dashing right along with her.

The group of runners grew closer and closer.

Suddenly, Alice was in the thick of the pack. She glanced this way and that, noting the chrome limbs and torsos, with bright racing patterns painted across skulls, shoulders, and hips. They all ran together for a few seconds, their mouthless faces pushed forward against the freezing salt air blowing off the tops of the swells that rose and fell much further to the west.

Then—*blink!*

Alice was back in the medical room. She reflexively jerked in her seat, giving off a small yelp of alarm.

"Uh oh," said a young man's voice to Alice's left. "Looks like we had an uplink auto-interrupt. That's the third time it's happened this week."

"Something about the combination of saltwater and multiple units in close proximity," muttered the young woman on Alice's right.

Alice groaned, and brought her hands up to her face—shaking unsteadily. Her fingers instead encountered the drawn-down optics of her visor.

"I was just starting to enjoy myself," Alice lamented, as the interface helmet was slowly lifted off her head.

"You okay, Missus Zee?" asked the young man who gently placed the helmet into its cradle beside Alice's high-backed, ergonomically-accentuated chair.

"Disoriented is all," she said. "For a split second, I could almost believe it was really me. That I was truly, actually out there. Goodness, what a rush."

"Sorry, Missus Zee," said the young woman, who was tapping her fingertips on a full-color computer pad projecting from a pylon sticking out from the chair's side. "Now that the company's been deploying these systems in large numbers across the country, we're running into certain problems—the usual stuff that has to be ironed out over time."

"Shoulda not let myself get caught up in the moment," Alice said, gently rubbing her eyes with her liver-spotted fists. "All I wanted was a nice, gentle trot by the water. For the first time in forever. Just to be *out* there again. Nobody told me it would be such a seamless experience. I could literally feel *everything*. Hear and touch! Even though the unit doesn't have a nose, nor a tongue, I could practically taste and smell the surf, too."

"We're glad you enjoyed the ride," said the young man, smiling. He put a hand onto Alice's shoulder, and squeezed firmly. "Once we get the units on that beach back to the shop, we should be able to sort the issue, and deploy them again. Feel like taking another morning jog tomorrow?"

"You'd have to beat me off with a stick!" Alice said, raising both arms, so that she could be helped up onto her feet, slowly rotated one hundred and eighty degrees, then deposited into her waiting wheelchair. "You kids should know that I was more than a little nervous when my daughter said she was moving me from the old facility to this new experimental rehab place. I kept telling her, when nerves get shot the way *mine* are shot, especially at this age, there's no help for it. But if I can take a run like that each day, if even for a few minutes ... I'll empty every penny out of my retirement account for the opportunity."

"Hopefully *that* isn't going to be necessary," the young woman said, checking to be sure that Alice's chair battery was still fully charged. "This technology is adapted from something the Air

Force and the Navy first put to use in orbit a few years ago. The engineering consortium that won the Avatar XPRIZE had most of its research funding provided by the Department of Defense. Now we're adapting the same system for civilian use—at a dramatically reduced cost. Consider it your tax dollars at work."

Alice merely grunted, and stared longingly at the ergonomic chair.

"When enough people my age get a taste of this, even the ones who can still walk will be demanding a piece of the action."

"That's what we're hoping for," the young man said, opening the door, so that Alice could roll her way out into the hallway. "The more facilities contracted with us to install and run this system, the less expensive each installation will be. Thus a net savings to you, the user. So don't be shy about telling people you liked your first try."

"Word of mouth advertising, eh?" Alice said, cocking her head to one side.

"See you tomorrow," the young woman said, nodding and smiling.

Alice weakly raised one hand to wave goodbye, then motored over the threshold—and back into the interior of the Harbor Lights Assisted Living complex. Other residents, all in various stages of decrepitude, scooted or shuffled their way between the rows of decorative potted plants and the artificial stream that ran down the middle of the concourse. Numbered doorways went up and down both sides of the concourse. Each with a first initial and a last name written across the top in elegant lettering. Alice took a moment to peer at the trout which lazily swam against the current of the stream, then she gently cruised along the stream's edge, taking her time getting back to her apartment. It wasn't yet ten o'clock, and they wouldn't be serving lunch for at least another ninety minutes.

With her adventure on the beach cut short, Alice had time to kill.

There was a silver-haired gentleman—also in a wheelchair —who zoomed out from behind a particularly large collection of ferns. His eyes went wide and he stopped, but not before Alice braked a bit harder than normal.

"Your pardon, madam," the man said, fidgeting with the little control mechanism on the arm of his chair. "Even after six months in this thing, I'm afraid I am not very good at driving."

"Took me the better part of a year to get comfortable with mine," Alice said. "Though, that was when I was staying at a different place."

"Have you been here long?" the man asked.

"Two weeks," Alice said.

"Three days for me," the man said, then reached a frail hand out toward Alice. "I'm William Cooper. You can call me Billy, please."

"Alice Zankanski," Alice said. "Though the staff around here have taken to calling me Mrs. Zee, for short."

The two shook hands slowly, and with much deliberation.

"Are you by yourself?" Alice asked.

"Unfortunately," Billy said, frowning. "My wife Julie passed about five years ago. I'd planned on staying put, until my son talked me into moving here. He said it was going to be less expensive if we used my veteran's voucher to try this new exper-imental program, versus hiring somebody to come to my house full time."

"I'm a vet too!" Alice said, her eyes brightening. "Army National Guard. Wound up in the desert for the first Gulf War."

"Marine Corps," Billy said in reply. "Full-timer. Saw the Gulf for the first round in 1991, then went back in 2004 for the second round."

"I regretted not being part of that," Alice said. "But by then I had a husband and kids, and figured I'd already done my bit for the country."

"You didn't miss much," Billy said, smiling. "Especially Fallujah."

"That's what my nephew told me," Alice said. "He was in Fallujah, too. Came back with some bad stories. He wouldn't even talk to my sister about it. But he *would* talk to me."

Billy merely nodded his head, then there was a stretch of awkward silence.

"Well ... at least we're getting *something* out of it, in 2036, eh?" Alice said, smiling and motioning with a shaky arm— taking in the whole of the concourse. "It's not home. But it'll do. And that new system they've got set up for us—"

"Have you tried it yet?" Billy asked, suddenly leaning forward—his eyes sharp with interest.

"Just this morning. After reading and hearing about it before moving in, I was a bit skeptical. You know how these places are. They love to make promises. But now that I've given it a go ... wow. That's all I can say."

"I'm on the list for tomorrow morning," Billy said.

"If it's anything like what I got to do a few minutes ago," Alice said, "you won't be disappointed."

"How does it work?" Billy asked. "Any poking and prodding?"

"Nope," Alice said. "You sit in this really plush, overworked kind of thing, a bit like a dentist's chair, but with more padding —and sensors that monitor your vitals—then they put a kind of helmet on your head. And after a few minutes in the dark, while the helmet reads and then adjusts to your nervous system, you suddenly find yourself staring out of a new pair of eyes. Almost as if you've got the gaze of an eagle! I could see for miles. Superb clarity."

"My eyes were never great, even when I was younger," Billy said, tapping a thumb on his spectacles.

"That's just for starters," Alice said. "My trip this morning was out to the coast. A nice, long run by the ocean. I could feel and hear everything. Run at least as fast as I used to, when I was still doing half marathons every year. And the best part was not losing my breath."

The corners of Billy's mouth had curled up in a wistful smile.

"What are you going to do?" Alice asked.

"The menu said there was climbing in the Rocky Mountains. I did that a lot, after I left the Corps. Julie thought it was too dangerous, though, once I got past age fifty-five. So I quit. But there's not been a day that's passed without me wishing I could be hanging off the edge of some rock somewhere."

"Well, if it's anything like what I've experienced," Alice said, reaching out to pat Billy's arm, "you won't be disappointed."

"Glad to hear it."

Then, a second stretch of awkward silence.

"Umm, I'm all the way down at the end," Billy finally said, clearing his throat. "You can find me in number 182."

"I'm further to the middle, in 150."

"Catch you for a meal, perhaps?"

"I'll look for you," Alice said.

"And I'll try to be *looked* for," Billy replied.

The two laughed—a good, hearty sound. Then the gentle whirring of their wheelchairs faded into the distance, as Billy and Alice parted company.

The dining hall was bubbling with conversation, as the several hundred strong mass of residents converged for their morning meal.

"You up for that climbing expedition you talked about yesterday?" Alice asked between bites.

"Woke up ready to go," Billy said, then sipped at a small glass of fruit juice. "Last time I got up into the mountains was in Colorado. I had chalk on me up to my elbows, and came down with a knee skinned almost to the bone. But I loved it. And that's when Julie talked me into being sensible."

"Did she always talk you into being sensible?"

"Sometimes," Billy admitted.

"I was never much of a fear junkie," Alice said. "Especially after I started having babies.

"Climbing is a calculated risk," Billy said. "It's all a matter of concentration. Keeping your mind focused on where you're putting your fingertips and your toes. The next ledge. The next lip of stone, just kind of presenting itself—each and every move. I never climbed competitively, though I know a few guys who did. For me, it was mostly about maintaining my edge. Once I was out of uniform."

"And when you couldn't climb anymore?" Alice asked. "What then?"

"Then ... well, I never let on with Julie much, but she could tell I wasn't thrilled about the situation. I think she tried to make it up to me in certain ways."

"Like how?"

"Like ... ummm, well, you know."

Alice stared at Billy for a second, while his cheeks turned pink.

Then she burst out laughing. Several heads in their immediate vicinity turned to look with annoyance. Then the residents went back to their food.

"I'm sure you didn't complain about *that*," Alice said, sarcastically.

"What sane husband would?" Billy said, chuckling.

"David and I just ran a lot," Alice said, teasing at her cereal with a spoon. "Even when the arthritis started to make things difficult, we kept after it. We figured it was either that, or time and inertia would catch us, and then ... well, I was the kind of stubborn person who swore she'd never wind up in a place like this. So naturally, I did. God has an evil sense of humor."

They ate quietly for several minutes, the mood having gotten sober.

"What time is your appointment?" Alice asked.

"Ten hundred, on the dot," Billy replied.

"Mine too," Alice said. "There are ten stations. Partitioned from each other. Rumor has it, there will be many more put in, but not before these ten have made a six-month trial run. You get sixty minutes per day."

"That's what they told me when I moved in," Billy said. "The two other residents I talked to—after you—liked it, too. One of them said he went kayaking, and the other said she went skiing. Better than having been there, each of them said. I am eager to find out for myself."

"If you decide you want a run on the beach, it's worth every second," Alice invited.

"Or maybe you can take a walk on the wild side, and come climbing with me?" Billy said, arching an eyebrow at her.

"I wouldn't know the first thing about doing it," Alice said. "I can't imagine the company who owns and runs those units would take kindly to seeing one of them smashed at the bottom of a cliff."

"Betcha they have safeties of some sort, to keep that from happening," Billy opined. "Waddya say?"

"Sounds like you're challenging me," Alice playfully accused.

"Maybe I am," Billy said, his eyebrow still arched.

"Fine," Alice said, slapping her hands down on either side of the table. "You're on. And if it turns out there are no safeties, the damage goes on *your* tab."

Billy laughed through a mouthful of sliced strawberries, then wiped at his chin with a napkin.

"Deal," he said.

As before, Alice allowed herself to breathe deeply and slowly. The imposed darkness of the helmet was mildly claustrophobic, until she could feel a pleasant sensation spread out from her spine and into her limbs. She began to hear things too. The gentle swishing of the breeze through the pine trees. The chirping of birds echoing off the rock face. People moving around, muttering checklists under their breath.

Then—

Blink.

The morning sky was bright, with a blue sky that was deep and breathtaking. Alice allowed herself to slowly pan her gaze around, noticing the half dozen other units all arrayed at the bottom of the stone bluff which they were due to assault. Company people were completing their inspections on each of the units, occasionally tugging on a limb or testing its range of motion. A woman wearing a beige campaign hat and khaki hiking shorts, with high-topped hiking boots, stood in front of them.

"Good morning everybody," she said. "I'm lead technician Lucinda Alvarez, and I'll be supervising you for this session. I know you're from different facilities scattered across the country, and have different levels of preexisting experience, but I believe you'll find this obstacle worth your time. Each of your units have been specifically modified for rock climbing, which will aid the beginners, and pleasantly surprise the rest. You will climb without shoes, chalk, or rope, and if any of you should lose his or her grip and experience a fall, the unit will immediately disengage you from the experience while deploying a landing-assist package which will prevent damage."

"Told ya," said a man's voice in Alice's ears. It was Billy.

"Shhh," Alice reflexively said—she'd never liked it when anybody interrupted a class of instruction.

"If you experience any technical malfunctions during the climb, just call for me, and either myself or one of my staff can assist. The weather is projected to remain dry during your ascent, and once you reach the top, there will be other technicians there to handle your units. So please take your time, enjoy the experience, and have a pleasant rest of your day."

Alice looked down at her body. Like with the units on the beach, this one was chrome-metal colored, with bright sport striping. The rubberized pads on the fingers appeared to be scuffed, but serviceable, while the pine needles beneath her toes actually seemed to tickle her feet.

She looked up to the very top of the bluff and could make out several figures peering down over the edge.

"Piece of cake," Billy's voice said.

"I don't even know which one you are," Alice remarked.

"I'm the guy with blue on him. You?"

"Green for me."

"Right. See, the others have already gotten started. Don't pay attention to them. Just pay close attention to me, and how I choose to use my hands and my feet. I'll go nice and slow. You mimic me, and you won't have any problem getting to the top."

"And if I panic and drop?"

"Then I will have a good time poking fun at you during lunch," Billy said.

"Well, I certainly can't let *that* happen," Alice said. "Lead the way, Marine."

While the other four units were already advancing up the rock face, Billy's unit walked over to stand in front of Alice's unit. He turned and began to run his hands along the rock, just grazing it with the tips of his mechanical fingers.

"Wow," he said. "You weren't kidding. It's amazing how I can feel even the slightest roughness. It's almost ... it's almost better than I remember it being. That lady said they modified these machines specifically for this task? She told no lies. Okay, I've been waiting for this since ... well, I'll try to contain my enthusiasm. Just be sure to talk to me as we go, so I don't look down and you're suddenly a hundred feet below me."

"Got it," Alice said.

Billy's unit—rather, he in the guise of his unit—reached over his head with both hands, and curled the tips of his fingers across a fairly visible lip. He pulled himself up to his elbows, then his toes engaged the stone surface, and within a few seconds he had spidered his way up to a small ledge perhaps a dozen feet in the air.

Alice reached for the same lip of rock, and tested her grip. The fingers of her unit were strong and sure, and she felt the fingertips gripping securely. Pulling herself up was no harder than running at full speed the morning prior—even though Alice's real body would never have been able to lift herself up the same distance in the same manner, no matter how hard she tried.

Alice hung there, her eyes staring directly into the rock, while her legs dangled beneath her.

"Push your toes into the stone," Billy said. "But *just* enough. You only want to get some leverage, not force so hard you lose the purchase you've gained with your fingers."

Alice's feet began to scramble on the rock, and then suddenly she dropped off, and collapsed to her knees in the bed of pine needles along the face of the bluff.

"Good try," Billy said. "But you don't have to be frantic about it. Just gently apply pressure along both sets of toes, until you can sense that you're not going to slip, and advance your way up. As you do, look for the next lip of rock. I found three of them within easy reach. You will, too."

Alice tried twice more, and then finally got the hang of what Billy had been describing. Even with overly sensitive fingers and toes, Alice was too instinctively nervous, and had to really concentrate on what she was doing—not the ground below—in order to make it up to Billy's ledge.

"See, that wasn't so bad, was it?" Billy said, clearly enjoying himself. His chrome-plated head was swiveling this way and that, surveying the scenery from their comparatively low perch.

"Damn, I've missed this," he said, with evident satisfaction in his voice.

"That took ten minutes," Alice said, exasperated. "We'll never get to the top at this rate. Maybe it was a bad idea for me to come along with you today."

"Nonsense," Billy said, standing up, and peering above himself—scanning for the next available fingerhold. "Let's just focus on your control and your form. Remember, everything is in the motion of your body. Learn to search for your safe purchases with not only your eyes, but your hands and toes as well. Climbing in this unit feels like climbing naked. There's literally no barrier between you and the rock. The mountain is not your enemy, it's your friend. The mountain will always be there for you, when you need it. Trust the mountain."

"Next thing I know, you'll be telling me to use the Force," Alice quipped.

"Yeah, well, as corny as it sounds, kinda," Billy replied. "If you do this enough, that's almost how it feels. You lose all notion of the space beneath you. It's just your mind, and your bones, and your muscles, and your blood, and the stone. Up, up, up. Hand over foot, over hand over foot. Okay, ready to go some more?"

"Yeah, go," Alice muttered, and then Billy was moving up the wall again. As he moved, Alice could see him testing different parts of the rock. Sometimes his fingers would explore two or three spots, before they'd curl down tight, and he'd be pulling himself up. Same with toeholds, where his mechanical digits would gently feel their way along the rock, until they found just enough purchase to allow him to engage his legs.

Every time Billy found a new ledge, he waited until Alice had made her way up to him. Generally, he waited several minutes at each stop, and had to keep himself from chuckling as Alice began cursing her clumsiness.

"You're doing great," Billy said. "Really, we've gone half a football field and you're acing it."

"Half a football field is fifty yards," Alice said. "And fifty yards is … *sixteen stories*?"

Alice suddenly froze where she was, just below Billy's latest ledge, and looked down.

The distance beneath her yawned like a chasm.

"Oh no, oh no, oh no," Alice began to repeat softly to herself, as the vertigo kicked in. She'd never been fond of window views out of tall buildings, but had assumed the detached nature of the units would somehow make this experience remote enough—for her hindbrain distrust of severe heights to not be a factor.

Alice seized on the edge of panic.

"Crap," Billy exclaimed, deadpan. "I should not have told you how far we'd come."

"Ch'yeah!" Alice practically shouted. "What happened to all that 'be one with the mountain' junk you were telling me?"

"Sorry."

"Sorry!" Alice exclaimed. "You're sorry? I'm probably taking a dump in my chair back at Harbor Lights!"

"Just pull yourself up a bit more, and I can help you," Billy suggested.

"No way!" Alice said, continuing to stare down at the tops of the trees far below.

Billy cleared his throat.

"Umm, Technician Alvarez?" he said, testing.

"This is Alvarez," said the woman's voice. "How may I be of assistance?"

"My name is William Cooper—Alice Zankanski and I are both here, out of Harbor Lights, from over in the Puget Sound area—and we've run into a bit of a problem. See, this is Alice's first time, and she was doing great! Except, she's now experiencing a case of vertigo, and I am afraid it might be best if we just cut the trip short. Can we do that?"

"It would be best if you both got to the top, or climbed down. Deliberately deploying a landing-assist package will cost your facility extra, which will in turn cost you extra as well. Is Alice's unit malfunctioning?"

"No," Alice and Billy both said in unison.

"Very well then," the technician said. "I will signal your facility that we're going to cut the link early. Just don't say I didn't warn you about the charges."

"Damn the charges, get me the hell out of here!" Alice screamed.

She waited—daring not to breath—for reality to reassert itself.

Beat. Beat. Beat.

"It's not happening," Alice said, her voice almost shaking.

"No, it's not," the technician said, sounding worried. "Let's try again. Hold on."

Beat. Beat. Beat.

"Still not working," Alice breathed, feeling the claws of genuine, life-in-the-balance terror beginning to close around her heart.

"Something's happened with the uplink," Alvarez said. "They can't seem to sever it. Live feedback is continuous."

Alice thunked her head against the rock wall, suddenly realizing that there would be no easy way out of her predicament.

"C'mon," Billy said, suddenly sounding angry. "You mean to

tell me this outfit can't find the 'off' button? Even my table saw back home has one of those! It's big, and red, and you can't miss it even when you're screaming because you took off the tip of your finger."

Alice got the distinct impression Billy was speaking from experience.

"It's not as simple as that," Alvarez said. "There could be adverse neurological reactions if your companion's connection isn't broken in the proper way."

"When I was running on the beach yesterday," Alice said feebly, "my connection was broken, and it didn't hurt me at all."

"The system's software is designed to cope with signal interrupt, bringing you back softly. Right now, the issue is not signal interrupt, but a feedback loop that's keeping the uplink open *despite* our people executing a command override. We'd have to get to your unit proper, to try to manually switch the unit off."

"Can I do it from here?" Billy asked.

"Not without the right tools, no," Alvarez said.

Now it was Billy's turn to curse. Then he was kneeling on his ledge and leaning out just enough to put one of his mechanical hands over the top of Alice's mechanical hand.

"Hey," he said.

"This isn't happening," Alice sniffed. "I don't want to die. Not like this."

"Nobody's gonna die this morning. And nobody's gonna get shafted with a giant bill, either. Here's what we're gonna do. We're gonna climb all the way to the top of this bluff. And then these people are going to use their tools to switch your unit off, and then you and I are both going to go find a couple of bottles of wine, and get drunk for the rest of the day. Do you hear me?"

"I can't move!" Alice said, feeling as if she were gritting her teeth in her skull.

"Yes, you can," Billy said, calmly. "You were moving great, all the way up here. You just need to get your focus back, start climbing again, and we'll get to the end of this thing before you know it. Okay? Just lift up your head, focus on me—on this metal suit I'm wearing—and get going. Got it? *Got it?*"

Part of Alice—the National Guard part—recognized the sound in the old Marine's voice.

Tapping her head against the rock three times, Alice closed out everything in the world except her desire to escape her predicament, then looked up at Billy's unit—his somewhat comical face staring down at her, with camera eyes—and began to push herself up with her legs. Then she grasped the ledge with her hands, and pulled herself up to where Billy had been.

He was already moving away from her, his movements sure and steady.

"Focus on me, all the way," he said. "Up, up, up!"

Slowly, and with much second guessing, Alice followed suit. Hand over foot, over hand over foot.

It took eighty-minutes before she finally pulled herself over the top of the bluff, and rolled onto her back, gazing up into the astounding blue sky above.

Without needing to be asked, several of the technicians scrambled to begin removing a plate on the side of Alice's head. Billy's unit—along with several others—leaned over Alice as she felt tools being inserted into her brain.

"There," said Alvarez's voice.

Blink.

Alice and Billy did go on a significant bender that day. Two old fools, slurring and talking loudly, while unsteadily steering their motorized chairs—each of them with a near-empty wine bottle perched in the metal basket in front of the handlebars. They were the source of much gossip for weeks, while the entire Harbor Lights virtual experience system was brought down for an exhaustive forensic technical check.

Meanwhile, both Billy and Alice were each comped for their day on the mountain—and credited with one hundred free trips each, by a supremely apologetic corporate officer who came to Harbor Lights in person.

"Nothing is ever bug-proof," Billy said one afternoon, while he and Alice both contemplated the virtual experience system being returned to working order. Not only had news of their fiasco not dissuaded interest, the Harbor Lights sign up list had been blocked out for weeks in advance.

Danger? Excitement? Adventure? Every resident in the place had looked at themselves in the mirror, and said, "Yes, please!"

"Bug, shmug," Alice said. "I'm not hanging off of any cliffs with you again any time soon."

"I didn't say we had to do that specifically," Billy said. "I thought maybe we could try the Catamaran trip that they're running off the coast of Mexico. There's hardly much danger in that, right? Especially since they said they fixed the problem this time. And gave us a ton of freebies for our trouble, too."

"I don't know," Alice said. "Seems to me like I've gotten into nothing but hot water since I met you."

Billy cracked a fiendish grin—the smile lines at the corners of his eyes crinkling up with mischief.

"You say that like that's a bad thing," he remarked.

Alice looked down at her lap—at the legs which had grown useless and weary with age—and remembered how much sheer joy she'd experienced pelting along like a cheetah, with seawater crashing at her knees.

"Fine," she ultimately said. "Catamaran it is."

"Great!" Billy said. "And then maybe—"

"But," Alice said, holding up a commanding finger, *"just*

Catamaran. For now. Until I feel like I'm ready for something else. You get any more bright ideas? You do them on your own."

"Which wouldn't be any fun," Billy said, his smile falling.

"That's the deal. You got it? *Got it?*"

There was a pause, and then Billy nodded his head in agreement.

"Roger," he said. "I'm with you."

"Good. Now, let's see when the next dual slot is open."

LITTLE AND SMALL

BY TODD J. MCCAFFREY

LITTLE AND SMALL

BY TODD J. MCCAFFREY

O nce I was big, but now I am small. I am tiny. The world is a scary place around me. Dark, hot, smoky.

I have a mission. Around me, there are sounds but I ignore most of them. I am only looking for one.

There is heat and sights, too, but I am focused, intent. I listen, I analyze.

There. *Thump-thump.* I triangulate. Identified. Heartbeat: 90%. Heart rate: 119 beats per minute—high stress range. Volume analysis: the target is five meters away, young, probably a child. I listen. I can hear no breathing.

I move forward, toward the sound.

It is a little girl. Her breathing is ragged and thready. She is maybe four years old. Near her is a larger mass, thermal readings show it to be below 37 degrees Celsius. Her mother: dead.

There is no one to talk to and no way to talk. I am not built to talk. I am built to find. I have found.

I pause. The little girl has heard my movements.

"*Mutti? Mutti wo bist du?*" I don't know this language. I am very limited. I look, I find. The girl starts crying. She must not cry, she'll breathe in too many toxins and die.

I am torn. She needs comforting, needs a sign. But I am small.

I am small. I move closer; not too close. I turn on my visible light.

"*Mutti? Wo bist du?*"

I waggle my light, making a little circle with it. The girl can't see me but she can see my light.

I keep my light on, monitoring my battery power and start back toward the entrance. I don't have enough power to transmit the coordinates, I need to deliver them in person.

Another tremor shakes the area. The little girl cries in pain. I pause, measuring. Her heart rate is higher but she appears alive. I must move quickly.

I increase my power. As I near the entrance, I see another rescuer like myself. Small. I train a beam on it, then direct the beam the way I came. The other beams back at me, message received.

I start toward the entrance but the other blocks me. I don't know why. I try to move around it but it blocks me again. Then I understand. I blink twice at it and turn back the way I came.

I shall go to the girl. I will be with her when help comes, even if my power runs out.

On the way down, I try to imagine the light shapes I can make to distract the girl until she is rescued.

I reach her again, shine my light. I have very little power. I will put it all into my light. I make tracks with my light, rising from the ground to the sky. Hopefully, she will understand.

———————

A harsh light disturbs me and there are sounds, loud. I blink and suddenly I am big again. My VR helmet is removed along with my headphones. A face is smiling into mine.

"It's okay, we got her."

It takes me a moment to recover and realize that I never left my base, that I was operating a remote on an earthquake site halfway around the world. The little remote was smaller than a mouse and had only one mission: find the living.

We had succeeded: the girl was found, I was home, the remote was dead, probably buried in the rubble that fell when they freed her. I gave a silent nod of thanks to my lost fellow traveler.

"We've got another run coming up in thirty," my boss told me. She gave me a measuring look. "You up for it?"

"Yes, ma'am."

IN THE HEART OF THE ACTION

JODY LYNN NYE

IN THE HEART OF THE ACTION

BY JODY LYNN NYE

"How much longer?" Portia Manolo asked, as they slogged down the road. *You couldn't really call a narrow dirt track a road*, she mused. The sun beat down on their heads, making sweat run down the back of her neck and pool between her ample breasts. They didn't even have hats. Why didn't they have hats? It had to be over forty centigrade. They had left the lab in the middle of the night. The sunlight was blinding as well as baking.

"You can't be tired," Professor Kelly Noble said. The head of the lead medic turned toward her. The android projected an all-over image that looked like the real woman, complete down to blonde, shoulder-length hair tied in a ponytail. "The servos are doing all the work."

Portia stuck out her lip, knowing full well that the silicon mask into which her face was pressed mimicked the expression on the avatar's face.

"I'm bored! Why couldn't we have landed right in the village?"

Noble looked amused. "Several reasons. One, that would be rude. The elders expect us to approach on foot. It's their custom. Two, it gives them a chance to get used to the way we look. They're terrified enough with what's going on. Three— aren't you enjoying the walk? You said you wanted to see Africa. Uganda is beautiful. Have you ever seen such green? It's not enhanced by your receptors. This glory is all natural." She swept a hand around at the open plain. Huge leaves, bigger than her head, hung from the black-boled trees, glistening with water droplets. The rainy season had just ended, so Portia had been told, and the hot season had yet to begin. "This is your only break before we get really busy. It gives all of us a chance to get used to the quirks of these bodies on this terrain. We're a lot heavier than humans. You'll have to watch your footing."

Heavy was no problem. Portia was used to hauling around extra pounds, maybe a lot of them on her five foot two frame. She thought she looked sexy, even if her mama kept making cracks about her starting to need two chairs. The court psychologist said that's why she stole things, to find comfort outside her family. But she resented having to work. She glanced back at the train of self-driving trucks carrying all of the heavy equipment and the power plant. They had ridden in them from the depot, but Dr. Noble made them all get down and continue on foot since they crested the last low hill.

"Aren't they *used* to robot doctors by now?"

"That's not the point," Noble said. "We're still human beings. Manifesting as androids doesn't make us less human. In fact, it makes it more necessary to exhibit those courtesies we owe one another, so the people we are *serving*," Portia winced at the emphasis Noble put on the word, "also don't feel less human. If that means walking a few kilometers and risking boredom, then so be it. That is part of our mission. You volunteered for this program."

Yeah, or go to jail, Portia thought. She kicked a clod of mud out of her way, shouldered the pack on her back, and kept walking. She had always hoped to get out of her neighborhood, and boy, was she way out of her neighborhood!

"And four, these bodies are stored in Kampala. We've got pods of android medics in place all over the world. We airdrop them and supplies close to the hot zone but not in it, so we can decontaminate before we enter. No sense in bringing more accidental pathogens into an area already suffering an outbreak of one virus. You're going to be in the thick of it before you know it. We're grateful to have you with us, Portia." The corners of the android's mouth lifted in the scariest smile she had ever seen. The robot bodies were just close enough to looking human to give her the creeps.

Portia tried not to imagine how many strings her father had pulled to give her—her, a cop's daughter—an alternative rehabilitation plan instead of getting locked up for shoplifting. True, it had been her sixth offense. True, she'd stolen a bracelet worth over a thousand dollars. True, Papi's friends didn't want to put his little girl in the lockup with chronic offenders, even if she deserved it. True, also, that her social media friends had been jealous to *death* about what she was doing. The XPRIZE had been around for twenty years, since it was founded in 2016. Dr. Noble and her husband had won it two years ago for their work there in Uganda and neighboring countries, serving the rural villages with advanced medical care through not one, but two deadly epidemics. They were heroes. They had shaken hands with the president and a bunch of world leaders. With the prize money, the Nobles had set up pods of android bodies all over the world, to step in where and when they were needed. Since the first mission, they had gone into emergency medical situations in rural China, Indonesia, and even Antarctica, when a scientist had needed lifesaving surgery during the long winter. One robot doctor could be operated by any of a dozen specialists. And the mechanisms were so cool! Portia had seen them on television and on the Internet, and wished she could try it.

The reality was a lot more ordinary than she thought it would be.

Portia had imagined that they'd be like gods, floating around and making patients better. Instead, she had to go to classes to learn how to operate the android body. The training 'bots looked like white robots with plain faces and big blue lights for eyes, like something out of Japanese anime. Then came the fitting.

The technicians were pretty matter-of-fact. Only Dr. Noble and the parole officer acted as though Portia ought to be more impressed with all the trouble and expense. The techs, who in spite of differences in gender and race were a sea of white lab coats, lathered her face with a kind of lubricant, then pushed it into a tub of silicone gel. When she surfaced a few seconds later, gasping, they took the mold away. The next time she saw the inside-out casting of her face, it was mounted on a framework with a million wires sticking out of it. A baggy white suit whose sleeves ended in gray, ridged gloves and festooned with more wires hung on a frame. Portia had stepped into it like a pair of trousers and fastened it over her shoulders with Velcro straps. It hung on her like a sack. The technicians had dived in to pull other straps tightly around her body, arms and legs, even her neck.

The moment they finished, she no longer felt its weight. Curiously, she moved her limbs, turned her head from side to side.

"It ought to be like a second skin," the lead tech told her. "This is your interface with any android body, anywhere in the world. You can do everything but eat, drink, or go to the bathroom. You can even smell the flowers."

Portia had tried to act as though it was no big deal, but the moment she wriggled her face into the mask, she was transported somewhere else. She was just barely aware as the technicians guided her onto the movement plate so she could walk in any direction without leaving the circle of wires and cables.

The test location was in a garden in the middle of the DWB facility. Portia had glanced at it on her familiarization tour. She had thought the white androids wandering around among the vines and trellises were only for display purposes. Instead, they must have been people like her, getting used to their new bodies. The air was warm and moist, heavy with the scent of growing plants. She reached out to pick a huge pink rose. She actually felt the stem between her fingers, sensed the faint crack as it left the plant, and experienced an ... awareness of the little prickly hairs in between the thorns. But when she raised it to her face to sniff, the sight of the stark white enamel hand—her hand—made her drop it with a squawk.

She could stand or sit, lie down, even dance in the body, although the floor thudded every time she hopped. She could hear, smell, touch and see, but not taste. In this body, her mouth was only for expressing herself. To her amusement, she could stick her tongue out, and people facing her android body would see that. Pressors and cameras embedded in the silicone mask mirrored even microexpressions. However nervous it made them at first, people started to relate to her in the body within a few minutes.

Once she was used to the suit, the real training had begun. Even though she wasn't going anywhere, she had to handle items that weren't there. They started with big, hulking things, like sacks of clothes hangers, which they wanted her to move from one place to another then stack neatly. As her dexterity improved, they decreased the size and increased the complexity, until the day she could deliver an injection with a hypodermic spray gun on an infant's arm.

"Be careful of your body language," Dr. Noble had warned her. "If you feel hostile, it will come across. An ordinary human isn't perceived as a huge threat, but you won't look completely human. Remember that."

So, Portia had to rein in her natural impulse to tell the authority figure to stuff it when they reached the first little house and Dr. Noble called, "Smile, everyone!"

A woman sat cutting up a pumpkin on a small table in front of the open door. Portia had lived in a mixed neighborhood all her life. She knew lots of African-Americans, but never met a real African. The woman wore a colorful flowered skirt, a plain yellow t-shirt, and brilliant orange sneakers. The tightly-knotted headscarf hid all of her hair. Her deep, dark, small face looked old, in contrast to the four little children in striped t-shirts and khaki shorts too baggy for their thin legs playing around her feet. Portia could no more picture her in the middle of Brooklyn than she could picture her friend Sasha in this village, cutting up pumpkins. The woman looked so tired.

"Are you well, mother?" Dr. Noble called out.

"My daughter has the fever," the woman replied, tilting her head toward the open door. "My son is late. These are his little ones. I pray to Jesus that we are spared."

Dr. Bruce Costain, a big man with thick black hair, dropped the bundle from his back with a deafening clatter.

"That's it. We set up here," he said. "This is the edge of it." The rest of the team scattered, heading toward the transports. They were already unloading themselves with mechanical arms. Portia hesitated. Costain waved a hand at her. Even though it was made of plastic and metal, its gesture had the same impatient authority of the real thing. "Get going! You know what to do. These people need us."

The decontamination bubble went up first. The white tent inflated with the noisy aid of a gas canister. Some of the medics pulled the extension flaps out and attached the hoses and tanks of antiseptic fluid to the spray heads. Portia set about her preas-signed tasks of hammering in the tent pegs and inserting filters into the ventilation tubes of the decontamination bubble and the big hospital tent. A hose insert stuck halfway out. She hit it with the side of her hand, and it popped audibly as it went into place.

"Where's the kids' mother?" Portia asked aloud.

Dr. Noble came close and dropped her voice.

"If she didn't mention the mother, she died first. The Kampeche virus moves like lightning. These children have probably been infected. We need to analyze samples, but first, we have to take care of the patients and try to save them." She stepped inside the booth. Hissing and a smell like daisies issued from the vents. When she emerged, Portia rushed inside.

The jets hit her from every direction. As she had been instructed, she lifted each foot to get the bottoms saturated. The overpowering odor of flowers made her eyes water, but she turned her face to the ceiling and got the full spray. When she came out, she heard a little boy crying.

"Mama!"

One of the children was leaning on the knee of the old-looking woman. From the dancing, romping imp that he had been when the medical team first came close, he suddenly looked like an old man, too weak to stand on his own. Dr. Noble dropped what she was doing, and went to scoop up the little one. Her hand brushed his forehead. Superimposed on Portia's eyeline, a red number appeared: 104°.

"He's burning up," Dr. Noble said. Because of the communication setup between the androids, her undertone was audible to the entire group.

"Hurry up," Costain said to the rest of the medics. "We have no time left."

Portia started hammering spikes as fast as she could. Every blow with her electronic muscles smashed the pegs into the hard, dry earth. Dust rose around her.

"Hey, take it easy," Devon Chun said, coming over and taking the mallet out of her hand. "Go help Kelly."

Portia stood up and raced over. The child had fallen limp in Dr. Noble's arms, and another, a little girl with her hair in six little braids tied with pink beads, started to waver. Portia knelt beside her.

"Hey, kid," she said. "Hold on, okay?"

The girl's eyes were too shiny. Portia wrapped her in her arms.

"Careful!" Dr. Noble said.

Portia felt like snapping at her, but she knew what she meant. She didn't know her own strength. She wanted to cure this kid, not kill her by squeezing her to death. Carefully, she made the arm loosen. The little girl's skin was hot, much hotter than the tropical air, and she smelled wrong, like someone had vomited on her.

"Bring them over here," Dr. Costain said. Portia looked up. He beckoned, gesturing to a low camp bed, a sheet of canvas held taut on the lightest of metal frames. Much stronger than they looked, like the androids themselves. The children looked so small, lying together on one cot. Costain moved in. A robotic IV followed him and lowered itself so he could attach drips to the children's tiny, thin arms.

Word spread faster than the wind that the medics had arrived. Before all the tents and beds were ready, a crowd had scrambled up the dusty hill. They gathered at the door, pushing one another to get in first.

"There are so many!" Portia said. Very thin men, their sable skin glistening with sweat, tried to climb over the women and children to get inside. Every one of them was crying, shouting, pleading for the doctors to save them, make them well. Chun pulled the folds of the tent closed, but arms reached in, clawing at the air. Portia froze. Then, a few of the men discovered the open side where the hospital tent had not been sealed yet. They charged toward the first white-bodied android, demanding to be seen. A cluster of women followed in their wake, pushing and elbowing one another.

Dr. Noble handed Portia a tablet and shoved her forward. "Take their names and vital signs, get them organized. Make them stand in line."

"How? They're bigger than me!"

Dr. Noble gave her a grim smile.

"You're here to help them. Do it. They'll respect you."

Portia hesitated. She smoothed her hands down her legs, felt the electrodes under her gloved palms. This was why she was there. She started forward.

"Look, guys," she said. The men turned and saw her. They looked scared, then the fear turned to determination. She stepped forward. "Give me your names and what's wrong with you."

"I feel sick to death," a man whose hollow cheekbones and temples made him resemble a skull. His irises were almost black. "Give me medicine!"

"No, me first!" a burly boy with a thin beard and mustache pushed forward. "I been puking all night."

An old man, with eyes with white film over them but with tightly-corded muscles in his arms and chest under his red button-down shirt shouldered forward. He punched the boy in the side.

"You let your elders go first! Show respect!"

"Hey!" Portia said, horrified. She pushed in between them. "Stop that! I need to take your names. You have to get in line."

"I don't listen to no woman-talk," the old man said. He tried to shove Portia. She wasn't even aware of it before the man grunted and dropped back. He couldn't push her over. She grabbed his wrist and saw him grimace.

"You're too strong!"

Portia immediately let go. She'd forgotten how strong she was. The man rubbed his arm. It must have really hurt.

"Sorry, but you have to take your turn!" she said. Behind him, she spotted Dr. Noble watching her and pulled back on her temper. This man was the oldest one she had seen. They were supposed to show respect to the village elders, and it looked as though she was the greeting committee. "Are you the head guy? I'm sorry you're not feeling good, but you have to stop pushing your way in here! We came to help all of you, but we need your help to do this right."

The old man nodded. He seemed to admire her attitude.

"That is more what I expect. You will make my people better. You must save all the others. I'm an old man. I will die soon."

"Don't say that!" Portia found she was more worried about him than mad. She brandished the tablet. "What's your name, sir?"

"Jendyose Nalubega."

"That's pretty," Portia said, seeing the words appear on the tablet screen. She held out her hand. "I have to take your blood pressure and pulse, okay, Mr. Nalubega?"

He seemed reluctant to let her touch him, but she did her best to look as friendly and open as she could. She circled his wrist with her forefinger and thumb. Sensors embedded in her palms took the readings, which were transferred to the spaces underneath his name. When she let go, she saw his wrist bump against something in the waistband of his khaki shorts. With a shock, she recognized the glint of blued metal.

"Is that a gun? You can't bring a gun in here!" She reached for it.

"We need protection," Mr. Nalubega said, shielding the butt with both hands. "The raiders, they come and steal everything valuable. I will not use it here and endanger my people."

She nodded, dissatisfied. A touch on his forehead brought

up another temperature in her display, 103.2°. Way too high. She glanced around for an open cot. She took him very gently by the arm.

"Come and sit over here, okay? You! And you!" She pointed an imperious finger at the other men who had pushed themselves in. "You stand there. Everyone line up!"

But the use of force, even if she didn't mean it, made the people show her the respect Dr. Noble had talked about. She strutted a little, then got into the rhythm of bringing people back to the examination room, taking names, temperatures and samples.

Around her, the sides of the tent were closed and sealed. Around her, the smells of antiseptic, stinky sweat, dirt and the sharp odor of the plastic tents were like more noises. She stopped being aware of the weight of the android's limbs and her touch became gentler.

Practically everyone she talked with was starting to run a fever. The kids caught it faster. She did her best to soothe them, brushing her hands softly over their hot faces, ruffling their wiry hair. Most of them tried to give her a smile, even if they were a little nervous about her weird appearance. They had her sympathy, them and the frightened mothers in tight headscarves who carried them into the hospital tent. The big, strong men who whined about feeling a little sick got no time from her.

"How come you not give me medicine to cure me?" A man with a bristling beard demanded as Portia rolled up the sleeve of his coral-colored button-down shirt to draw blood.

"Because we don't have one yet. We're working on finding a cure," Portia said, running the needle into the bulging vein in his dark chocolate skin. She made the clicking noise out of the corner of her mouth that brought the briefing about Kampeche fever up onto her screen and scanned down the bullet points. The first thing the virus did was make its victims tired and cranky. He sure fit into that category. She tapped the vial with her fingernail and withdrew it carefully from the rear of the needle. The blood looked brown inside the plastic tube. She glanced up at him. "Look, we don't know everything about it. The doctors will do all they can for you. Just cooperate, okay?"

His eyes flashed. "You spacesuit people gotta know! Fix me!"

"I don't know!" Portia said, feeling her temper rise. "And I'm not a spacewoman. I'm just a helper. Don't be such a baby."

He clamped his jaw shut and glared hard. She bit her tongue. He was scared. He knew he could die. Since he was showing signs of the fever, he probably *would* die. Kampeche was horribly contagious. In fact, everyone around her might fall over dead. The plague could spread through Africa, across into America, and kill everyone!

Portia clutched the blood sample in both hands. What was she doing there? She didn't have any real skills. Every one of them could catch the fever. Anyone with a temperature was considered infectious. She had to decontaminate herself, right there and then.

She hurried over to put the blood samples into the frame of the analyzer, a big rectangle about six feet tall by three feet but only two inches deep. The front panel clicked shut, and a series of little red lights shot up the screen above it.

"Portia!" Costain called. "Come here. I need your help."

She turned to see the dark-haired doctor with a wisp-thin woman in his arms. Her head lolled back against his white-shelled body.

"Give me a hand," he said. "She's bad. This is the advanced stage of the fever."

An infrared reading gave the woman's temperature as 105.5°, the highest yet. Portia hurried over and held out her arms, ready to help set her on one of the beds. Then she saw the yellow pustules on the woman's face. They looked like drops of wax. She flinched away. Costain nearly dropped the patient.

"What's the matter with you?" he snapped, gathering the woman back. He set the woman down on the cot by himself and rounded on Portia with his hands on his hips.

"She's ... what's in those blisters?" Portia asked, feeling ill. "Can ... can they make us sick?"

She touched her own face, feeling for the outbreak.

"You can't catch it," Dr. Costain said. He leaned forward, willing her to understand. "You're not *there*. This is why we can help them."

"But I am here!" Portia wailed. How could he say she wasn't right there? The heat baked her, making her feel lethargic and frustrated. She smelled the urine, sweat, blood and disinfectant. Her hands twisted together in frustration. Costain grabbed her wrists and put her hands in front of her face. For a moment, the projection died away and she saw the white ceramic material beneath the illusion. Portia caught her breath.

"No. You're not here," the doctor said, in low, urgent tones. "Don't get distracted. This is critical. If we give her antibiotics and keep her hydrated, we might be able to nurse her through this stage. If not, she'll die. Pull yourself together! You can do good here, girl. This is your chance to step up and help society instead of being a burden on it. *We're trying to save lives.* Forget about yourself. You're safe! Now, help me!"

The illusion returned, clothing the android's hands with her brown skin, her nails brilliant with the teal polish she had applied that morning, and the gleam of the silver ring on her right hand which her boyfriend had given her.

She took a deep breath.

"Okay. I'm sorry." She pulled out of Costain's grasp. He nodded, and knelt down beside the woman. Portia looked around. A woman in a striped skirt was being towed toward the flap of the tent by two boys. They were too small to support her. The woman stumbled on the plastic threshold. Portia scurried forward and caught her. The boys had tears running down their faces. They didn't show signs of the hot sweats.

"Sit here," she said. "I'll take her." Portia swung the mother up in her arms. The woman was so light. The boys clung to her skirt for a moment. Portia tried not to be impatient. "Look, *chicos*, I get it. She'll be close by. You concentrate on staying well yourselves, right?"

The bigger of the boys looked at the other with the somber eyes of a man. "We understand."

Portia's eyes went out to him. She had seen that look in her own neighborhood when a father got shot by gangbangers, and the eldest son had to step up. She wondered what had happened to the woman's husband. But that had to come later. The woman's temperature was over 103°. Portia laid her on the last of the available cots, took blood samples, then started antibiotics through a drip. She was proud that she only had to take one stab with the needle to get it in place. The woman didn't move at all, except for the shallow rise and fall of her chest.

"Make sure you lock the drug storage whenever you take a dose out," Peggy, an Asian-American nurse, said. Portia thought her name was Nissa. "We get a lot of thieves coming in."

"So what?" Portia said, turning her chin up in defiance. "I can drop them. No one crosses me."

"I'm from Brooklyn, too, honey," Nissa said. "This isn't like that. They have machine guns."

Portia refrained from telling her, "So do the gangbangers," but she kept an eye on the locked cabinet from then on.

The crowds just got bigger and bigger over the next couple of hours, the tent got dustier, and the patients who arrived were sicker. Lots of them had those yellow blisters on their skin. Portia rushed from one cot to another, making sure that the IV bags hadn't run out. She did rounds of all the patients every half hour, timed by an alarm that went off in her ear, taking blood pressure and making sure the people on the cots and those that took care of them had water.

The two boys sat by their mother's bed, their eyes wide and solemn. Portia didn't like the look of the woman. She lay too still. Portia saw that her face was covered by the yellow blisters, more than any she had ever seen. According to her briefing, that was the terminal stage of the fever. No! There had to be something they could do for her.

"Dr. Noble!" she said into the communications link.

"She's busy," Dr. Costain said. "What is it?"

She found the tall physician at her elbow. He edged past her and looked down at the woman. To Portia's horror, he drew the sheet up over the patient's face.

"Time of death, two forty." He wrote something on the tablet at the end of her bed, set it down and walked away. Portia thought he couldn't have cared less about a woman he had known for about a minute, but she caught a glimpse in profile of his downcast eyes and drawn face. The brusque man was suffering for the loss of a patient. He *cared*. She liked him a lot more from that moment on.

It was up to her to comfort the kids. Portia knelt down between them and put her arms around their shoulders. They put their heads down. The little one started to sob. The alarm went off in Portia's ear to start her next round, but she ignored it, rocking the boys until the bigger one squirmed loose. He took his younger brother by the hand and led him out of the tent.

"Where are you going?" Portia called.

"Home," the bigger boy said. "We will make arrangements."

Portia shook her head. No one in her neighborhood would ever be so mature so young. She guessed they had to learn.

One of the young men sitting nearby raised his eyebrows. Despite the fever sweat, he inched out a hand toward the computer screen. Portia almost jumped toward him.

"Leave that alone! We're trying to save your miserable life!"

She snatched up the tablet. He glared at her. Portia glared back. She realized he had a gun, too. This was as bad as the projects. His hand moved toward his waistband, then relaxed.

"You're right." That was all the apology she was going to get.

Portia deliberately turned her back on him. Dr. Noble wanted her to get onto rounds. She threw herself into the disgusting tasks she had been assigned. Bed pans had to be emptied into the sanitizing chute that led to a sump at the rear of the main tent. A young girl vomited all over herself, the cot she was lying in, and two other patients close by. Portia's eyes watered from the stinking mess, and she had to disinfect her hands over and over again so as not to spread the contagion. She had never known what the international volunteer medics did. As far as she was concerned, they were heroes.

As she washed out a stack of reeking, crusty metal emesis basins, doing her best to stifle her gagging, Portia heard the sound of engines revving outside. Probably, more patients were being brought in. How was the team going to manage anymore?

But instead of a plea for help, a rattle of gunfire erupted.

Men in short-sleeved shirts and shorts poured into the tent. Each of them clutched a machine gun to his chest. Some had a second one slung on their backs. Their jaws were set, white teeth clenched in dark faces. The people around her screamed and dove for cover. Portia hurried at once to the drug machine. Dr. Noble had warned her not to let anyone touch it.

Just as she suspected, two of them headed straight for it. She stood with her back to the device, spreading her arms out to protect it.

"No, you don't!" she said, fiercely. "You get these medicines over my dead body!"

They paid no attention. To her astonishment, they didn't try to get past her to the drug dispenser. Instead, they went for her arms. With loud grunts, they picked her up off the ground.

"Let me down!" Portia bellowed.

All of her long-honed instincts of living in a crappy neighborhood reared up. She kicked out with her left foot, taking the left hand man in the chin. He fell over. The other man tried to wrap his arms around her. She grabbed his wrist and squeezed, kicking back with both feet. When he let go, she dropped into a crouch, her hands out in defensive mode, fending off his attempts to seize her again.

"They're trying to kidnap me!" she shrieked, opening all her communication channels with a twist of her jaw. "Help!"

The man she had felled jumped up and sprang onto her back. She staggered forward, into the arms of the first man. He locked his hands around her chest. No matter how she bucked and struggled, he held on.

"Run, Portia!" Dr. Noble cried. Portia scanned the room. Crowds of armed men were herding the families to one side of the tent. Others were fighting with each of the doctors and nurses, trying to pull or push them toward the outdoors. Dr. Costain smashed one man over the head with his joined fists. He dropped, but there were four men behind him, trying to find an opportunity to grab one of the physician's arms or legs. Beyond the tent flap, Portia saw a big truck with its rear gate down. Two men were hauling Peggy toward it. She drooped between their arms. The gang wasn't after drugs. They were trying to steal the androids!

The first man dropped his gun and took a taser out of his pocket. Miniature lightning bolts danced between the tines at the end.

"Come quiet, or we kill everyone else here," he said. An old woman had fallen to the floor next to an overturned cot. He brandished the taser at her. She tried to crawl away, but she was too weak to move fast. The man grabbed her by the neck.

"No!" Portia shrieked. She looked around for a weapon and seized a sloshing bedpan from the floor. "You'll get this!"

The two men circled her from both sides. She knew she couldn't hold out forever, but what could she do against dozens of attackers?

"Emergency override!" A deep male voice said in her ear. "Commencing!"

Suddenly, Portia found herself gasping, her sweating face cold from the touch of air conditioning. She tried to tear off the body suit, but she was shivering. Beside her, the others acted like marionettes, dancing on the strings attached to their masks and suits. None of what had just happened seemed real.

But it was more real than anything else she was doing—had ever done. Hands grasped her arms and legs. An arm around her torso pulled her backward. Some low obstruction hit her in the back of the knees. Against her will, she sat down.

She looked up. A team of technicians helped her out of the tangle of wires around the silicone mask and the tight jumpsuit.

"You have to let me get back there!" Portia exclaimed. "My patients are in danger!"

"We're doing everything we can," said the senior tech, a man with sandy blond hair and round glasses. "Come on, you need a break. You've been at it for over four hours. Don't you have to go to the bathroom?"

"I ... uh, yeah," Portia said, suddenly aware of a full bladder and sore feet.

"We brought you some lunch," said a young Latina woman with black hair tied back in a ponytail. "You're doing awesome for your first day."

Portia stared at them. They had to be out of their minds. Her heart pounded, worrying about the people, all the sick people. They *trusted* her.

"How are you feeling, Portia?" Dr. Noble said, detaching from her own mask. Her blonde hair was slicked back with sweat. Portia touched her own head. It was damp, too.

"They're stealing us!" she said. "How can we let them get our androids?"

Dr. Noble sat down on the bench beside Portia.

"We aren't. One of the wonderful things about the Avatar Program is that anyone can be slotted into the bodies, from anywhere on the planet. We have a strike force on call for times like this. Experienced soldiers from nine different Geneva Convention countries. Right now," her mouth creased in a tiny smile, "your street moves are being replaced by *krav maga* and some compact weapons."

Portia gawked. "I saw everything that went in those trucks! We didn't bring in any weapons!"

Dr. Noble sighed. "Yes, we did. They're locked inside the bodies. Since the avatars have no need for lungs or digestive systems, we carry extra equipment inside them, things that require high-security clearance to access. It's one of the reasons the bodies are so heavy. I hate having to take those precautions, but it's turned out to be necessary more times than Mark and I like. Those bodies are worth hundreds of thousands of dollars and they're capable of saving lives every day."

"Damn," Portia said, her heartbeat slowing at last. "Good thing I didn't know it."

She had a chance for a shower and joined the others for a colorful, good-smelling lunch. Being back in her own body, her senses felt heightened. Deep red chili with all the fixings, crisp, golden corn bread, creamy, pale coleslaw—it could be a picnic in her own family's back yard. How strange it felt to sit at a Formica table with the people she had just seen up to their elbows in vomit, diarrhea and blood on the other side of the world. Dr. Costain, who outside of his suit wasn't any taller than she was, gave her a smile as he passed a bowl of potato salad her way.

"You're doing well," he said, scooping up a spoonful of chili with white chunks of onion scattered on it. "With a little train-ing, I wouldn't mind having you on my future teams."

"What do you think of the pathology so far?" Dr. Noble asked him.

"It's a bacterium, thank God," Costain said, swinging back to business in a heartbeat. "I don't see any signs that it's weaponized, but it means it can move faster and farther than a virus. We've got to keep infected patients from leaving the area. Harold Russell said there's already been a few who escaped on foot when the shooting started. We've got to find them and bring them back if we can. If they haven't succumbed. I programmed the computer to find us a cocktail of antibiotics that might work. I say, might. We've got to throw everything we have at it, and hope something sticks."

Portia watched this exchange with growing annoyance.

"How can you discuss this so calmly?" she demanded. "We're not there! We ought to be taking care of our patients. They could all be being shot up by those gangbangers!"

Dr. Noble's smile quieted her. "Two personalities can't occupy the bodies at the same time, Portia. We have to give the strike force a chance to do their job. They have to restore peace before we can go back in and help those people."

Portia nodded. She had heard her father give similar talks during riots.

"Okay," she said. "I admire them having to do the hard part."

"Oh, no," Dr. Noble said, a sad look in her lovely blue eyes. "We have to do the hard part. When we go back in, we have to get the townspeople to trust us again."

Portia let the techs strap her in, then leaned forward to put her face into the silicone mask. All her sweat and spit had been wiped out in her absence, so the transition and adaptation was effortless. The moment she could see through her avatar's mask again, though, she gasped in horror.

The tidy but crowded hospital tent that she had left behind was a ghost town of waving flaps. Most of the machines lay tipped over on the floor. Spatters and pools of blood covered the dirt floor. At the far end of the enclosure, next to the disposer chute, a heap of bodies had been partially covered with a tarpaulin.

Not all of the medics had returned yet. The android avatar that had been Peggy was occupied by a broad-faced black man in a camouflage cap. He held a machine gun upright against his hip.

"All under control," he said to Dr. Noble. "There were fifteen of them. Two of them survived. We're questioning them now. I'm sorry, but they shot four of your patients. We tried to save them, but they were too weak. This fever's a bitch, isn't it?"

Tears stood in Dr. Noble's eyes. "Thank you, Colonel Russell. I know you did your best."

"That's why we're here, ma'am," Russell said. He unfastened the magazine from the bottom of his weapon. A weird, sharp noise sounded, and the front of his torso opened wide. Portia couldn't help but stare at the arsenal hidden in the recesses of the android body. A stack of magazines, two vicious-looking knives, and other riot gear were neatly packed, wasting no space. He cleaned out the barrel of the gun and tucked it away. The panel snapped shut, accompanied by another off-key tone. "Hope we don't see you again for a long time."

"I hope the same," Dr. Noble said. Russell gave her a curt nod. In the next second, his face vanished, and Peggy's pale gold features returned.

"Wow," Portia said, trying to absorb what she had just seen.

From the huddled crowd of the sick and their families,

Jendyose Nalubega stood up. His face was covered with sweat, but he held himself with dignity.

"So, you turn into another gang now?" he asked, spitting every word. "Are you going to kill the rest of us now?"

Dr. Costain started to speak, but Portia cut him off and stepped forward, ignoring the blood on the floor.

"No. We're here to cure you. We can't help it if those men wanted to steal us. Please, let us do what we can. That's why we came."

After a lot of pleading and apologizing, she persuaded Mr. Nalubega to sit down and submit to antibiotic therapy. She watched Costain's experimental formula flow down the translucent tube into the old man's ropy-muscled arm. Nalubega maintained an aloof attitude, keeping his chin in the air in spite of the pain he had to be feeling. Once he had agreed to be treated, his villagers also left the huddle near the wall, and let the medics do what they could for them.

"They come all the time when there is anything to steal," the chief said. "Vultures. I'm glad you can be a warrior, too."

Portia kept his words in her mind as she made her rounds. She helped Peggy and the other nurses clean up the blood and patch the bullet holes in the walls. The surviving patients needed to be fed and cleaned and turned.

She needed to be fed and cleaned, too. Every few hours, the techs pulled each of them out of their avatars to take a break. Portia submitted to the ministrations with impatience, eager to get back in there. She was determined to give all the effort she had to the people who had once again granted their trust.

Night came on fast. She had never been in a place that didn't have street lamps. The village was as dark as a closet. The only light source was the round blue lights lining the tent.

Portia walked through the aisles of low camp beds, checking IV bags, picking up used bedpans and placing new ones, and just smiling at the people. She noticed that the other doctors' avatars seemed to glow from within, like angels. Guardian angels. She wondered if she looked like that, too. She wanted to protect these people, hold them to her heart and keep them safe.

A hand dropped onto her shoulder.

"How are you doing, Portia?" Dr. Noble asked. "Are you sorry you asked to do your community service with us?"

"No way!" Portia exclaimed. "It's been hard, but I feel really good. Do you think, when I'm done with the court-ordered hours, that I could join the team and be a real part of it? I'll study in school, whatever you want."

The blonde doctor smiled. "You'd be a genuine asset to us. I think you'd make a wonderful doctor or nurse, but you'd have to stay a nurse's aide until you graduated medical school."

"That's great," Portia began, wrinkling her nose. "Only, is there any way we can turn off the smelling part of my android's programming when I have to clean bedpans? I can put up with anything except everyone else's ... stink."

Dr. Noble laughed. She put out her hand, and Portia squeezed it, feeling the click as the two ceramic hands met.

"It's a deal," the blonde physician said, her smile projected on her android face. "As long as you bring your heart, we can leave your nose back at headquarters. The avatar won't mind."

ABOUT THE EDITORS

Kevin J. Anderson has published 140 books, 56 of which have been national or international best sellers. He has written numerous novels in the Star Wars, X-Files, and DC Comics universes, as well as unique steampunk fantasy novels *Clockwork Angels* and *Clockwork Lives*, written with legendary rock drummer Neil Peart, based on the concept album by the band Rush. His original works include the Saga of Seven Suns series, the Terra Incognita fantasy trilogy, the Saga of Shadows trilogy, and his humorous horror series featuring Dan Shamble, Zombie PI. He has edited numerous anthologies, written comics, games, and the lyrics to two rock CDs. Anderson and his wife, Rebecca Moesta, are the publishers of WordFire Press.

Mike Resnick is, according to Locus, the all-time leading award winner for short fiction. He has won five Hugos (from a record 36 nominations), a Nebula, and other major awards in the USA, Poland, France, Catalonia, Japan, Croatia and Spain.

He is the author of 75 novels, almost 300 stories, and three screenplays, and the editor of 41 anthologies, and is currently the editor of *Galaxy's Edge* magazine. Mike was the Guest of Honor at the 2012 Worldcon.

Harry 'Doc' Kloor is CEO and Co-Founder of Beyond Imagination – a company that will bring general purpose humanoid avatars to the world enabling near instantaneous transportation. He is an American scientist, inventor, film producer, director, writer, and entrepreneur. Kloor was the first (and still the only) person to be awarded two PhDs simultaneously in two distinct academic disciplines. He holds PhDs in Physics and in Chemistry, both earned at Purdue University.

Dr. Kloor is a recognized leader in bringing science to the public, and science consultant for NASA, CIA, and fortune 500 companies. In 2016, Kloor returned to XPRIZE Foundation, as Bold Innovator bringing his decades long mission of advancing avatar technologies to XPRIZE. As Bold Innovator he created the Avatar X Prize, raised 22M commitment from ANA to fund this prize, which was formally announced on March 12th, 2018 at South by South West. Dr. Kloor has advised in the area of Blockchain and crypto-currency for many years, and serves as advisor on several ICO offerings.

OTHER TITLES FROM WORDFIRE PRESS

Decision Points

edited by Bryan Thomas Schmidt

Resurrection, Inc.

Kevin J Anderson

Club Anyone

Lou Agresta

Our list of other WordFire Press authors and titles is always growing. Join our WordFire Press Readers Group and get free books, sneak previews, updates on new projects, and other giveaways. Sign up for free at <u>wordfirepress.com</u>

OTHER WORDFIRE PRESS TITLES FROM THE EDITORS

KEVIN J. ANDERSON & MIKE RESNICK

Kevin J. Anderson

Alternitech

Blindfold

Climbing Olympus

Clockwork Angels: The Comic Scripts

Dan Shamble, Zombie PI Series

Dan Shamble 1: Death Warmed Over

Dan Shamble 2: Unnatural Acts

Dan Shamble 3: Hair Raising

Dan Shamble 4: Slimy Underbelly

Dan Shamble 5: Tastes Like Chicken

Working Stiff

Gamearth Series

Gamearth 1: Gamearth

Gamearth 2: Gameplay

Gamearth 3: Game's End

Hopscotch

Million Dollar Series

Kevin J. Anderson & Neil Peart

Clockwork Angels

Clockwork Lives

Drumbeats

Mike Resnick

Away Games

The Dark Lady

First Person Peculiar

The Outpost

Million Dollar Writing Series

The Science Fiction Professional:

Volume 1 Expanded and Updated

Q&A for Science Fiction Writers: The Science Fiction Professional: Volume 2 Expanded and Updated

Our list of other WordFire Press authors and titles is always growing.
To find out more and to see our selection of titles, visit us at:

wordfirepress.com